Ann Barker was born and brought up in Bedfordshire and currently lives in Norfolk with her husband who is a clergyman. She enjoys spending time with her children, Sally and Ralph, and her pet dog. For more information about Ann Barker and her books visit www.annbarker.com

THE SQUIRE AND THE SCHOOLMISTRESS

When Flavia Montague arrives to take up employment as a schoolmistress in the village of Brooks, she learns that the school has been closed for some months and that the previous teacher, Miss Price, has been involved in a scandal. Flavia is given welcome assistance in establishing the school by the handsome landowner Paul Wheaton, who seems attracted to her. It becomes clear that one of the pupils, Penelope, has been ill-treated by her guardian, Sir Lewis Glendenning — a name linked with the notorious Miss Price. But is Sir Lewis the brute that he appears to be? And what is the truth about Miss Price?

Books by Ann Barker
Published by The House of Ulverscroft:

HIS LORDSHIP'S GARDENER
THE GRAND TOUR
DERBYSHIRE DECEPTION

ANN BARKER

THE SQUIRE
AND THE
SCHOOLMISTRESS

Complete and Unabridged

ULVERSCROFT
Leicester

First published in Great Britain in 2005 by
Robert Hale Limited
London

First Large Print Edition
published 2005
by arrangement with
Robert Hale Limited
London

British Library CIP Data

Barker, Ann
    The squire and the schoolmistress.—Large print ed.—
Ulverscroft large print series: historical fiction
1. Women teachers—England—Fiction 2. England—
Social life and customs—Fiction 3. Large type books
I. Title
823.9′14 [F]

ISBN 1–84617–057–5

Published by
F. A. Thorpe (Publishing)
Anstey, Leicestershire

Set by Words & Graphics Ltd.
Anstey, Leicestershire
Printed and bound in Great Britain by
T. J. International Ltd., Padstow, Cornwall

This book is printed on acid-free paper

For Ralph, my talented son.

1

'Well, this is it, Miss Montague — Brooks village school. I trust that it comes up to your expectations?' The Revd Brian Steeple's tone was anxious, and a slight frown furrowed his brow.

He was right to be anxious. The village schoolroom in which they were standing was a far cry from the establishment in which Miss Flavia Montague had been working until recently. She had been a teacher in a select school for young ladies in Bath. Situated in Queens Square, and boasting among other things a music master who had studied with Herr Beethoven and a headmistress of awe-inspiring gentility who was distantly related to an earl, Miss Bredale's school for young ladies attracted the highest families in the land. The single room which constituted Brooks village school, with its benches and desks pushed against one wall, its teacher's desk on a platform at the front with a sturdy-looking cane lying across it and its blackboard resting on an easel to one side was certainly very different from the well-appointed house in which Mr Steeple had first made her acquaintance.

Much to his relief, however, after a swift look around she said, in the low-pitched decisive tone which in the short time in which he had known her he had come to realize was very much characteristic of her, 'Thank you, Mr Steeple. This appears to be entirely satisfactory.'

The lines on the vicar's rather high brow cleared a little. 'Miss Montague, you cannot think how happy this makes me,' he said earnestly. 'But let me show you the cottage.' Behind the teacher's desk, at opposite sides of the room and facing directly forwards were two identical doors. 'The right-hand one leads into a cupboard,' the vicar went on. 'In it you may keep pencils and paper, chalk, slates, globes, books and so on.'

He led the way to the other door and opened it. At first glance, it appeared that this was just another cupboard, for in front of them was a plain wooden panel, but with a murmured word of apology, Mr Steeple reached past and pushed the panel, and it was seen that in fact they were standing in a small lobby with another door straight ahead. The vicar politely gestured for his companion to go ahead of him.

'This is the schoolmistress's cottage,' he said, looking anxious again.

Miss Montague looked around. The room was small and plainly furnished, containing a modest dining-table with two upright chairs tucked beneath it, and two easy chairs placed either side of the fireplace. Evidently, she gathered, the schoolmistress was not expected to entertain very extensively. But there was a neat bookcase against one wall, where she would be able to put all her books and another little table in the window which would be well set off by a vase of flowers.

'The kitchen is through the door over there,' the vicar indicated. 'For water, I think that you will find the pump in the yard quite convenient.'

Miss Montague walked over to the staircase which was to the right of them and led directly out of the room in which they were standing. 'May I go up?' she asked him.

'Why, yes . . . yes, of course,' replied the vicar, colouring a little. 'You will forgive me if I do not accompany you. Our reputations might not . . . It might not be quite seemly if . . . But pray, go up, Miss Montague.'

She went upstairs, a little amused at the vicar's obvious embarrassment. There were two rooms, one at the front of the house, which was clearly the main bedroom, and a tiny one at the back which might be a box room, but which could equally well be a servant's room. That would do for Grace, she decided. As for the larger room, like the room downstairs it was plainly furnished, containing just a simple tester bed, a tall cupboard with drawers with a jug and a basin on top of it, and a cupboard in the corner in which clothes could be hung. Obviously, the schoolmistress was not expected to have many clothes, either. She looked down at the floor. Like the floor downstairs, it was bare of any covering, but that could soon be remedied. Her father's sea chest, she decided, could come upstairs. It would provide her with extra storage space.

When she came downstairs, she saw that once more, the vicar was looking anxious. Repressing an urge to tell him not to worry so much, she said instead in bright tones, 'It all looks perfectly acceptable, Mr Steeple. I am very pleased with it.'

'Then you are willing to come and be our teacher here? That is, subject, of course, to everyone's agreement.'

'Of course,' she replied, thinking that this was rather a strange way of putting things. 'Did I not make that clear when I accepted the post in Bath?'

'Oh yes,' he agreed. 'But I did wonder how you would feel when you saw the place for yourself. It is not everyone's idea of what is comfortable, and for someone who has dwelt in a city, our little village can seem a trifle remote.'

She smiled ruefully. 'It is possible to be in too close proximity to one's fellow man,' she told him. 'I assure you that a little solitude will be very welcome.'

'I will send our outdoor man from the vicarage. He can help your maid with the luggage,' said Mr Steeple. 'My wife and I dine at five. You will think that a very old-fashioned hour, I'm sure, but we keep a country table here. I hope that you will dine with us tonight, since you have had no opportunity of making any other arrangements here.'

'You are very good,' she replied. 'I shall certainly need someone to cook for me, and maybe a manservant; neither of them to live in, of course.'

'My wife will be able to advise you on that score,' he said. 'Today is Thursday. You will need a day or two to settle in. Shall we say that school will start on Monday? Then after a short time we may review the situation to make sure that it is satisfactory to all parties.'

'That sounds a reasonable suggestion,' she said, privately thinking that he was being rather pompous.

'Then I will bid you goodbye for now,' said

5

the vicar, bowing politely, before leaving the cottage by the main front door, which stood a short way along from the door which led into the schoolroom.

She waited until his footsteps had faded away completely before flopping down into one of the armchairs and saying out loud, 'At last! A home of my own!'

★　★　★

For as long as she could remember, Flavia Montague had never had such a thing. Her mother was a squire's daughter who had been widely held to have married beneath her when, in the teeth of parental opposition, she had joined her life to that of a junior naval officer, dependant upon his pay. Throughout the short marriage of Lieutenant Clive Montague and the former Miss Stephanie Prowse, her family had refused to acknowledge their existence, and the death of delicate Mrs Montague when her only daughter was five had done nothing to change their attitude.

Thereafter, Flavia had lived with her father in lodgings when he was not at sea, and had stayed with a series of aunts when his duty had called him away. On attaining the age of eighteen, she was taken to London by one of her aunts, and put through what she referred to ever after as the misery of a London season. At the close of those unhappy weeks, which had seemed more like years, she had declared emphatically, 'Never again!' She was not pretty enough, nor rich enough, nor flirtatious enough to attract any man's attention, and had spent much of her time sitting next to her chaperon and growing increasingly bored whilst other young ladies enjoyed themselves. Others might be prepared to go to such trouble and expense only to be ignored and discounted, but Flavia was not of their number. After her unsuccessful debut, she had informed her father that since she had never had a suitor, and never expected to have one, she had decided that she might as well have a profession instead, and become a teacher.

Her father had protested at first, but he soon realized that another London season would only be more punishment for her and an inordinate expense for him with little expectation of a result, so he had allowed her to have her way.

At that time, Lieutenant Montague had just been given his first captaincy and had recently come into some prize money; not a large amount, but enough for his daughter to be a schoolmistress as an independent woman, rather than as an indigent spinster with no alternative. Thanks to a good word from one of the aunts with whom she had resided, she obtained a post as junior mistress in a select school in Bath, and had quickly discovered in herself an ability and a willingness to communicate with the younger ones, and especially with those who found learning hard. She also developed her own ways of discipline, which enabled her to keep order, and usually her temper at the same time.

This existence had continued for seven years until, just before her twenty-fifth birthday, her father had been killed in action. Her grief had been sincere but limited, for after all, she had only seen him when he had been on shore leave, and that only if he had been able to make the journey to Bath, which had not always been possible.

Her father had never really been interested in anything other than the sea, and was frankly perplexed at having a daughter to consider. He was not a man to be tempted by expensive vices and had found very little reason to spend his money on anything other than his basic needs. On not one occasion had he ever gained a large amount of prize money; but what he had won from time to time had been carefully banked, and upon his death, Flavia, as his sole beneficiary, had found herself the mistress, if not of a fortune then certainly of a very pretty competence. Strictly speaking, it was not necessary for her to work at all, but she enjoyed her teaching and in the classroom discovered an assurance and an ease of manner which tended to desert her in social situations, and in particular in encounters with members of the opposite sex.

Her father's death did, however, enable her to make a change if not in the nature of her employment, certainly in her situation. Although father and daughter were never close, they were sincerely attached to one another, and Flavia had always been reluctant to do anything that might cause him distress. Whilst she was a teacher in a school in Bath, he could be sure that she was protected and safe. Had she taken a position such as, for instance, village schoolmistress in Brooks during his lifetime, he would have been extremely anxious about her. Such anxiety might have meant that he would have enquired further into her desire to do such a thing. Then all the business about her not having a home might have come out, and he would have started blaming himself for not providing for her adequately.

She had waited until her year of mourning

was over before making her move. In truth, she had not been entirely sure what it was that she wanted. She only knew that suddenly Bath had become stifling and the very atmosphere of the place was making her feel restless.

Then one day, visiting the Abbey over the Christmas period when all the girls had gone home to their respective families, she had bumped into a friend. At one stage, when she had been staying with her aunt Drusilla, she had shared lessons with a girl called Pamela Beech. Pamela had a sister much older than herself who was married to a clergyman, and so since she was now to all intents and purposes an only child, she was very glad of Flavia's company. The two had got on so well together that after Flavia's father had returned from his latest voyage and taken his daughter to share yet another set of lodgings with him, they had continued to correspond.

They had not met in person for some years, and in truth, the correspondence had dwindled a little. But as Flavia was taking in the well-known sights of the Abbey and, for once, finding them dull and irritating rather than comforting and familiar, she heard a voice saying 'It is! It *must* be Flavia Montague!' Flavia turned and was delighted to see her old friend, who informed her that since her last letter — and indeed, she was dreadfully behind with her correspondence, she must apologize — she had got married, and she and her husband were staying in Bath — 'at the Pulteney, my dear! You cannot imagine how grand! Come back now and have some tea with us! I am longing for you to meet Edgar!'

Edgar Graceforth was a friendly, unassuming man with a humourous light in his eye, and the three of them spent a delightful afternoon together. Mrs Graceforth begged Flavia to dine with them at the Pulteney the following day and knowing that Miss Bredale would have no need of her at the school, she had no hesitation in accepting.

That occasion was as enjoyable as the previous one and Flavia began to feel more at ease with her contemporaries than she had ever done.

Eventually, Mr Graceforth said to her, 'So you are dedicated to education then, Miss Montague.'

'I think I must be,' she replied seriously. 'The satisfaction of feeling that knowledge has been imparted and understood cannot be equalled. But . . . ' She paused.

'But what?' asked Pamela curiously. 'Do you secretly hanker after a post in London? Perhaps a governess to royalty, or at the very least, to the children of a duke?'

'By no means,' laughed Flavia. 'I cannot think of anything I would want less. In fact, to tell you the truth . . . '

'Well?'

'I think I would like to be a village schoolteacher. Oh, you may laugh,' she went on, when Pamela did that very thing. 'But you have always belonged somewhere. I only belong in the school in term time, and nowhere during the holidays, unless I visit my aunts, and they have a habit of making sure that I am kept busy and useful, and introduced to dull widowers. So you see, I should very much like to be part of a community, to share in its joys and sorrows and to feel that I had made a difference to the lives of some of its inhabitants.' She spoke a little defensively, but Pamela leaned forward and placed a hand on her arm.

'I wasn't laughing at you,' she said earnestly. 'I was laughing because I have been struck by an amazing coincidence. In fact, I think that I may be able to help you find the very situation you are seeking.'

'Truthfully? You are not jesting?'

Pamela shook her head. 'Do you remember that I had a sister who married a country clergyman? Well, in his parish he has a school that he is obliged to maintain, and I happen to know that a short time ago he was looking for a teacher, the previous one having left rather suddenly. Would you like me to find out whether he still needs someone?'

Flavia nodded her head, her eyes shining.

It had not taken long to arrange the whole business. In fact, it could have taken even less time, for Mr Steeple was anxious for her to start immediately. But Flavia did not want to leave Miss Bredale without giving her plenty of time to find a replacement. She had been too considerate an employer for her to be treated in such a casual manner.

'Steeple,' Miss Bredale had murmured in a thoughtful manner, when Flavia had spoken to her of the matter. 'We had a young lady here a few years ago by that name. Do you recall?'

Flavia nodded. 'Yes, I do,' she replied. 'Mary Steeple. I wonder if she could be from the same family?'

'Your friend would surely have said so, if that had been the case.'

'Not necessarily,' replied Flavia, with wry amusement in her voice. 'Would you want to tell all your friends and relatives about the antics of Mary Steeple?'

Miss Bredale smiled in return and conceded the point. Mary Steeple had been one of their more difficult pupils, being

13

reluctant to learn any of the subjects offered from Miss Bredale's excellent curriculum, but more than willing to learn all about evading chaperons in the town, flirting with visiting teachers, talking after lights out, and climbing out of windows in order to rendezvous with unsuitable young men in the Sidney Gardens. Only Miss Bredale herself, and Flavia to a certain extent, had been able to inspire any respect in the wayward young madam; her departure at the age of eighteen had been a great relief to all.

'Even if she is a relation, I am sure that you will seldom if ever encounter her,' Miss Bredale said reassuringly. 'She is probably married by now and far too busy caring for a husband and children to even remember her youthful folly.'

Mr Steeple had visited her in Bath, and when she took the opportunity to mention the name of Mary Steeple, he admitted that there was a connection. 'She is my sister,' he said, his tone a little defensive. 'My parents always hoped for more children, but sadly, after my own birth, there were two brothers and two sisters who all died in infancy. Mary was born late, and as she was younger than myself by twenty years, I fear that she was a little spoiled.' He flushed slightly. 'She did attend this academy — I do not know whether you were a teacher here at that time, or whether you had just heard her name by . . . by . . . ' His voice tailed off.

'Yes, I was a teacher here, and I remember Mary,' answered Flavia. Seeing his expression, she felt emboldened to say, 'She was always a handful, I'm afraid.'

The vicar's anxious expression became a little more relaxed. 'Yes, but she is married now, to an army officer, and living in the north of England. I do not suppose that you will see her very much, if at all.'

The bargain was soon sealed, for they had liked one another on sight. His unassuming diffidence had appealed to her, and for his part, he had been glad to find that the young woman that had been recommended to him was neither glamorous nor sophisticated. When he had said as much she had laughed.

'Surely you did not expect such a person to apply for a post as village schoolmistress?' she protested.

'Not in the general way of things,' he admitted. 'But the last person was unsuitable; most unsuitable!'

Flavia would have liked to have heard a little more about her predecessor's unsuitability, but she restrained herself. There would be time enough to find out about that when she arrived at Brooks. No doubt in such a close-knit community, someone would tell her. For now, she would simply rejoice that she could at last escape from Bath, and that she had found a situation so easily that seemed as if it would be very much to her liking.

2

'Well, Miss Flavia, I never thought I'd say this, and heaven knows it gives me no pleasure to do so, but it's my belief that you've run mad.'

Grace's fierce loyalty would never have permitted her to say such a thing within the hearing of the man who had helped with the luggage, but now that he had gone, she did not hesitate, speaking with all the freedom of one who having been with her mistress for ten years looked upon herself as an old retainer. She was the twin sister of a man who had served at sea with Captain Montague and, like her brother, she was stout, broad-featured and sandy-haired, with a somewhat phlegmatic disposition. She had been employed by Flavia's father at Aunt Drusilla's insistence when Flavia was sixteen, and her solid presence at Miss Bredale's academy for young ladies had ensured that her mistress was treated with respect by even the most highly born of pupils. Essentially a town person, she found Flavia's longing to be in the country quite inexplicable, and she had grumbled from the first moment when the idea had been mooted.

'You have already said it several times,' replied Flavia calmly, as they tidied away the rest of her clothes in the bedroom. 'I know that the country is not to your liking. I may yet find that it is not to mine, but this is something that I feel I must try.'

'Well, don't blame me when you fall flat on your face,' answered Grace.

Flavia laid a hand on her arm. 'We can always return to Bath if we don't like it,' she said soothingly. 'Remember that Miss Bredale said that there would always be a place for me at the school. And if I *do* fall flat on my face, I promise not to blame you. But I expect I shall come running to you, just as I always do.'

Grace said nothing, made a hrumphing sound, and carried on with her work, but Flavia could see from her expression that she was a little mollified.

After they had finished putting everything away, Flavia tidied herself up in readiness to go to the vicarage for dinner. Critically, she examined her expression in the mirror. She was short, with a neat figure, but her brown hair was unremarkable, of a mousy shade and neither riotously curly, nor glossy and straight. Her features, though pleasant enough, were neither sufficiently regular for beauty, nor sufficiently strange for ugliness. Eventually, satisfied that every stray lock was fastened back and that she looked the image of the efficient schoolmistress, she turned away from her reflection. It would be a very bold person indeed who found any fault with her appearance, she decided.

Grace firmly rejected the suggestion that she might accept any hospitality that the vicar's housekeeper might have to offer, declaring that she would manage very well on the provisions that they had brought with them. But she did state her intention of walking with her mistress to the vicarage. As it was only just the other side of the church from the school, and therefore barely three minutes' walk away, Flavia rejected this offer.

'For goodness sake, Grace, don't treat me as if I were one of Miss Bredale's pupils out in Bath for the first time,' she said laughingly. 'People are much more free and easy in the country.'

'Humph,' grunted Grace, thereby expressing her disdain for the countryside's free and easy ways.

Because her anxiety sprang from real concern, Flavia relented and said, 'Remember that it's still daylight. I am sure that Mr Steeple will make sure that I am accompanied if it should be dark before I leave.'

Very seldom in Bath had Flavia ever walked anywhere on her own. It was not that she had felt the need to be accompanied there. At the age of twenty-six, she had considered herself to be past the need of a chaperon. But since none of the girls was permitted to go out alone, a rule which was most strictly enforced, it seemed wrong for her to set a contrary example by going about here, there and everywhere unaccompanied when the girls were on the premises. It frequently happened that one of the girls would want her company for a visit into town, and very early on in her teaching career, she learned to combine her own shopping expeditions with such outings. Furthermore, some of the girls came from quite a distance and only went home at Christmas, and so it was only during that period that she felt able to go out and about, only consulting her own wishes. So to stroll through the churchyard without having to tell anyone else not to dawdle and not to look at strange men, or simply feeling obliged to make conversation with them, was luxury indeed.

The vicarage was a handsome building constructed from dark-red brick, and Flavia could not help smiling as she compared its generous proportions to those of the little cottage that was now her home. But the schoolmistress's dwelling place was far more suited to her needs than this fine house, she told herself. Why, if she had all of this to attend to, she would never find any time to teach!

The front door of the vicarage was opened by a smiling maidservant, who bobbed a curtsy, relieved her of her bonnet, and conducted her to the drawing-room which was situated at the back of the house. Glancing swiftly round her before Mr Steeple came to greet her, Flavia could see that the furnishings, although modest as befitted the home of a clergyman were of excellent quality. Clearly, the Steeples had private money in addition to the vicar's stipend.

Mr Steeple greeted her civilly and made her known to his wife, Mrs Phyllis Steeple, a slender, rather careworn-looking woman, a little younger than her husband. As Flavia looked at her, she seemed to recognize her; or perhaps it was just that Mrs Steeple was an older, rather less pretty and more anxious-looking version of her sister Pamela, with whom Flavia was much better acquainted. When the vicar enquired as to how she had found everything, they both looked at her with such similar anxious expressions that Flavia decided that they were visible proof of the theory that those who live in close proximity for any length of time grow to be like one another.

She replied that everything was entirely satisfactory, but restated her need to find a cook who would come in daily, and an outdoor man who would come in from time to time as and when needed. Mrs Steeple, as her husband had suggested, knew the very people who would be able to help, and promised to speak to them. In this pleasant, undemanding way the time passed until dinner was announced.

This was a well-cooked but simple meal, consisting only of a meat pie, a chicken, and a fricassee of vegetables, followed by an apricot tart, a blancmange and some stewed pears from the vicarage garden, which Mrs Steeple had bottled the previous year.

'We are fortunate in having a number of fruit trees here. Indeed, sometimes I find it difficult to use all the fruit that we have,' said Mrs Steeple. 'Have you ever lived in the country, Miss Montague, or are you a town person?'

Flavia explained about her father's occupation and how consequently, she had never really had a settled home. 'So you see that I count myself very fortunate to have secured this position,' she concluded. 'Do you expect there to be many pupils for the school?'

'I think quite a number,' replied Mr Steeple. 'The village is quite a good size, and since there are two estates very nearby, no doubt some children will attend from both of them. May I offer you a little more wine, Miss Montague?'

Sadly, the wine which had been chosen to go with this meal was very inferior stuff and Flavia, who had inherited her father's excellent palate, refused any more after the first glass. The vicar smiled approvingly. Her apparent abstemiousness did her no disservice in his eyes. 'Does the village belong to either of the two estates?' she asked.

The vicar shook his head. 'Not entirely, although both Mr Wheaton and Sir Lewis Glendenning own property in the village.'

'And are both Mr Wheaton and Sir Lewis supportive of the school, or am I to expect some opposition?' Flavia asked.

'Mr Wheaton has been very helpful in the past,' said the vicar, 'and no doubt will be so again. Sir Lewis is . . . less so.' His voice tailed away.

Flavia waited for him to say more, and when he did not do so she murmured, 'I do trust that he will not be actively hostile. That would make matters a little difficult.'

'Oh no, I do not think that he will be that,' replied Mr Steeple, perhaps a little too hastily. 'But he can be a difficult man.'

'His treatment of that poor idiot son of his is positively brutal, apparently,' put in the vicar's wife.

'Yes, but who knows how any of us might react given the presence of a similarly afflicted person in our own family,' responded the vicar. Obviously Mrs Steeple was not going to indulge in the impropriety of brangling with her husband in front of a visitor, so she said nothing, but she looked less than convinced.

After dinner was over and they were sitting once again in the drawing-room, Flavia said, 'You have already given me to understand, sir, that the school has been without a teacher for over six months. Can you tell me, if you please, whether you think that the children will welcome a resumption of their studies?'

'I believe that they will be very eager to learn, going on past evidence,' replied the vicar. 'With the last teacher, they . . . that is to say . . . I must not speak ill of her, but . . . '

'Well *I* am not bound by such constraints,' declared his wife with a forthrightness that was so much at variance with her customary meekness that Flavia almost jumped. 'She was a hussy, only using the school for her own ends, and we were very glad to see the back of her!'

Flavia found herself very intrigued by this description and she would have liked to request further enlightenment, but she decided regretfully that curiosity about such a person would not be considered seemly. And after all, as she reflected later, if the previous schoolmistress had been notorious locally, no doubt some other person would take the opportunity of enlightening her. Surely, in a close knit community such as Brooks, *someone* would not be able to resist doing such a thing!

When it was time for her to return home, she firmly refused Mr Steeple's offer to escort her. 'My dear sir, I am less than five minutes from my own front door,' she declared. 'I shall be perfectly safe, I assure you.'

It was a bright, moonlit night and, as she strolled home, she relished the peace and the beauty of the scene. Never would she have had the freedom or the opportunity to enjoy it in Bath. Grace eyed her suspiciously as she came in, but although she muttered, 'I hope that vicar brought you home,' she made no further enquiries when Flavia replied, 'Mr Steeple is a gentleman, Grace. Of course he offered to bring me home.' After all, that was perfectly true, she reflected. The fact that she had refused Mr Steeple's offer was beside the point. She needed Grace to make it possible for her to live alone; in any case, she was very fond of her and would not know what to do without her. But she was certainly not prepared to allow Grace, or anyone else, to dictate her actions.

'Pour me a glass of wine, would you, Grace?' she said. 'The stuff that was served this evening was barely drinkable.' While Grace was fetching the wine, Flavia went upstairs and extracted a small box from her father's sea chest. She brought it downstairs, and opened it. Then, after first making sure that all the curtains were closed, she prepared to indulge in her second and far more scandalous vice. With a smile and a sigh of contentment, she took out and lit a long, slim cigar.

3

The following day, Flavia was awake in good time, conscious of having had a most restful night's sleep. She had heard that for those accustomed to town living, the countryside often seemed very lonely and quiet, but she had found no difficulty whatsoever in getting off to sleep. After all, she reflected, her childhood had been spent in a variety of locations, and this early preparation probably meant that she would be able to sleep almost anywhere. Furthermore, the previous day's travelling had been long and tedious, and she had fallen asleep almost as soon as her head touched the pillow. She found it very refreshing waking up simply to the noise of bird song as opposed to the clatter of traffic in the street. Not so Grace, who came in grumbling with her mistress's morning chocolate.

'I don't know how long I shall be able to endure this, Miss Flavia, I'm sure I don't,' she said, putting down her tray and opening the curtains. 'It's spooky, that's what it is. And every time I was about to drop off to sleep there was a terrible hooting outside my window. Enough to wake the dead, it was!'

'That would have been an owl,' replied Flavia.

'Oh, would it,' answered Grace. 'I'll give it ''owl' if it does that again. I hope you don't mean to stay here long, Miss Flavia, for I don't know how I'll be able to stand this, and that's a fact.'

'But you'd never leave me, would you, dear Grace, for I don't know how I should manage without you,' replied Flavia placatingly.

'That's as may be,' returned the faithful Grace. But the tone of her voice told her mistress that she was soothed, at least for the time being. How to explain to her, though, the feeling of exquisite luxury, knowing that they were the only persons in the house at that time? Grace would never understand it. She liked a house to be full of people.

It was not that Flavia was averse to company. It was just that she wanted to enjoy the freedom of being able to choose the company that she kept, at least for the time being.

After she had washed in the water which Grace brought her, she dressed in one of her oldest gowns, for it was her intention to clean, tidy and sort out her schoolroom that day.

There had as yet been no time for Mrs

Steeple to arrange for someone to cook, but there was bread, butter and jam in the kitchen, and after Flavia had breakfasted, served for the first time by Grace at her very own dining-table, she made her way into the porch and through the connecting door which led into the schoolroom. She realized immediately that her delight in escaping Bath and securing another position so easily had caused her to paint the schoolroom in rosy colours. Now, in the clear light of day, she could see that apart from anything else, since it had not been used for six months, there was at least that much dust on every visible surface, and the windows were grimy too. She was not afraid of hard work, but if the whole schoolroom needed dusting and washing down — and it looked very much as if it did — there was probably too much work for one person if the school was to open on Monday, since, of course, working on a Sunday was out of the question.

In order to make the place more light and airy, she threw open the front door of the school and then went to investigate the cupboard. She was hoping that it might contain rags that could be used as dusters and — perhaps less likely — that there might be a scrubbing brush in there. Moments later, Grace came through the doors that led into the cottage and stood on the threshold.

'Oh, my Lord,' she exclaimed. 'What Miss Bredale would say I can't imagine.'

Flavia smiled ruefully. 'Exactly my sentiments,' she replied. 'Well, I'll certainly need some help for I can't do all this by myself.'

'You know I'll do what I can, Miss Flavia,' said Grace doubtfully.

'I know you will,' replied Flavia warmly. 'But you still have plenty to do in the house, and besides, I doubt if we will be able to lift those desks. Will you go over to the vicarage and see if Mrs Steeple can spare anyone to help, or perhaps recommend someone?'

While Grace was gone, Flavia made the unwelcome discovery that since some of the furniture in the room was pushed against the cupboard door, it was quite impossible for her to open it in order to find out whether or not it contained any cleaning equipment. This purpose frustrated, she returned to the cottage kitchen, made sure that there was water heating in order to clean the room thoroughly, and sought out a broom so that she might at least begin her endeavours.

When Grace returned, it was with disappointing news. 'Vicar and his wife are away all day,' she said. 'There's only the housekeeper there.'

'Bother,' declared Flavia. 'Now I do recall

that Mrs Steeple said that they would be away from home today. What shall we do? Did the housekeeper have any suggestions to offer?'

'She did mention one or two people we could ask, but I feel a bit awkward asking such favours of someone I've never met,' Grace admitted.

They were standing in indecision when they heard the sound of horse's hooves outside, and Flavia, going to the door, was in time to see a tall, handsome man get down athletically from his mount, secure it at the school railings and walk towards her. By his air of fashion, even in country clothes, and his assured manner, she was immediately convinced that this must be either Mr Wheaton, or Sir Lewis Glendenning. Since he was smiling in a friendly manner, she concluded that he was more likely to be Mr Wheaton.

He bowed politely and proved her assumption to be correct by saying, 'You must be the new schoolteacher. I'm Paul Wheaton, ma'am, and come from hereabouts.'

'How do you do, Mr Wheaton,' replied Flavia, dropping him a curtsy. 'Yes, I'm Flavia Montague.'

'Flavia!' he exclaimed. 'That's unusual; charming, too.'

'It's the greatest trial to me, I assure you. I

was named to please an elderly relative with classical tendencies, in the hope that he would leave me his fortune, but all to no avail. I would invite you in, Mr Wheaton, but I fear that you would only become covered with dust.'

'As bad as that, is it?' he said, peering in. 'Well, I'm not altogether surprised. It hasn't been used since the school closed six months ago. When do you hope to start?'

'On Monday,' replied Flavia. 'But, as you have observed, there is a great deal to do, and the vicar seems to have gone out for the day, so I cannot ask for his help in finding someone to do the heavy lifting.'

'I can put you in the way of some help,' he answered. 'What do you need? Will a couple of men to do the lifting, and two women to clean suffice?'

'That would be ideal,' said Flavia honestly. 'I will pay them, of course.'

He gestured dismissively with his hand. 'By no means,' he replied. 'You must allow me to see to that as part of my service to the community. And in any case, a number of the children from my estate will benefit when the school is open.'

'You do not object to the presence of the school, then.'

'No, I don't object,' he said. 'I'm doubtful

of the benefits. I think, also, that you will find that many people will consider it to be a waste of time. But I'll do my best to encourage parents to send their children, at least to start with. After that, it will be up to you to keep their interest.' He left soon afterwards, in order to find some people to help her. 'But I shall return later to see what progress has been made,' he promised.

Flavia watched him get back on his horse with the same athletic grace that he had shown when dismounting. So far, he had impressed her favourably. He had understood her problem and had offered the help that she needed without having to be asked. Furthermore, she was pleased rather than otherwise by the frank avowal of his uncertainty with regard to the merits of the school. At least she knew where she was with him. She could only hope that Sir Lewis's disapproval would be expressed in as honest and open a manner.

Within half an hour, the helpers he had promised appeared. Neither of the men was very communicative, but they both touched their forelocks respectfully, listened carefully to her instructions, and made nonsense of moving the furniture out of the way. Since the day was fine, Flavia decided that the best idea would be to have the furniture carried out into the yard and cleaned there, whilst the floor of the schoolroom was being thoroughly scrubbed. Once all the furniture was outside, therefore, she sent the men off to their usual work, asking them to return at the end of the day in order to take the furniture back into the schoolroom.

One of the women sent by Mr Wheaton was middle-aged and taciturn, and from her unsmiling demeanour, Flavia gathered that she would have infinitely preferred to have been elsewhere. She worked hard, however, and made no complaints about even the dirtiest jobs. The other was very much younger, and she treated Flavia with open friendliness, telling her that her name was Sara Briggs, and that she was the youngest of her family, all of whom worked on her father's farm, which he tended as Mr Wheaton's tenant. Flavia toyed with the idea of asking her whether she liked her landlord, but deciding that this would encourage the girl into impropriety, contented herself with asking whether she had ever attended the school.

'Oh yes, miss,' replied Sara cheerfully, as she finished scrubbing one of the last desks, her sleeves rolled up to the elbow. 'I came here while Miss Gordon was the teacher — not Miss Price, but the one before her.'

'Did Miss Price not stay for long, then?'

Flavia asked, vaguely remembering that she had already heard as much.

'Couldn't hardly, in her condition,' put in the other woman, whose name was Jean Gray.

'Her . . . condition?' repeated Flavia.

Jean smiled for the first time, but it wasn't a pleasant expression. 'Expecting, she was, so she had to leave.'

'Jean that's not fair,' put in Sara. 'You know that Miss Price was engaged to be married, and a married teacher wouldn't be able to stay.'

'Ah, but what came first, the chicken or the egg? That's what lots of folks would like to know,' answered Jean, in the same unpleasant way.

Flavia would have liked to enquire further, but was suddenly aware that she would be taking part in rather scurrilous gossip, so instead she said, 'Thank you, Jean,' in quelling tones, and changed the subject by asking Sara what she had learned when she was at the school.

'I learned all my letters, miss,' replied Sara. 'I think I might even be able to remember some of them.'

'And will you come back to school to learn with me?'

Jean gave a derisive laugh. 'I'd like to see your ma letting you,' she said.

Sarah nodded. 'And besides, I'm too old,' she said, with no noticeable tone of regret in her voice. 'Do you want me to help Jean with the windows or shall I start scrubbing the floor now, miss?'

By the end of the afternoon, the schoolroom had been transformed and all that remained for Flavia to do the following day was to turn out the cupboard and clean and catalogue its contents. A glance inside had not given her any grounds for optimism. Mr Steeple had told her that she might keep paper, pencils, chalk, slates and books in there, and this had encouraged her to believe that there must be at least some of those items there already. But an initial look had revealed what seemed to be mounds of rubbish on the shelves and spilling over on to the floor. As for a globe, there certainly was one, but it hung drunkenly from its stand. Its condition, which appeared to be none too clean, did not lead Flavia to suppose that even a well-travelled explorer would be able to find the most familiar place on it without considerable difficulty.

Both helpers offered to return the next day, Jean with her usual sullen expression and Sara with enthusiasm.

'I shan't need you both,' Flavia said, 'since there's only the cupboard to sort out. Sara, perhaps you could come back?' Sara readily agreed and even Jean looked slightly less sullen when Flavia pressed two shillings into her hand.

She was preparing to lock the school when Paul Wheaton returned. He was just as handsome as Flavia had remembered, and she was conscious of a feeling of regret that because of the work she had done that day, she was looking a little grubbier than her normal self. 'This is looking much better,' he said, looking round approvingly. 'Were my people of service to you?'

'I couldn't have managed without them,' she owned frankly. 'Sara offered to return tomorrow and I ventured to accept her offer, for I was certain she would not have done so had she not been sure that you would give her leave.'

'It's not really for me to say,' he replied. 'But I can't see Mrs Briggs objecting. Will you not need the others as well?'

She shook her head. 'There is only the cupboard to do, and it does not look to be very well filled,' she replied. 'Was all the equipment cleared out when Miss Price left?'

'That I cannot say,' he answered shortly, a shadow falling across his handsome face. 'It's possible, I suppose. I do not recollect your saying when you intended to open the school.'

'Mr Steeple would like me to open it on Monday,' she replied, tacitly accepting his change of subject. 'But as to whether Monday's session will be very long will depend very much on whether I find anything useful in that cupboard!'

He looked at her hesitantly, seemed about to speak, changed his mind again, but eventually said in somewhat constrained tones, 'There is something I feel I must say to you, if only because no one else will dare to say it. I would keep well clear of Lewis Glendenning if I were you.'

Flavia did not like to say that she had already been warned about the baronet. Instead, she merely remarked, 'Is he likely to be hostile to the school?'

'That I could not say,' he replied carefully. 'But he is not a man whom it would be wise to cross.'

'Will he be against any of his people coming to the school?' she asked, a hint of anxiety in her voice. Nothing that Mr Steeple had said had led her to suppose that any of the local landowners would be actively hostile.

Again Mr Wheaton said, 'That I could not say.'

His vague answers were beginning to irritate her, and forgetting the difference in their stations, she said, in the masterful tone that her pupils at Miss Bredale's academy would have recognized, 'Mr Wheaton, it seems to me that if you cannot speak to the purpose then it would be better for you not to speak at all! Is there, or is there not anything to Sir Lewis's detriment that might be relevant to me?' He almost jumped back in surprise, and she felt obliged to ask his pardon. 'I fear that I have been a schoolmistress for too long,' she confessed.

'Not at all,' he replied smiling faintly. 'Lewis is not an easy man to deal with. As for Miss Price, who was the teacher here before you; well, it is said that he was not entirely unconnected with her obligation to leave.'

'I thought that she left because she was engaged to be married,' said Flavia, then she blushed as she remembered what Jean had said about Miss Price's condition.

Mr Wheaton, who had himself coloured a little, ran a finger inside his collar. 'I see that you have heard that there was something of a scandal connected with Miss Price, but that is over and done with now, and is best not enquired into.'

Privately thinking that if the affair was to be forgotten about, it would be far better if so many people did not keep mentioning Miss Price at all, Flavia simply added 'I have no interest in gossip, but if the children are gossiping, it would be as well for me to know something of what they are talking about. Is the young lady married now?'

'As far as I know,' he answered.

He was clearly not going to say any more on the subject, so Flavia asked, 'And what of Lady Glendenning? Does she take an interest in the school?'

'Sir Lewis is a widower,' replied Wheaton. 'His wife died giving birth to their son. But anyway, before I leave, to more pleasant matters. My sister is to come and visit me shortly; indeed, she will be here by next weekend. I know that she will be very pleased to meet you, and I would be glad if you would dine with us to give her that opportunity. Do say that you will.'

Flavia felt her heart sink into her boots, but she endeavoured not to let her feelings show as she said, 'Thank you. I should be delighted.'

'Probably next Saturday, then,' said Mr Wheaton, bowing slightly and putting his hat back on. 'I'll send you word. Good day to you.'

After he had gone she wandered back inside the school with dread in her heart. She had never felt at ease in social situations, and whilst she had played her part in preparing young ladies to take their places in the fashionable world, it was a world from which she had very happily withdrawn. At ease and confident when teaching children or discussing her work or other practical matters, she became awkward and tongue-tied at balls and parties where polite small talk and flirtation were the order of the day. Her chosen work as a schoolmistress had meant that she could almost always avoid such occasions.

She found herself wondering whether Miss Price had ever been invited to the Wheatons' table during her short time in office. He had certainly changed the subject quickly when her name had been mentioned, and when he had spoken of her again, it had been to refer to her possible connection with Sir Lewis.

She began to review what she had heard of Miss Price so far. The young woman had not stayed long. Mrs Steeple had called her a hussy. Her husband had indicated that she might be worldly and sophisticated. Mr Wheaton had said that Sir Lewis had been implicated in her need to leave the school; and, most damaging of all, Jean had hinted that she might have been with child. If so, whose child was it? Sir Lewis's? And did the gentleman whom she had married know that there was doubt being cast over the paternity of his wife's child?

In the meantime, whatever Miss Price's fate, there was the forthcoming dinner party to be endured. She consoled herself with the thought that in inviting her, Mr Wheaton was probably just being polite to a newcomer to the area, and that when he discovered what poor company she was at table, he would certainly never invite her again.

4

The following day's survey of the schoolroom cupboard was no less depressing than Flavia had feared. There were indeed some slates, but a large number of them were broken into such small pieces as to render then unusable. There did not appear to be any chalk at all, although from the evidence of its having been trodden into the floor, there had been some at one time. There was a small quantity of paper but it was in very poor condition, and only one or two pencils. The writing on the globe, when looked at more closely in the clear light of day, was just as illegible as it had seemed at first, and furthermore the globe itself was badly dented on one side. The few books that were there nearly all had pages missing. Those that were complete, she took outside, clapped together to get rid of the dust, then set on one side to be looked at later.

'There seems to be very little here that is not fit for the bonfire,' Flavia said decisively to Sara who had arrived in good time, and as cheerful as the day before. 'I defy anyone to learn anything with this load of rubbish. We might as well pile most of it up in the school yard and have it burned there. Then we can start again.'

This they did, after which they scrubbed the cupboard out thoroughly. They were not finished by midday, so Flavia invited Sara to come into the cottage for a drink and something to eat. Sara accompanied her inside rather shyly, and when invited, sat down at the table, where Grace had laid out bread and cheese. 'I'll be glad of a drink, miss, but I shan't need anything to eat, as I've got my clanger with me.'

'I beg your pardon?' asked Flavia.

'My clanger,' Sara repeated, putting a package on the table. 'It's a Bedfordshire clanger, miss. It's a pasty with meat at one end and jam at the other and it's real tasty.'

'I'll have to ask Jane to make me one,' answered Flavia politely, thinking that it sounded rather an unusual mixture.

'What'll you do on Monday, miss, without books and slates and all?' Sara asked, as they ate.

'Oh, there are plenty of things that we can do,' Flavia replied. 'I shall need to make a list of all the children's names to start with, and ask them what they know already. Then we might do something all together from the blackboard, or learn something by heart. But

44

I shall have to find the means to travel to Bedford and purchase some new equipment. The children cannot possibly learn very much with no equipment to help them.'

'Vicar might lend you his pony and trap, miss, if it's to get things for the school,' Sara suggested.

'That's a good idea,' replied Flavia, and as soon as their work was done — Sara having very gratefully received another shilling for her efforts — she wandered around to the vicarage.

The maidservant who opened the door looked a little surprised, and it was only then that it occurred to Flavia that it might have been as well to change her dress after the exertions of the morning. At least she had stopped to wash her hands and take off her filthy apron, she reflected thankfully.

Mrs Steeple looked just as surprised as her maid, but she greeted her visitor cordially enough and offered her tea. 'No doubt you have been very busy,' she remarked.

'Yes indeed I have,' replied Flavia, 'and a cup of tea would be very welcome.' While they were waiting for the tea, Flavia said politely, 'I hope that your outing was an enjoyable one.'

'My outing?' repeated Mrs Steeple in a puzzled tone.

'You were out all day yesterday.'

'Yes thank you,' Mrs Steeple said, in such a tone as seemed to imply, and none of your concern. 'Are the curtains in the bedroom windows satisfactory, Miss Montague? If not, I have some spare ones here that may do.' Flavia assured her that the curtains were perfectly suitable, and reflected on the merits of minding her own business. However close neighbours they might be, something told Flavia that she and the vicar's wife were never going to be exchanging girlish secrets.

When the tea had arrived Flavia said, 'By the way, thank you for sending Jane and Henry to me. I think that they will do very well.'

The cook and the odd job man had both arrived that morning for their orders. Much to Flavia's relief, Grace had pronounced Jane to be a 'sensible body' and Henry to be 'a good sort of man'. Grace had given up so much that was familiar to come with her mistress into the wilds of Bedfordshire that Flavia would have been hard put to it to justify hiring servants of whom she could not approve.

'I'm glad that you are satisfied with them,' replied Mrs Steeple.

'Oh certainly. Henry is very busy even now

burning the rubbish that had been left in the cupboard.'

'Rubbish?' questioned Mrs Steeple as she poured the tea. 'I thought that there was quite a lot of valuable equipment in there.'

'Perhaps there was at one time,' Flavia concurred. 'But I can assure you that with the exception of a few books, practically all I found there was rubbish.'

'I do not think that Brian will be quite pleased that you have burned it without consulting him,' replied the vicar's wife.

Flavia took a deep breath, counted slowly to five then said, 'I am very sorry if he wanted any of it. Had I known, I would have had Henry put it in boxes and bring it round here for Mr Steeple to sort through.' Then before Mrs Steeple could reply to this admittedly rather provocative speech, she said quickly, 'I shall need to purchase new equipment immediately. I wonder, might I speak to the vicar about getting it from Bedford?'

Mrs Steeple shook her head, and Flavia could not decide whether she looked regretful or pleased. 'I am afraid the vicar cannot be disturbed today,' she said. 'He always writes his sermon on Saturdays.'

'Then perhaps *you* could help me,' Flavia suggested. Mrs Steeple looked very doubtful as to whether she could do anything of the sort. Nevertheless Flavia went on, 'I shall need to go into Bedford on Monday in order to purchase, or at least order, new equipment, and I was wondering whether I might borrow the pony and trap for that purpose?'

'Oh I'm not sure,' replied the vicar's wife.

'I do know how to drive if that is what concerns you,' Flavia said. 'My father taught me when I was thirteen.'

'Did he? How interesting,' answered the other, somehow managing to make the word 'interesting' sound as if it meant 'unladylike and inappropriate'. 'I'm afraid that I don't know whether Brian will want it himself,' she concluded.

'Could you possibly ask him?' said Flavia, hoping that her voice did not reveal how close she was to losing her patience completely.

'No, I'm afraid not. Not whilst he is writing his sermon, and he will be doing that in his study for most of the day. Perhaps you could ask him tomorrow after the service?'

'Very well,' responded Flavia. She would have liked to leave immediately, so annoyed was she by Mrs Steeple's unhelpful attitude, but there was her tea still to be drunk. In any case, it was very early days in her time here to be making an enemy of the vicar's wife. She therefore settled back in her chair, ready to take part in whatever topic of conversation her hostess might choose.

'I understand that Mr Wheaton has called upon you,' Mrs Steeple said.

'Yes, he came yesterday,' Flavia replied. 'He seems to be very pleasant.'

'I believe that he actually came into the school,' Mrs Steeple continued.

'He did,' agreed Flavia. 'And I was very glad that he did so. He offered me some much needed assistance with cleaning and tidying the school, and sent round two men and two women who helped me considerably. I doubt if the task would have been accomplished without them.'

'Might I counsel you to exercise a little caution there?' said the other. 'Such an action might easily be misconstrued.'

'Misconstrued? In what way?' asked Flavia, honestly puzzled.

Mrs Steeple coloured. 'I thought it had been made plain to you that the last teacher, Miss Price, had behaved disgracefully. It would not do for anyone to suppose that you were going to do the same. Perhaps you have not understood perfectly, Miss Montague, what qualities are required of a village schoolmistress. It would be a pity if you had given up a perfectly good appointment in Bath before you were certain that this job was for you.'

At this point, Flavia very nearly wavered in her resolve to remain on good terms with the vicar's wife. Again, she counted to five in her head before speaking. 'Mr Wheaton was simply being a good neighbour,' she said eventually, as calmly as she was able, 'and he offered me help when I was very much in need of it. There is no more to be said on the matter.'

Mrs Steeple looked as if she might have liked to add a good deal more, but Flavia must have appeared rather formidable, so instead she simply said, in rather nervous tones, 'I will pass on your message about the pony and trap to my husband when he emerges.'

After having said all that was polite, Flavia returned to her cottage, but resolved to have as little to do with Mrs Steeple as possible. She was clearly not very similar to her sister Pamela in character, and had she been the younger of the two it seemed unlikely that she and Flavia would ever have struck up a friendship. As for the suggestion that she, Flavia, might go back to Bath, it was hard to know what to make of it. Had there been any other candidates in view, Flavia might almost have suspected Mrs Steeple of favouring the other applicant over herself.

Feeling rather restless and somewhat stifled

after this conversation, she decided to walk back to her cottage by a longer way. In fact, it was possible to travel to the vicarage from the school and back using any of three different routes. The shortest, as she had already discovered, was through the churchyard, entering by one gate, walking up the path and around the church, then out of another gate which opened at the top of the vicarage drive. It was possible, however, to walk round the outside wall of the churchyard in either direction. The rougher path of the two led from the back of the school, and over a little bridge and beside one of the brooks from which the village got its name. Later on, it was necessary to cross the brook again, and then walk all the way around the vicarage to the front, unless one was a member of that privileged group permitted to enter the vicar's residence by the back door.

The other route led across the school yard and then into the main village street, which, for the length of the churchyard wall, had houses only on the other side of the road. The houses nearer the church tended to be those of the better sort, one being occupied by the doctor and another by a genteel spinster of uncertain age and limited means. A little further down the street, beyond the vicarage, there were houses on either side, and at the very end of the street was the village inn, The Kings Head. The sign outside depicted a be-wigged Charles II, who gazed benignly across at the village pond upon which a number of ducks were usually to be found.

On this occasion, Flavia decided against walking through the village. It was one thing for Mrs Steeple to see her when she was not looking her neatest. After all, Mrs Steeple had met her before, and knew how she had been spending her morning. But she was anxious that she should give a good impression to the village inhabitants when she made her first public appearance. Turning left out of the vicarage gates, therefore, she walked around the perimeter wall of the garden and back to the school by the rough path, lingering a little beside the brook as she went.

Two things occurred to her as she was walking back. The first was that someone must have observed her meeting with Paul Wheaton and had passed that information on to Mrs Steeple. She was not at all ashamed of her encounter with the local landowner, and fully intended all her behaviour to be capable of public scrutiny. But she had forgotten the fact that in such a small community, everyone would know everyone else's business. It was a side of village life that she was not sure she liked.

The other thing that came to her mind was that she had now been warned about two men. Mr Wheaton had warned her about Sir Lewis Glendenning; now Mrs Steeple had warned her against having too much to do with Mr Wheaton. Could it be the case that Mr Wheaton had blackened the other man's name just for his own ends? Suddenly realizing what she was doing, she smiled to herself. Only a short time ago she had condemned village gossips. Now, she was speculating about others in exactly the same kind of way.

Although she had worked hard that day, Flavia felt a certain reluctance to retire that night, so she sent Grace off to bed, telling her that she would look after herself, and then stayed up for a while. The teacher's house had a small, enclosed garden, in which there were a few flower beds, one or two shrubs in pots and a rather handsome climbing rose which had been trained to cover the arch into which the back gate was set. There was also a wooden bench set against one of the walls, and it was to this bench that Flavia went in order to enjoy the one cigar which she had now decided to permit herself each evening.

It was a habit which she had acquired on one of the rare occasions when she had gone to sea. She had once travelled briefly with the eccentric sister of an older sea captain, in order to bear her company. This lady, born and brought up in Jamaica, had acquired the habit of smoking, and had introduced Flavia to it. Flavia's father had never known about this little eccentricity, and at Miss Bredale's she had seldom had the opportunity to indulge it. Now, she sighed with contentment as she blew the smoke into the air; and for a time she sat there, enjoying the peace of the summer evening. This was yet another reason for her to be glad that she had her own establishment, she decided, when her cigar was almost finished. A sound of hoofbeats aroused her from her reverie, and hastily, she put out the cigar and hurried indoors. It would never do to be caught indulging in that habit!

Once inside, she paused and looked around her. The luxury of being able to be in her own sitting-room without having to make conversation with anyone was still sufficiently novel for it to be relished. At Miss Bredale's academy there had been a teachers' sitting-room, in which all the staff had tended to gather at leisure times. When Flavia had first arrived at the school, there had been one teacher who could never admit that she was wrong. Her manner of imparting information to her pupils was dogmatic in the extreme, and her approach towards other members of staff was similarly self-consequential. Flavia had found her to be so tiresome that sometimes, rather than put up with her conversation, she had retired to bed early. With these thoughts in mind, it was delightful to be able to select a book and look at it without anyone asking what she was reading, or expressing an opinion upon it.

She picked up the three books that she had rescued from the schoolroom cupboard, and sat down to look at them. One was a book of sermons, and another was a rather old manual of etiquette for young gentlemen, with careful instructions as to how to stand elegantly whilst wearing a sword, and how to retire from a room in good order when there was more than one lady present. Both of these volumes seemed to her to have very limited application in her present situation.

The third was a book of poetry by William Cowper, and appeared to be quite new. Thinking that it might have been left there by mistake, she looked inside the front cover and found written there: *For Sylvia, loveliest of teachers, from your adoring L.*

'Sylvia'; could that have been Miss Price's name? Of course, Miss Price had not been there long, and before that, the teacher had been Miss Gordon. It would be interesting to discover which, if either of them, had the Christian name Sylvia. If the book belonged to Miss Price, then perhaps her husband-to-be had given it to her. But what if her husband's name did not begin with L? Could the book have been given to her by Sir Lewis Glendenning, and was there any way that she could find out? Chiding herself for vulgar curiosity, she shook off these thoughts and settled down to read until she felt tired enough to sleep.

The following day, Flavia attended church with Grace, and was conscious of many curious eyes upon her. Paul Wheaton came in alone when it was almost time for the service, and took his place in the pew reserved for his family. The pew which was level with his remained empty, and Flavia decided that this was probably Sir Lewis Glendenning's. If so, then either he was away from home, or he did not attend.

Mr Steeple preached adequately, but Flavia could not help thinking that given that he had taken the best part of Saturday to write his sermon, he really ought to have come up with something more effective.

After the service, Mrs Steeple approached Flavia and both ladies, conscious of the not entirely cordial nature of their last exchange, made a special effort to be friendly.

'The vicar is very happy for you to borrow the pony and trap tomorrow afternoon,' said his wife. 'When you come to collect it, he will discuss with you the nature of the supplies needed.'

As they were talking, Mr Wheaton approached them, touching his hat. 'A fine day, ladies,' he said, to which they both agreed. He turned to Mrs Steeple. 'Your husband must be very pleased to have found a teacher at last.'

'I believe so,' replied that lady. 'It is to be hoped that Miss Montague will prove to be suitable.'

'I'm sure she will,' he said smiling warmly. Then, turning to Flavia, he added 'I trust that all will go well for tomorrow.' He touched his hat again, then turned away to speak to another lady and gentleman. Flavia was pleased that he had spoken but, in view of all that had been said the previous day, she was glad that he had not singled her out for any special attention. Such an attitude on his part might easily link her in people's minds with the last schoolmistress whose misdemeanours had obviously made her the talk of the neighbourhood.

5

The following day, Flavia woke up feeling very excited and at first she could not think why. Then she remembered that it was today that her school would really begin. She had always enjoyed teaching, and at the end of every holiday from Miss Bredale's had looked forward to the return of the girls, and the chance to impart more knowledge. But never before had she been conscious of such a keen sense of anticipation as she felt today. Perhaps, she mused as she washed and dressed, it was because this was her very own school where she would employ her own methods and ideas. Perhaps she would fail: then so be it. At least she would have had a chance to try. But deep down in her heart, she was convinced that she would not fail. Her enthusiasm could not help but communicate itself to her pupils.

She hesitated for a moment on the stairs as she recalled that she had virtually no equipment with which to work. But then she continued down briskly as she thought about how she would proceed. She need not keep them for long, she decided. She would compile a register with their names and ages; she would also try to find out if any of them had been to the school before and if they remembered anything that they had learned. Then perhaps they might learn a song or a poem or say the alphabet together. That would be quite enough for the first day. After that, she would spend the afternoon seeking out and buying or ordering supplies for the school.

When she got downstairs, a pleasing savoury aroma told her that Jane was cooking bacon for her breakfast. Breakfast seemed to Flavia to be one of the most enjoyable meals of the day, and without a good start to the morning, she always felt slow and sluggish. Jane had therefore been carefully instructed to make sure that breakfast was always tasty and filling. It was as she was finishing her breakfast that a sudden thought occurred to her.

She called Jane through to thank her for her efforts, and the pleasantly plump, fair-haired countrywoman came in, smiling and smoothing down her apron.

'You seem to have mastered the kitchen very quickly,' Flavia added when she had thanked her.

'Oh, well, that's on account of my knowing it already,' Jane volunteered. 'I was here cooking for Miss Price *and* for Miss Gordon before her; not that Miss Price stayed for long, of course.'

'No, I've heard it said that she left after a short time,' remarked Flavia, in a carefully casual tone. She had suspected from the ease with which Jane and Henry had settled in that they had worked in the schoolteacher's cottage before. 'For how long was she here?'

'Only for a few months, miss. A very pleasant lady, she was; very pretty and well-spoken, but not really suitable for a teacher, if you know what I mean.'

'No, do explain,' prompted Flavia.

'Well, she wasn't strong; I mean, not a strong-minded person. She was a bit, well, fluttery like.'

Flavia longed to ask more, but reflected that she did not want to earn a reputation as a gossip. So, conscious that she had a good reason for asking at least a few of her questions, she said, 'I have found a book, nearly new, which I think may have belonged to a previous teacher, and the dedication inside indicates that it is a personal possession which ought to be returned. Can you tell me, I wonder, if either Miss Price or Miss Gordon had the Christian name of Sylvia?'

'Oh, that must be Miss Price's,' said Jane.

'Miss Gordon's name was Margaret. Will that be all, miss?'

'I don't suppose you know the name of the gentleman she married?' asked Flavia hopefully. 'Her maiden name will not find her now.'

'No, I don't, miss,' answered Jane. 'He wasn't from around here. I think he was a French gentleman.'

Well that answered one question, reflected Flavia as she went into the school to unlock. The book belonged to Miss Price. But only half of the mystery was solved, for the name of the donor remained unknown. A perfectly simple explanation did occur to her. She could always ask Sir Lewis, when she knew him well enough, if he had given the previous schoolmistress a book. The only problem with that solution was that it would very likely resurrect the scandal that everyone seemed anxious to bury. Furthermore, if he had been rejected in favour of another suitor, he might not relish the idea of talking about the lady who had let him down. She would just have to wait and see if any other ideas occurred to her. If Miss Price — as she must still call her, for she did not know her married name — had managed without the book for so long, then she could surely manage without it for a little while longer.

As nine o'clock drew near, she became conscious of some noise outside, and on opening the door, she was pleased to see that there were about twenty-five children, all running about, laughing and shouting.

She then became aware of another dilemma. There was no bell for her to ring in order to attract their attention. She now recalled that amongst the contents of the cupboard there had not even been a cracked or broken one. Clearly this was another purchase which would have to be made. In the meantime, however, she would have to resort to other methods. Smiling to herself, she recalled a boyish trick that she had been taught by one of her father's junior officers, much to her aunt's disgust. Putting her fingers to her lips, she blew through them, making a piercing whistle which stopped every child in its tracks.

'I want two lines by the door, one of boys and one of girls, in order of height,' she said firmly. She smiled to herself again as they complied meekly. Heaven only knew what Miss Bredale would have said had she witnessed that display. Flavia was never to know how much that whistle had impressed her new pupils from the very start. In discussing the day later, several of them agreed that a teacher capable of that must surely be capable of anything!

She counted them as they walked in. There were nearly thirty children, sixteen girls and thirteen boys, and the age range which they represented was quite large. She estimated that the oldest present, a girl, was probably thirteen, whereas the youngest was another girl of about six. The key factor would be how much they knew already. As they progressed, the older ones would have to help the younger ones.

She told the boys to be seated on one side and the girls on the other, but apart from that, she allowed them to sit very largely where they wanted for the time being. She could sort them out later when she had discovered how much they knew.

She had just written the first child's name down in the register, when the door opened tentatively and a thin, anxious-looking girl came in, holding a small boy of about seven by the hand.

'Please, I am sorry we are late,' said the girl in a cultured voice. 'But we would very much like to attend your school.'

Looking at them carefully, Flavia could see that, like most of the other children who were present, they were spotlessly clean, but, unlike the others, they were well, even expensively dressed. 'Yes, of course you may join us,' replied Flavia, smiling. 'Girls sit over there, and boys over here.'

'If you please, miss, may Philip sit next to me?' the girl asked. 'I don't think he will want to stay if he cannot do so.'

Flavia thought for a moment. She wanted to maintain her own standard, but at the same time, she did not want to lose two pupils, for she had a feeling that if the boy did not stay, the girl would go too. 'Sit in the middle,' she said at last. The girl led Philip to a place on one of the middle benches, and made sure that he was seated on the boys' side.

All the children gave their names in a soft country burr, but when it came to the turn of the latecomers, the girl said politely, 'My name is Penelope Lynton and this is Philip.'

'Can he not speak for himself?' Flavia asked her gently.

She was a little shocked when the girl said 'No, he never does so.'

Flavia was mystified. They were plainly from a genteel enough family for a governess to be teaching them privately. Why, then, were they attending a village school? Of course, she had not been in the village for many days, but Lynton was not a name that she had heard mentioned by anyone. She said no more at that stage, but resolved to speak to the two of them after school was over, and try to find out more about them.

On this occasion, however, her purpose was frustrated. After she had done all that she felt she could do, given her limited resources, she dismissed the children, and fully intended to catch Penelope and Philip before they left. Before she could do so, however, one of the other members of the class, a ten-year-old boy came up to her.

'Are you staying, miss?' he asked her.

'Certainly,' she replied. 'Why do you ask?'

'Miss Price didn't.' Miss Price again! Flavia wondered what some of the children might be able to tell her about the infamous Miss Price. Such a pity that it would be entirely unethical to ask them!

'Well, I certainly intend to stay,' she said firmly. The boy looked pleased and ran off, and smiling, she watched him go. Then suddenly, she remembered that she had intended to speak to Penelope and Philip. Of course, they had gone. Never mind, she told herself. She would speak to them another day. There was no rush. She could always ask the vicar about them when she collected the pony and trap.

'Lynton,' he said, wrinkling his brow as he escorted her round to the stables. 'No, that name does not mean anything to me, I'm

65

afraid. A well-bred family, you say? I will try to make enquiries. Now, about these supplies that you need. My wife tells me that you burned the contents of the cupboard, Miss Montague.' He sounded disapproving.

'That is what one does with rubbish,' replied Flavia pleasantly. 'Did you look inside the cupboard in the schoolroom, Mr Steeple?'

'Why no,' he admitted. 'But there must surely have been something useful in there?'

'Certainly,' Flavia agreed with a smile, but with a note of steel in her voice. 'There was some excellent kindling and paper for lighting fires, but very little else, I assure you.'

'Miss Montague, to be plain with you, I should have valued the chance to inspect it for myself.'

Flavia decided that by the time she had finished dealing with the vicar and his wife, she would not only have mastered her temper, but would also have mastered counting from one to five in order to keep it in check! Of course she did not want to antagonize Mr Steeple, for after all, it was he who had decided that she should have this post. But she had no patience with the kind of attitude that gave a person responsibility then prevented them from exercising it.

'I am very sorry if you think that I acted too hastily,' she said placatingly, 'but knowing how keen you were to get the school started, I thought that you would rather I got on as quickly as possible. And besides, I felt certain that you would be far too busy to go through the contents of the cupboard when you had surely employed me to perform that task.'

'Well, there is that,' replied the vicar, slightly mollified. 'What were you thinking of purchasing today? I cannot let you have a very large sum of money, I'm afraid.'

Flavia told him what her chief requirements were, and he handed over a very modest sized purse. 'You can bring me any change when you return the pony and trap,' he said. Flavia smiled. She suspected that it would be far more likely that she would have to add money of her own in order to purchase what she needed.

She was about to drive away when Mr Steeple said to her, 'There is one thing about which I think I should perhaps warn you.'

'Warn me?' queried Flavia, wondering if he was going to tell her about the existence of highwaymen in the locality.

'Sir Lewis Glendenning has returned,' he said. 'Mr Wheaton told me this morning.' He paused for a moment. 'It was also he who suggested that you should be informed. Sir Lewis is a . . . a man of uncertain temper. You would be wise to avoid him, particularly until your position is established.'

'So I have already heard,' she replied. 'But thank you for the warning.' After this exchange, she set off for Bedford, and in the excitement of the outing, she put Sir Lewis Glendenning out of her mind.

6

The drive to Bedford took her down some very pretty lanes with overhanging trees covered with blossom, and greenery of every possible shade, and she enjoyed the freedom of driving herself in the gig. This kind of outing had been unheard of in Bath, and she relished the independence that resulted from running her own school in a place where she was less governed by society's rules. Having driven for some years she was very confident with the reins and she would have relished a more lively animal than Dobbin between the shafts. This was a very minor consideration, however, when set against the pleasure of driving again.

Unfortunately, although the drive itself was enjoyable, the visit was not as productive as she might have wished. It proved to be impossible to procure everything that she needed during the one visit to Bedford. Paper and books were easily obtained, but paper was expensive, and she had no intention of using it for anything but the very best work. She had been obliged to order slates, but at least she had been able to purchase chalk for her own use on the blackboard. Before she left, she made arrangements for the slates to be delivered by carrier's cart, which she was assured would happen the following week.

It was not until she was halfway back from Bedford that it occurred to her that before purchasing anything at all, it might have been wise to communicate with Miss Bredale and ask for the name of her supplier. Miss Bredale was quite an astute businesswoman, and had been known to drive a very hard bargain when it came to obtaining equipment for her school. The thought was an infuriating one, especially now that she had ordered what she needed, and would make herself look very foolish if she decided to cancel.

'Bother!' she exclaimed out loud, and dropped her hands. Dobbin, the days of his vigorous youth suddenly and unaccountably returning to him, leaped forward and at the same moment, a horseman came around the next bend at speed, and only just managed to avoid an accident by superb horsemanship.

'Damnation, woman, what are you about?' he exclaimed angrily, whilst he was still settling his mount. He glared down at her, his furious expression accentuated by the livid scar that ran from his temple to the corner of his mouth.

'What am I about?' she replied, bringing

70

Dobbin back under control with ease. 'I was not the one negotiating that bend far too fast!'

'And I was not the one who had dropped my hands in order to coax a greater speed out of that miserable animal.'

'Dobbin is *not* a miserable animal!' she declared indignantly, quite forgetting that only a short time before she had been thinking much the same thing.

'Is that Parson Steeple's horse?' the man asked suddenly, narrowing his eyes. Her astonished expression gave him his answer. 'I assume you must have borrowed it,' he went on. 'Only a completely deranged person would think of stealing it.'

'Are you accusing me of being deranged?' she demanded, too angry at the whole encounter to take in his words properly.

'Why? *Have* you stolen it?' His tone had become sardonic rather than angry.

'No I have not! How dare you even suggest it.'

'If you will only remember accurately what I said, you'll know that I suggested no such thing,' he replied. 'But perhaps Parson Steeple should be told to have a greater care with regard to whom he gives permission to borrow his horse and trap.' Then, with no further acknowledgement and before she could make any response, he wheeled round and rode on his way.

'Detestable man!' Flavia declared. 'Quite detestable!' It was some minutes before she felt sufficiently composed to drive on. It was a mercy that she had not managed to obtain any slates, she thought wryly to herself, as she arrived back at Brooks. Had she been carrying them in the back, then the sudden jolt occasioned by the encounter with the unknown horseman would undoubtedly have broken some, and she might have been very little better off than she had been when she had set out.

On her arrival back at the school, she unloaded her purchases from the trap and put them on her desk, then took the pony and trap back to the vicarage. There was no sign of the vicar or his wife, so she left them with the groom with a word of thanks, resolving to go back and thank Mr Steeple in person at a later time.

That done, she walked back to the school and opening the cupboard, began to put her purchases away. Yes, it was true that she had not been able to obtain all the things that she needed, but she had made a start, and now at least she had something to work with.

Because she was happy at seeing the cupboard now containing useful things, as opposed to rubbish, she began to whistle. Again, it was a habit that her aunt had deplored, and she had naturally had to keep it a secret when she was at Miss Bredale's academy. But these days, she did not have to refer either to her aunt, or to Miss Bredale. She chirruped her way through a melody by Mozart, and was not aware that she was no longer alone until, as she was stacking books tidily on the shelf, she sensed rather than saw a shadow fall across her, and heard the sound of a voice speaking from immediately behind her.

'Good day to ye . . . schoolmarm,' it said. The tone was sneering, rather than angry, but the voice was unmistakable, and with a sinking heart, Flavia recognized it as being that of the man whom she had encountered on her journey home. She remembered some of the things that she had been told about someone who lived in the neighbourhood and whom she had not yet met, and suddenly, there were no doubts at all in her mind as to who this might be.

'Good day . . . Sir Lewis,' she said calmly, leaving precisely the same insolent gap in her words as had he, before turning to face him.

He was standing in the doorway, his hands resting on the frame on either side. It would be quite impossible for her to leave the cupboard without an undignified tussle unless he chose to allow her to do so. The sneer in his voice was reflected on his face, and his tawny brown hair fell loosely to his shoulders, with one lock flopping over on to his brow. On horseback, he had appeared to be a tall man. Now that he was standing level with her, she could see that he was broad, and taller than she was by about a foot. One more fact became clear to her, namely that he had been drinking.

'You have guessed my identity, then,' he said.

'I have,' she replied, turning her back on him once more. Her present vulnerable position favoured him. Obviously he wanted to intimidate her, and the rapid beating of her heart told her that he was succeeding, but she was determined that he should not know it. She played for time by tidying the things on the shelf.

'Clearly, my reputation went before me,' he remarked.

'It did,' she agreed, turning towards him once more. 'Sir Lewis, will you please step aside so that I may come out of the cupboard?'

He did not move. Instead, he bent down a little, and said, 'Find me hideous, do you?'

She stared at him. 'Not particularly,' she replied truthfully.

'You lie,' he retorted, his eyes glittering. 'I can see disgust in your very stance.'

'You might well,' Flavia replied. 'You are possibly the rudest man that I have ever met, and furthermore I dislike the smell of spirits on a man's breath. Now will you allow me to leave my cupboard?'

He paused for just a moment, then stepped back and made her an elaborate bow. Quickly, before he could change his mind, she emerged from the cupboard and dropped him the smallest of curtsies, before walking back to her desk.

'You're a damnably annoying woman; did you know that?' he asked her. Out of the corner of her eye, she observed him follow her, and noticed that he walked with a slight limp.

'I would be interested to know in what way I have managed to annoy you, considering that I met you for the first time today,' she said calmly. There were a few items on her desk still to be put away, but she had no intention of returning to the cupboard until she was sure that he had gone.

He picked up his riding crop, which he had laid upon one of the front desks. 'Firstly, the fact that you have re-opened the school at all is an annoyance to me,' he replied. 'Secondly — '

'Wait a minute,' she interrupted. 'Why should my opening the school be an annoyance to you?'

'Because it makes my people dissatisfied with their lot and breeds discontent amongst them,' he retorted. 'The ones who attend it think that they're entitled to something better, and they want to come here so they are tempted to skimp their work. The ones who can't come resent those who do, or pour scorn on them for wasting their time.'

'Or perhaps they are jealous because they wish they could learn,' put in Flavia swiftly.

'You prove my point, schoolmarm,' he replied. 'If some are jealous of others, then that will be just another cause of resentment that will build up between those who go to school and those who do not. And when you leave, as no doubt you will when the weather gets cold and the room is filled with the smell of wet children and mud gets trod all through the place, they will be disappointed.'

'And what makes you think that I will leave?' she asked him.

'Previous experience,' he said briefly. 'What good do you think it'll do, anyway? None of them has any books to read in order to exercise this new skill.'

'Well of course they haven't,' replied Flavia scornfully. 'What would be the point of having a book if you couldn't read it?'

'You're wasting their time, you're wasting mine, and you're wasting your own,' Sir Lewis said forcefully. 'And the other reason why you annoy me is because you damn near made me fall off my horse today.'

'That was entirely your own fault,' replied Flavia. 'You were going much too fast.'

'At least I know how to ride,' he responded provocatively.

'Meaning, that I do not know how to drive?' she challenged him.

'If the cap fits, then who am I to prevent your wearing it?'

Choosing not to respond to this, she said instead, 'I can see how you might believe that I am wasting my own time and that of my pupils — although I think that you are mistaken in that view — but I would very much like to know how you have managed to conclude that *your* time is being wasted.'

'It's being wasted now,' he declared, 'having this very stupid conversation.'

'Well, you can end it by going away if you like,' said Flavia bluntly. 'You will find the door behind you.'

Sir Lewis did indeed move, but it was towards her and not towards the door. He

77

retrieved his crop and stepped up on to the dais on which she was standing, and she realized afresh that he was much taller and more powerful than she was. In his eye there was a malicious gleam, rendered even more diabolical by the scar on his face. 'I'll go when I'm ready,' he told her. 'Devil take me, but you take a mighty high tone for a village schoolmistress, especially when your position has not yet been confirmed. In my opinion, it's high time someone taught you a lesson.' So saying, he slapped his riding crop against his boot in an ominous way.

Flavia stood firm, resolved not to move by so much as an inch. 'Am I to understand that you are to be the one to do so — with that?' she demanded, determined not to be intimidated by him. 'I am impressed by your effrontery, sir — but not by your courage.'

'With this?' he said scornfully, dropping the riding crop again, this time on the floor. 'There are other ways of schooling head-strong women!' So saying, he pulled her against him, and, to her amazement, for such a thing had never happened before, bent his head as if he were intending to kiss her! But before he could do so, had such been his intention, the schoolroom door opened, the baronet stepped back hastily and they both turned their heads to see Paul Wheaton standing on the threshold.

'Good afternoon, Miss Montague — Lewis,' he said politely. 'Miss Montague — is there any way in which I may serve you?' From his expression, it seemed possible that he had seen her in the baronet's arms, and Flavia could have screamed with vexation.

'There, schoolmarm,' said Sir Lewis turning back to her, his expression as malicious as ever. 'Are you quite recovered, now? You must not step back so hastily. I was afraid that you were about to tumble off the dais.'

The two men were very much of a height. Sir Lewis was perhaps a little broader, but Flavia surmised that Mr Wheaton was the younger, possibly by as much as ten years. She glanced from one to the other. It seemed probable that if she disclosed what had really happened and asked Mr Wheaton to throw the baronet out, then he would be able to do it, not least because the older man was somewhat the worse for drink. But if she made such a disclosure, there was always the possibility that Mr Wheaton might suppose that she had done something to make the baronet take her in his arms. After all, she would not be the first schoolmistress in the village to be involved in scandal! Like it or not, she would have to go along with Sir Lewis's story.

'Thank you, Sir Lewis,' she replied, through clenched teeth. 'The edge must have been closer than I thought.' She turned to Mr Wheaton. 'I am very fortunate indeed today. I have been . . . saved from a fall by Sir Lewis and now you have offered to help me also. I believe my tasks are now done, however, and must ask you both to leave me so that I may lock up the school and return to the cottage.'

The baronet stared at her from under his brows. His eyes still gleamed, but the malice had now gone, leaving pure amusement. 'It was my pleasure, ma'am,' he murmured. 'Pray let me know if I may be of service again — perhaps in a similar way.' So saying, he sketched a bow and left.

'He *saved* you?' asked Wheaton incredulously, after Sir Lewis had gone. His tone could not have been more surprised if Flavia had announced that the other man had been teaching in the school.

'Certainly,' answered Flavia calmly, as she picked up the rest of the things in order to put them in the cupboard. Mr Wheaton, she was certain, would not attempt to imprison her in there as Sir Lewis had done. 'He came while I was putting the things away,' she went on. That statement was true enough, she reflected.

'Well I must say, you do surprise me,' Mr

Wheaton said frankly. 'Miss Montague, you will have a care, won't you? He's not the easiest of men to deal with.'

'Yes, so I've been told more than once,' replied Flavia, as she emerged from the cupboard. 'In fact, that's practically the only thing that I *have* been told about him. Is there nothing more to tell?'

She had intended the remark half-humorously, but Wheaton did not smile. 'Well, he has an idiot son,' he said, after a moment's thought.

'That, too, I have heard,' she replied. They were both silent for a few moments.

'Let us turn to more pleasant matters,' Mr Wheaton said at last, his brow clearing. 'My sister is arriving tomorrow. May I bring her to the school to meet you?'

'Yes, of course, I would be most happy,' replied Flavia, hoping that this visit would not mean an interruption to lessons that had only just begun.

'And I wanted to confirm with you that you will dine with us on Saturday. Just a small family gathering you know — perhaps Steeple and his wife and one or two others.'

'Thank you. You are very kind,' answered Flavia.

He smiled warmly. 'I have written to tell my sister how charming you are,' he murmured. 'I don't think she believes me.' He had taken her hand; now, he half raised it to his lips, but seeing how grubby it was, he contented himself with squeezing it gently before releasing it. Then bowing politely, he left.

She watched him leave in some confusion. The afternoon had seen several unprecedented occurrences; so many, in fact, that she was very glad that she had not had prior warning of any of them. First of all, she had been shouted at by a baronet, then trapped in a cupboard and almost kissed by the same man.

She had never been kissed by a man other than her father. When teaching at Miss Bredale's academy, she was very well aware that some of the girls, among them the notorious Mary Steeple, had allowed men to behave towards them with too much familiarity. No doubt they would have been quite scornful of their teacher, who had never experienced a man's embrace. For her part, Flavia had been faintly contemptuous of those who were prepared to grant such favours so easily. Today, however, she was conscious of a novel idea which had affected her mind, and subtly changed her attitude. She had not enjoyed being seized and manhandled in such a way, but oddly enough, neither had she been afraid. She blushed as she realized that what she chiefly felt now was curiosity. What would it have been like, to have had the baronet's lips pressed to hers?

She shook herself abruptly, and forced herself to recall that that had not been the only unusual experience that day. After all, she had later been treated by a handsome landowner as if she were a blushing debutante. Village life was turning out to hold quite a few surprises. She wondered whether she would be able to cope with them all.

She thought about the forthcoming dinner at Mr Wheaton's house. She knew that she did not shine at social occasions, and had hoped that he had forgotten the matter. Never mind. It would soon be over, and at least there was one thing to be thankful for; living in the teacher's cottage, she would never be expected to reciprocate.

7

In the event, Mr Wheaton's sister did not visit the school before the Saturday of the dinner party. Her brother sent apologies on her behalf. She begged to be excused, but she was tired from the journey and she needed to rest. She had travelled down from Harrogate where she had been visiting an aunt, and had most unfortunately succumbed to a chill. She looked forward very much to meeting Miss Montague on Saturday at dinner, and she would give herself the pleasure of visiting the school at a later date.

These kind words filled Flavia with misgivings. She would naturally be grateful for any kind attention, since it clearly indicated local support, but she hoped that too much would not be expected of her. She had heard very little talk of other young ladies in the neighbourhood, and she feared that Mr Wheaton's sister might want to take her up and make a kind of companion of her. This was no doubt flattering up to a point. If, however, the young lady wanted someone with whom she could exchange frequent visits and go shopping every week, then she would be sadly disappointed. It was to escape precisely that kind of tedious social round that Flavia had come to be a village schoolmistress, rather than take her place in society, as she could so easily have done. She would just have to hope that when it was revealed what unpromising material she was, the lady would transfer her attentions elsewhere.

She might have known that she would not be able to escape the social round completely. On the Thursday morning, a servant from the vicarage came to the cottage with a note for her from Mrs Steeple. In this note, the vicar's wife advised her that some young ladies would be taking tea at the vicarage that afternoon, and that Flavia was invited to attend.

She put the note down with a little sigh. She would have given a great deal to be able to refuse, but she knew that it would not be wise, certainly until she was established in the neighbourhood. In any case, she did not have the excuse of afternoon school to attend to, for she had decided not to keep the children on after midday, certainly until the slates had been delivered.

Needless to say, Grace was very pleased about the invitation to tea and the forthcoming dinner at Wheaton House, although only those who were well acquainted with her would have known it. 'It's taking your place in society just as you should,' she said, determinedly arranging her mistress's hair in a slightly looser and more becoming manner than usual.

'Well we don't feel the same way about that and never shall, so I shan't argue,' replied Flavia. 'But I'll be glad to be home again.'

'You ought to be going in a carriage,' said Grace, as Flavia left the cottage.

Flavia burst out laughing. 'A carriage? From here to the vicarage? I would take as long climbing into it as I would travelling from here to there!'

When Flavia arrived at the vicarage, entering by the front gate in deference to the importance of the occasion, there was indeed a very pretty equipage outside, and it was obvious that the occupants had only just gone into the house. Once Flavia was in the drawing-room, Mrs Steeple begged leave to present her to Mrs Bell and her two daughters, Lucy and Evelina. 'Mr and Mrs Bell live in Stagsden, which is a village not far from here,' explained Mrs Steeple. Lucy, who was the elder, was tall and slender with a fine head of golden hair and blue eyes. Her sister was a little shorter, and not quite so conventionally attractive, but they could both be called very pretty women without any fear of contradiction.

'I am sure you will think it vastly amusing, Miss Montague,' tittered Mrs Bell, 'but our name has given rise to a number of witty comments, especially in recent years. Probably, with your high standard of education, you will be able to guess what they may be!'

'Something about striking the right note?' hazarded Flavia.

Mrs Bell looked blankly at her. 'Why no,' she replied in puzzled tones. 'Why should you suppose that it would be that? It is the girls, you see. They are called the Stagsden Belles, you know. 'Belle' with an 'e' on the end. It is not how our name is spelled, of course, but the girls are so pretty! I forget who it was who first said it. Do you remember, Mrs Steeple?'

'Do I remember what, ma'am?' asked her hostess, who had been distracted by the maid coming in with the tea tray.

'Do you remember who first called our girls the Stagsden Belles? It was so amusing at the time, and I have thought so ever since.'

'No, I am afraid I do not,' replied Mrs Steeple. 'Will you take tea, Mrs Bell?'

'Yes, thank you. Oh, I do wish I could remember, but it has quite gone out of my mind. Lucy, Evelina, do you remember who first called you the Stagsden Belles?'

'No, Mama,' they replied in chorus, looking a little sulky, and Flavia wondered, with a sudden rush of sympathy, how many times they had had to sit through this performance.

'Well, it is very vexing not to be able to remember. I wonder if your Papa might do so? We must ask him as soon as we get home.'

'Have you always lived in Stagsden, ma'am?' asked Flavia, guessing that this topic would not easily be laid to rest unless she deliberately found another.

'No, I am from another county, but my husband's family have lived there for several generations. I understand, Miss Montague, that you are from Bath.'

'That is correct,' answered Flavia.

'It is surely quite unusual to find a lady as educated as yourself taking up the post of village schoolmistress,' remarked Mrs Bell.

'My appointment is of very recent date,' Flavia replied. 'Before that, I was teaching at Miss Bredale's academy.'

'Miss Bredale's academy? In Queen's Square?' queried Mrs Bell, a new respect in her tone. 'Was that not the seminary which Mary attended, Mrs Steeple?'

'It was,' agreed Mrs Steeple shortly, as well she might, Flavia reflected, remembering Mary's behaviour.

'And what caused you to make the

change?' asked Mrs Bell.

'Simply a longing to do something different in different surroundings,' answered Flavia. At this moment, a flutter was created in Mrs Steeple's prim drawing-room by the entrance of Mr Wheaton. He was dressed in a blue coat with buff breeches and highly polished boots, and he had never appeared more handsome. The effect upon the two young ladies was instantaneous. From resembling slightly wilting blossoms, they now seemed much more like plants half an hour after a much needed watering, and their expressions as they looked up at him were unashamedly admiring. Mr Wheaton made his bow with all the elegance at his command, accepted Mrs Steeple's offer of tea, and took a seat close to the young ladies, who now exerted every effort to please. Mrs Bell looked at them fondly.

'There, you see, Miss Montague,' she said, in a very audible whisper. 'Now you see why they are called the Stagsden Belles, do you not? There is not a young lady anywhere around to touch them for beauty, or even for accomplishments!'

'How interesting,' murmured Flavia, reflecting that it was a good thing that she was not vain, or she might have taken Mrs Bell's remarks somewhat amiss. 'Perhaps, as they are so accomplished, they might like to come and help me one day in the school. I am sure that there are all kind of useful skills which they might pass on to others.'

Mrs Bell turned a little pale. 'My girls? In a village school? Oh no no no, Miss Montague. They are far too delicate!' Then obviously feeling that talking to Flavia was rather a disturbing business, she turned away to speak to Mrs Steeple, and Flavia was left for a few moments to observe Mr Wheaton and the two young ladies.

He did not appear to favour either one over the other, but on the contrary, he divided his smiles and his conversation equally between the two of them. As if suddenly conscious of being observed, he looked up and smiled at Flavia, gesturing to her to come and take his chair so that she might join in the conversation. Doing as she was bid, she reflected that she had been the recipient of just the same kind of smile as he had been bestowing upon the Stagsden Belles. The two sisters were very ready to carry the main burden of the conversation, and by the end of the visit, Flavia was left wondering whether Mr Wheaton was simply a very friendly person, or whether he was naturally flirtatious and did not know when to stop.

Mercifully, she had been spared any further visits from Sir Lewis Glendenning. No encounters with parents of pupils, benefactors, other members of staff or even naval officers at their most frisky had prepared her for her encounter with him in the schoolroom. Had he really intended to kiss her? She had asked herself this question over and over again, but not come up with a satisfactory answer. On one level she found it very hard to believe. Her mirror had always told her that she was plain; at her come-out, no gentleman had ever attempted to be so bold as to even press her hand. And yet, if she were honest with herself, she would have to admit that his intentions had been quite clear. He had obviously wanted to punish her by humiliating her in that way. Well, she would make very sure that he would never again have the opportunity of doing so. If she were alone in the schoolroom, then she would leave the communicating door open, and ensure that Grace was within call. Ugly customer he might be, but she was determined that he would not have the satisfaction of besting her!

It was only a short walk from the school to Mr Wheaton's house, accomplished in half an hour with a good pace, but for Mr Wheaton's dinner party, Mr Steeple offered to take Flavia up in his carriage. She accepted very readily. Even though she did not attach very much importance to social occasions, she did not want to arrive on a warm summer evening hot, flustered and dishevelled.

Knowing that a plain woman will always look worse in fussy attire, Flavia studied the simple in her dress and now, tonight, she put on a grey silk gown made high at the neck. It was almost new and of the finest fabric, but she hoped that it gave a clear indication that she was not in pursuit of a man, or of any social advantage. She would hate Miss Wheaton to think that she had designs upon her brother. But she did allow Grace to dress her hair in the less severe style in which she had worn it on the day of Mrs Steeple's tea party.

The gown certainly had the desired effect upon Mr and Mrs Steeple, who both eyed her very approvingly, and then went on to ask her about the success of her shopping expedition to Bedford.

'The carter will bring the slates when they are ready,' she explained, after telling them about the shops she had visited in Bedford. 'The most expensive item to replace will be the globe, but that need not be done just yet.'

'It is a thousand pities, then, that it was thrown away,' said Mrs Steeple with a pointed look.

'It is a thousand pities that it was ever broken and thrown into the cupboard,' Flavia replied pleasantly.

Since there was no obvious answer to this, it was perhaps as well that at this point they arrived at the front of Mr Wheaton's house. It was a handsome, brick-built structure, probably about fifty years old. The gardens, or at any rate what could be seen of them, appeared to be neat but not too formal and altogether, it bore the appearance of a place that was well cared for.

They were admitted into an airy saloon in which Mr Wheaton was waiting and standing with him was a young woman, dressed in the height of fashion. Undoubtedly she was his sister, for her likeness to him was unmistakable. It was clear, however, from her dove-grey gown that she was in half mourning, and when Mr Wheaton introduced her as 'my sister, Mrs Retford', Flavia came to the conclusion that she must be a widow. She was a little too sharp-featured for beauty (having most unfortunately, a rather prominent nose and teeth) but she could without fear of contradiction have been called a handsome woman.

'Miss Montague,' exclaimed Mrs Retford, smiling and holding out her hand. 'How I have been longing to meet you. Paul has been telling me all about your skills and abilities.'

Repressing the urge to say that in less than a week, it would have been very difficult if not impossible for him to discover anything about any gifts which she might or might not possess, Flavia merely said, 'That is very kind of him.'

'And, of course, you will remember Mrs Bell, Miss Bell and Miss Evelina Bell,' said Mr Wheaton. 'But I don't believe that you have met Mr Bell.'

Flavia made polite acknowledgement of this introduction, but before Mr Bell could say anything, Mrs Bell spoke. 'Yes, indeed, I remember Miss Montague. Such a lovely chat we had at the vicarage, did we not? And I tried to remember who had first called the girls the Stagsden Belles, but I could not do so. Do you remember, my love?' she asked her husband.

Flavia was conscious of a horrible feeling that somehow she had strayed backward in time and would be forced to relive the same conversation with Mrs Bell over and over again. Thankfully, however, Mrs Retford spoke at that moment, giving the subject another direction.

'And how are you liking being schoolmistress and living in that dear little cottage?' the widow asked. 'I am sure I should be quite content to live there for ever!'

Mr Wheaton burst out laughing. 'More than three months away from London, and

94

I'll wager you would be screaming for someone to come and rescue you,' he declared.

'No, I protest,' she answered with mock indignation. 'Just think, no demands upon one as to how one should dress or where one should go or with whom. It must be absolute heaven!'

'Well, there are the children of course,' replied Flavia. 'They do make a demand or two. And after all, they are why I am here.'

'Yes indeed,' agreed Mrs Retford. 'But they aren't there all the time, are they?'

'No, that is the one good thing about it,' Mrs Bell interposed. 'Miss Montague, I have been thinking that such gifts as yours are wasted in a village school. You would do far better to come to me and give Lucy and Evelina instructions as to how they should go on when they come out. Do you not think so, my dear?' she added, speaking to her husband who was exchanging a few words with their host. Lucy and Evelina were now both talking to Mr Wheaton, who gave every indication of being well satisfied with his lot.

Not wanting to find herself drawn into yet another conversation in which she was obliged to defend her choice of occupation, Flavia went to look out of the window, and was thus standing near to the door when it opened and the butler announced 'Sir Lewis Glendenning.'

He was correctly attired for evening, with his hair tied back; but the lock that had fallen across his brow at their previous meeting was doing so again, and there was about him the faintest air of untidiness, which she suspected was probably an essential part of the man. He paused briefly on the threshold, then, catching sight of the Stagsden Belles, he muttered under his breath 'My God! The Bedfordshire Clangers!' Glancing swiftly around, he caught Flavia's eye, grinning maliciously, and Flavia, remembering Sarah's explanation of the term, was overcome with an almost irresistible desire to giggle. Then, with a nod in her direction, he strode forward to greet his hostess.

His limp was less pronounced than when she had first met him, but he moved with a kind of insolent swagger that seemed to be characteristic of what she had learned of the man so far.

'Here you are, Lewis,' exclaimed Mrs Retford, hurrying to meet him and tucking her hand into his arm.

'Yes, here I am, Celia,' he replied in the same drawl which Flavia remembered, which was almost a sneer.

'I declare, you look more disagreeable

every time I see you.' answered Mrs Retford. 'Do you not think so, Miss Montague?'

'As I do not know how Sir Lewis looked when you last saw him, I cannot possibly say,' replied Flavia.

The baronet gave a crack of laughter. 'Miss Montague is only temporizing,' he said. 'I'm sure that she agrees with you, and with every justification, no doubt.'

'You are a bear, Lewis,' exclaimed Mrs Retford, laughing. 'Is he not a bear, Miss Montague? You must not take any notice of him!'

'I should not dream of ignoring bears,' replied Flavia, looking the baronet straight in the eye. 'It sounds like a very unwise thing to do.'

He looked straight back at her. 'Quite right,' he murmured. 'Most unwise.'

Dinner was well served and well chosen, but Flavia found herself somewhat ill-at-ease. In sparring with Sir Lewis, she had forgotten her fear and dread of social occasions. Once they were all sitting at table, however, those fears returned.

To her surprise, she discovered that she had been placed on Mr Wheaton's left, with Mr Steeple on the other side of her. She had not expected to be put next to her host, but concluded that she had earned such a position by virtue of her novelty. Miss Bell, who was seated on the other side of Mr Wheaton, looked at her as if she could not imagine how she came to be there. For all that she was a superior schoolmistress, she was still just a schoolmistress.

Clearly, Mr Wheaton had noticed the expression on Miss Bell's face, for when she began to speak to Mrs Steeple, he turned to Flavia and said, 'You mustn't take any notice of her. She is very young, after all, and she isn't very confident with people she doesn't know.'

'Neither am I,' confessed Flavia. 'It's always been a trial to me.'

'But you seem to get on well with the children in your care — or so I'm told.'

'Children are different,' she answered him.

'In what way?' he asked her curiously.

She thought for a moment. 'They do not expect you to be fashionable or beautiful, or witty,' she said eventually. 'All they want from you is that you be truthful, genuine and consistent. They aren't fooled by someone who is putting on an act.'

'But surely, being witty, or beautiful, or fashionable need not be part of an act,' he replied. 'They could all be part of a person's real character.'

'They wouldn't be part of my real

character,' she replied frankly.

'Then we will just have to put up with your own charming self, will we not?' murmured Mr Wheaton with a smile. Flavia forced herself to smile back, but from that moment on, she could feel her expression becoming more wooden and her replies becoming more mechanical as she found herself embroiled in the kind of conversation which she had always found almost impossible to maintain. And as she grew more silent, and Mr Wheaton turned more of his attention to Miss Bell, who was all too delighted to indulge him in a modest flirtation, she could hear Mrs Retford's laughter trilling from the other end of the table. Sir Lewis was obviously keeping her very well amused.

After the meal was over, Mrs Retford got up from the table and the other ladies followed suit and left the dining-room with her. The gentlemen rose at their departure, although it seemed to Flavia as if for two pins, Sir Lewis would have remained lounging in his seat.

Once they had entered the saloon, Mrs Retford caught hold of Flavia's arm, exactly as if they had been bosom friends and insisted that Flavia tell her all about herself. When the ladies present were given to understand that she had actually chosen to be a teacher, Mrs Bell and Mrs Retford both expressed surprise.

'How very peculiar,' Mrs Bell said frankly. 'I cannot imagine anyone choosing to do such a thing.'

'Neither can I,' yawned Miss Bell. 'I am sure, I would rather die. Evelina, will you play the pianoforte if I turn the pages?'

The two young ladies went over to the instrument, whilst Mrs Retford said to their mother, 'Do remember that Miss Montague has been living in Bath. Such a delightful place! Just think of the Abbey, and all the assemblies, and the Pump Room! I never tire of the Pump Room! I am sure you do not either, do you, Miss Montague?'

'I'm afraid I seldom saw it,' admitted Flavia.

'But, my dear, that is the only place to see and be seen in Bath,' protested her hostess. 'Such charming men that one can flirt with under the guise of drinking the waters, too!'

This was exactly the kind of conversation in which Flavia had never known how to participate, so she was pleased when Mrs Bell responded to Mrs Retford's words with a comment of her own about the shopping to be had in Milsom Street. As they chattered, she reflected with inward amusement that recalling the behaviour of some of the girls at

Miss Bredale's academy, including Mary Steeple, a place where young men might be found to flirt with would be the very last place to which she would have wanted to take them.

Glad to be relieved of the necessity of indulging in polite chit-chat, she turned to Mrs Steeple to ask her about the possibility of starting a 'sewing for the poor' basket. Not long after this, they were joined by the gentlemen.

'Lewis!' Mrs Retford exclaimed. 'You wicked man! I am convinced that all that lingering over the brandy and the port was entirely your fault.'

As the gentlemen were behind them by only a quarter of an hour, Flavia felt that this was hardly fair comment, and she wondered, not for the first time, whether there was some special reason why Mrs Retford was bent on attracting Sir Lewis's attention.

The baronet did not defend himself against this attack on his reputation, however, and merely raised his brows and said, 'If we lingered, then the excellent quality of your brother's brandy is to blame.'

'Well, we have not missed you at all,' declared Mrs Retford, tossing her head. 'You must not be thinking that you are the only gentleman in the world. In fact, we were just talking about how agreeable it is to flirt in the Pump Room at Bath, were we not, Miss Montague?' Flavia started, looking completely nonplussed at this reference to herself taking part in a conversation, some of which had not included her and some of which had not taken place at all.

Sir Lewis looked at her with what she had come to think of as his diabolical expression, and replied, 'I can imagine.'

'Now that I am here, we can have some splendid outings,' said Mrs Retford. 'You must not think that you need feel bored or neglected, Miss Montague. I shall make sure that you are very well entertained.'

'That is very kind of you, Mrs Retford,' said Flavia, on surer ground, 'but I am here to work and my opportunities for socializing will be somewhat limited, I fear.'

'But it is only a village school for village children,' replied Mrs Retford. 'Surely one day more or less here or there will not make any difference to them.'

'I'm afraid that it will,' replied Flavia.

'Lewis!' exclaimed Mrs Retford. 'Tell Miss Montague that she need not apply herself to her work all the time. It will make her ill.'

'I fear I'm really in no position to give Miss Montague instructions as to what she should do,' was the reply.

'But surely you do not feel that the school would suffer if she took a day or two off here and there,' she pursued.

'To be honest, the fate of a school for village brats is a matter of complete indifference to me,' said the baronet. He then turned to Mr Bell to speak of other matters.

Mrs Retford pouted and began to talk to Mrs Bell of the season that had just passed, and of her visit to Harrogate. From the glances that she kept casting in the baronet's direction, however, Flavia gained the distinct impression that she wanted Sir Lewis to know exactly with whom she had flirted and when.

From the lack of response that she got it seemed clear that he was as indifferent to her success in London as he had been to the fate of the village school, and while Flavia could not help applauding his attitude to the one, she found his approach to the other infuriating in the extreme.

Upon entering the room, Mr Wheaton had wandered over to the pianoforte to listen to Miss Bell's playing. Now, the two young ladies pressed him into singing with them, and whilst Miss Evelina took the pianoforte stool, her older sister warbled a duet with their handsome host. Sadly, her voice, although well-trained was not of the most tuneful, and when she had finished singing, no one begged her for another song. So much for the accomplishments of the Stagsden Belles, she thought to herself, with not very admirable but entirely comprehensible satisfaction.

Now that she had had a chance of observing them for a whole evening, it seemed to her that of the two, Mr Wheaton slightly favoured Miss Evelina, but Miss Lucy did not seem to mind. She would be a good match for him, Flavia decided, if he could but control his tendency to flirt with almost every woman in sight.

This idea was completely banished, however, with Mr Steeple's next words. 'Well, Miss Montague, you have been with us for a week now, so I suggest that since both Mr Wheaton and Sir Lewis are here, we arrange to meet together so that your appointment can be formally approved.'

'Formally approved?' echoed Flavia hollowly.

'Why yes,' answered Mr Steeple. 'Since both Mr Wheaton and Sir Lewis are bound to be so closely concerned with the school, they must give their approval for the appointment of a new teacher.'

Flavia became aware of the lowering presence of Sir Lewis standing behind her. 'You have forgotten to mention a matter which is of some importance,' he said. 'Were you aware, Miss Montague, that the school is built on my land?'

She turned to look at him, all the consternation that she was feeling written on her face. She heard Mr Wheaton saying, 'You mustn't worry, Miss Montague. I am sure that you can take our consent for granted. This interview will only be a formality.'

But as Flavia looked at the baronet, she could see from the malice in his expression that it would not be anything of the sort.

8

Since there had to be an interview at all, Flavia wanted it to be held as soon as possible. In her heart, she was convinced that Sir Lewis would argue vigorously against her staying, but he was only one out of three. Of the remaining two, Mr Steeple would most likely vote in her favour, since he had been the one to appoint her. The fact that the school was built on Sir Lewis's land might make a difference to his attitude, however. Mr Wheaton had also seemed to support her, but there was no telling how much he might be influenced by the opinions of the baronet. On one thing she was determined: if the decision went against her, she wanted to leave as soon as possible, before she became any more settled.

Now, the comments which Mr Steeple had made about her appointment being confirmed or about its being agreeable to all made perfect sense. She supposed that at their first meeting he must have said something about the interview being necessary, but in her excitement at gaining the post she had failed to take it in. She wished that she had done so. She feared that already she was becoming very settled in her little cottage, and she did not want to go back to the noise and busyness that would await her in Bath, should she return to Miss Bredale. She had no doubt that there would still be work for her, but that was beside the point.

On the day for which the interview had been set, Flavia dressed with particular care, and set out to walk to Mr Wheaton's house, where she was to meet with the others. She was glad that Mr Steeple had not suggested that they walk together. She felt that she would rather spend the journey in quiet reflection.

As she walked, she became more and more despondent. She felt sure that Mr Wheaton had decided in her favour, but Sir Lewis was a strong character and might be able to sway his neighbour's opinion. The fact that the school was built on his land might also mean that his vote would carry a little more weight. As for Mr Steeple, he certainly appeared to approve of her at the beginning, but since then, she had burned the contents of the cupboard, and spent quite a sum of money on the school. There was also the lack of sympathy between herself and Mrs Steeple to be taken into account. True, the vicar's wife would not be at the interview, but it would be too much to hope that her opinions would be ignored by her husband.

These dismal thoughts so absorbed her that she was surprised to find that she had reached the house without taking in any of the surrounding scenery. She looked around her before ringing the bell. 'Oh please let me stay,' she said out loud, her voice sounding rather more plaintive than usual. 'I like it here.'

She knew that she was a little early, so she was not surprised when she was shown into the book-room, to find that only Mr Wheaton was present. He bid her a civil good morning, offered her refreshment, which she declined, then told her not to worry. 'You look very anxious, but really there is no need,' he said. 'Steeple makes the appointments, and Lewis and I just agree with whatever he says. Apart from the last teacher, of course.'

'I suppose that that was Miss Price,' Flavia remarked. 'Who appointed her?'

'Oh, she was Lewis's choice. She didn't stay long, but then I don't suppose . . . ' He stopped speaking, his face colouring up a little.

'You don't suppose . . . ' Flavia prompted.

'Forgot what I was going to say,' he mumbled. At that moment, Mr Steeple was announced, but Flavia was able to hazard at the ending of Mr Wheaton's sentence. He had intended to say that he did not suppose that she had been hired to be a schoolteacher at all. Flavia had expected as much, and her lip curled. No doubt it had seemed reasonable to the baronet to install his mistress in a house on his own land. Probably the needs of the village children had not even occurred to him.

Unlike Flavia, Mr Steeple did not refuse refreshment, and Mr Wheaton rang for wine to be brought. It was as the butler was bringing in the tray that Sir Lewis strolled in, nodding carelessly at the assembled company. 'Nervous?' he said to Flavia, showing his teeth.

'Why should she be?' asked Mr Wheaton. 'She is among friends, after all.' The baronet inclined his head, but Flavia was not deceived. He might have said that the fate of a school for village brats was a matter of indifference to him, but he had every intention of tormenting her. She must not allow him to succeed.

When wine had been served to all the men, and Flavia had once more declined, Mr Wheaton invited them all to be seated. 'Mr Steeple, would you be so good as to conduct this meeting?' he said.

'I? Oh, well . . . well, yes, of course,' replied

the vicar diffidently. 'Well, it seems to me that Miss Montague has made a very good start at the school. The children are minding her, and making progress already. Perhaps the destruction of the contents of the cupboard was a little hasty, but no doubt she had very good reasons for taking such a course of action. In short, I recommend that her appointment be confirmed immediately.' Flavia breathed an inward sigh of relief. Whatever reservations Mrs Steeple may have had, they certainly did not seem to weigh with her husband.

'Well, in that case, if Miss Montague herself is willing — ' Mr Wheaton began; but Sir Lewis interrupted him.

'One moment,' he said. 'I am not entirely sure that Miss Montague is suitable for this post.'

'Indeed?' Flavia replied, her tone indignant and a little imperious. 'And what are your reasons for this belief?'

He smiled, and leaned back in his chair, his quizzing glass swinging from his right hand. 'Miss Montague is accustomed to teaching social skills to well-bred, wealthy young ladies. I cannot suppose that the same kind of teaching would be either necessary or appropriate for village children. Or are you proposing to teach my farm-hands how to dance the minuet and flirt with their fans?'

'By no means,' replied Flavia, striving to keep her tone pleasant. 'I am well aware that the needs are very different. But I must assure you that I have also taught younger children the rudiments of reading, writing and mathematics, and am quite capable of teaching village children basic subjects. If, however,' she added out of sheer devilment, 'you feel that they need to learn the minuet, then I am quite happy to oblige you.'

'Then if you are quite satisfied — ' began Mr Steeple, but he was interrupted before he could finish his sentence.

'I have some further objections,' said the baronet, raising his hand. 'Miss Montague, I fear, is somewhat rash and excitable by nature. I have seen this in her at first hand, and am not sure that it is an appropriate trait for a teacher. A teacher should be calm and rational, not impulsive and passionate.'

Flavia gave a tiny gasp, and with difficulty held her peace. A sudden outburst would only confirm what he had said of her; and looking at him she could see by his wider smile that he knew exactly what she was thinking. Mr Steeple was looking at her doubtfully, as if he expected her to burst into flames at any moment. 'Miss Montague, this is a grave matter,' he ventured. 'Do you have

111

anything to say in response to Sir Lewis's comments?'

'I have never been aware that this was a failing of mine,' she replied carefully. 'Probably Sir Lewis is referring to the time when he was riding with so little consideration for others that he caused Dobbin to shy, and as a consequence I lost my temper. But I cannot think it a failing to be angry at appropriate moments.'

'No, no indeed,' agreed the vicar, looking nervously at Sir Lewis. 'Well, if that is all — '

'Not quite all,' put in the baronet.

'Oh, for goodness' sake,' began Flavia; then realizing how her interruption was confirming everything that he had just said, she turned bright red.

'Yes, for goodness' sake, and even for the sake of those charming children whom you are so anxious to serve,' he said piously. 'I have one further objection; perhaps the most serious of all.' Once more, he grinned widely. 'Miss Montague is a young woman. Who is to say that some man will not . . . ah . . . lure her away? All unbeknownst to those around her she might already have formed a secret attachment. She is, after all, very attractive.'

'Attractive?' exclaimed both Mr Steeple and Mr Wheaton in astonished tones, almost as though they had been scripted to do so.

'Don't be so absurd,' declared Flavia, blushing again. How she longed to slap that grin off the baronet's smirking face!

Meanwhile, realizing the infelicitous nature of his exclamation, Mr Wheaton, his colour also a little higher than usual, said, 'Naturally, some gentleman might indeed have enough sense to appreciate Miss Montague's gifts and . . . er . . . attractions. But this might be the case with any lady, surely. After all,' he went on, pursuing his theme with more confidence, 'Miss Stokes, who was governess to the Misses Bell, was married to a clergyman only a year ago, and she must have been quite fifty!'

'You relieve my mind,' murmured Sir Lewis. 'In that case, we may reckon on having Miss Montague with us for nearly twenty years?'

'Twenty-four,' Flavia put in swiftly, then could have kicked herself for speaking so hastily.

'Mathematics is obviously secure,' remarked the baronet, getting lazily to his feet. 'Well, Steeple, the lady is clearly suitable in my opinion. I should snap her up if I were you. You'll forgive me if I take my leave of you. I have some business that must be seen to.' He sketched a bow to the assembled company, and then, turning to Flavia, he grinned maliciously. 'Welcome to the neighbourhood,' he said.

'What a strange, unaccountable man he is,' remarked Mr Steeple. 'Do you know, Miss Montague, I actually thought for a moment that he was opposed to your appointment? But it seems that after all, he was simply satisfying himself that you were entirely suitable. I take it, Mr Wheaton, that you are agreeable to Miss Montague's remaining with us?'

'Yes, I am quite satisfied,' replied Mr Wheaton.

Mr Steeple stood up. 'Well, I must be going as well,' he said. 'We have had some surprising news. My sister, Mrs Glenn is coming to stay with us for a time, and she will be arriving today. I think you already know my sister, Miss Montague,' he added, looking at Flavia a little anxiously.

'Yes, certainly I do,' replied Flavia, standing as well. 'I shall be pleased to renew my acquaintance with her.' She turned to Mr Wheaton. 'Thank you for allowing us to meet here, and for your hospitality.'

'Not at all,' he replied, with his usual charming smile. 'And lest you suppose that only Steeple is glad to see you stay, let me say that I am delighted — more than delighted — to have you here.' Flavia smiled and allowed him to take her hand. He was certainly a charming man, though why he should choose to exercise his charm on a plain village schoolmistress was a mystery to her. Mr Wheaton then turned to the vicar. 'Pray give my compliments to Mrs Glenn, and assure her that I shall call upon her very soon.'

Had Flavia been given the choice, she would probably have preferred a solitary journey after the events of the morning, but she could scarcely refuse to walk back to the village with Mr Steeple when he was leaving at exactly the same time. In any case, his rather anxious-sounding monologue about his only sister Mary, much younger than himself, whose husband, an army officer, was on exercises, did much to calm her spirits, and by the time they parted at the school, most of Flavia's longing to hurl breakable things had disappeared.

Looking back on the interview, she had absolutely no doubt that the baronet had spoken out of sheer devilment. He had had no reason to think that she could not teach basic subjects, his comments about her age and attractions had been frankly nonsensical, whilst his criticism of her temperament had simply been designed to enrage her. The most infuriating aspect of the matter was that, by and large, she was a very even-tempered person, able to cope calmly with the most recalcitrant of pupils and the most demand-ing of parents. It was only Sir Lewis Glendenning who seemed to bring out this fiery side of her nature. She was convinced that he had annoyed her on purpose, hoping that she would lash out and thus condemn herself out of her own mouth. Well, he had not succeeded; she could congratulate herself on that score; and in the end, he had been obliged to admit that she would be very suitable for the position.

'Attractive, indeed!' she muttered to herself as she took off her bonnet. She was plain; she had always known it, but as she looked at herself in the mirror, she wondered for a moment what it would be like to have a man say that she was attractive and mean it.

★　★　★

Flavia had thought that Mrs Retford's supposed desire to visit the school was probably a fiction, invented by her brother for the sake of being polite. She was, therefore, very much surprised when two days after the interview, Mrs Retford arrived with her brother during the morning class in order to observe the school at work.

The children who had come on that first day had for the most part remained faithful.

Occasionally some would be absent if needed elsewhere, for Flavia had learned that the school came quite low in most people's list of priorities, but they tended to come back as soon as possible. Flavia counted that as a small personal triumph.

Those who had attended the school under Miss Price's leadership seemed to have learned remarkably little. They did, however, have a healthy respect for the cane, to which Flavia had not yet had to resort.

The sewing-for-the-poor basket was quite popular. The children who attended the school did not appear, for the most part, to come from the very poorest families, and Flavia found that they were quite responsive to the idea of helping those less fortunate than themselves.

The pattern of working which she established quite early on was to conduct lessons in the more demanding subjects during the morning, leaving the sewing and other handicrafts to be done in the afternoon. In this way, she found that more of the children were likely to continue to attend, if it was known that they could be free to help at home after midday.

Of great use was Penelope Lynton, the slender, well-dressed girl who had appeared with Philip on the first day. She was an intelligent, well-behaved girl, with a ready willingness to try to grasp all that Flavia was teaching her, and she was always ready to give help with the slower ones if necessary. One thing that did surprise Flavia was that she never returned to help with the sewing group, for she would have expected Penelope to have been able to sew, and keen to pass on her skill to others.

Flavia had found Penelope to be entirely accurate in her assessment of Philip's behaviour. He did not speak at all, but he seemed content to be amongst the other children, as long as he was near Penelope. Sometimes he would get up from his place during a lesson, and wander over to a window to look out, and the others present soon learned to take no notice of him at such times. On other occasions, he would stand close to Flavia whilst she was giving instructions.

The slates were soon delivered and on one occasion, acting on impulse, she gave a few to Philip to pass to other members of the class. Without the slightest hesitation, he followed the example of the other child who was helping, and when he sat down, he kept a slate for himself. Flavia had already noticed that when she wrote anything on the blackboard, he watched her with close attention. On this occasion, he observed her writing some letters for the class to copy, then, because he had no chalk, he licked his finger then carefully traced a shape upon his slate. Hurrying over to him, she saw that he had made quite a fair copy of the letters that she had drawn on the board.

'Philip, well done! You clever boy!' she exclaimed, beaming. He looked at her a little apprehensively and then, for the first time, a slow, tentative smile crossed his face. She took a piece of chalk and placed it in his hand. 'Try with this,' she said. From then on, he drew everything that was written on the board, although during stories, learning by rote, or at other times, he would wander about and pay no attention to what was happening.

Flavia had not found a chance to catch Philip and Penelope after school in a casual way as she had hoped, so one day she said quite deliberately, 'Penelope, will you stay behind today to help me clear up, please?'

Penelope nodded warily, but stayed willingly enough. Philip wandered around in his usual fashion after the others had gone.

Flavia had gone over and over in her mind how she might begin to question Penelope in a gentle, unthreatening way. In the event, however, their conversation was sparked off by an incident which meant that it took a very different turn to that which Flavia had expected. It so happened that during the course of the morning, the cane had fallen from its usual place on top of the blackboard, and there had not been the opportunity to pick it up. Flavia bent to retrieve it then turned to speak to Penelope with it still in her hand. The young girl's reaction was immediate and instinctive. She cringed away, whimpering, her hands coming up to cover her face and her head. Immediately Flavia dropped the cane.

'Penelope, no!' she exclaimed, horrified. 'I would never hit you. How could you suppose it?' She paused, then went on slowly, 'Someone has, though, haven't they? Who was it?'

Penelope's hands had dropped to her sides. She never had a very rosy complexion, but now all the colour in her face seemed to have drained away. She turned her face aside, shaking her head. 'No, no,' she said. 'It . . . it's all right now, really . . . '

Flavia took a step closer to her. 'My dear, this cannot be allowed,' she said. 'I will help you in every way that is in my power, but you must trust me. Who is it who has done this? I will speak to them for you.'

'No,' Penelope said again. 'There's no need.'

'Forgive me, but there is every need,' said Flavia very firmly. 'This cannot be allowed. With whom do you live?'

Penelope looked at her anxiously, then looked round for Philip. 'Come, Philip, we must go. Miss Montague, I'm sorry, we . . . we really can't stay. We must go . . . I'll . . . I'll see you again soon.'

The next day, Penelope and Philip did not come to the school. Flavia was angry with herself. She knew that she had approached the matter clumsily, but she had been so angry that anyone could beat a gentle person like Penelope that her anger had got the better of her and she had forgotten to be cautious. She could only hope that they would come back eventually, and if they did so, she told herself, she would be more careful in her approach. She was determined to find out who was ill-treating Penelope, and to put a stop to such contemptible behaviour.

The day when they were absent was the same day on which Mrs Retford made her promised visit to the school accompanied by her brother. The scholars were all awe-struck by this august visitation, and behaved impeccably as a result. Mr Wheaton impressed Flavia by asking some of the children about their work, but Mrs Retford seemed less interested in the school's activity than in the stitching on her riding gloves, and was clearly pleased when Flavia dismissed the class at twelve o'clock.

'Well thank goodness for that,' she exclaimed. 'What a relief to see the back of them, is it not?' She beamed sunnily at Flavia as if she could not imagine anyone holding a contrary opinion. 'Paul, you may take yourself off now. Miss Montague is going to take me into her sitting-room and give me a cup of tea, and we are going to talk secrets.'

Firmly repressing the thought that it would actually be a relief to see the back of Mrs Retford and drink a cup of tea in agreeable solitude, Flavia made ready to usher her guest into the cottage.

'Well, if you are going to talk secrets, I shall go to the vicarage and make a visit there,' said Mr Wheaton. 'Thank you for showing us the school. You have indeed achieved a great deal over a short period of time. I am all admiration.'

As soon as he had gone, Mrs Retford said 'I did not think that it would be very long before he would be hurrying off to see Mrs Glenn. She and Paul had a bit of a thing between them at one time, but instead, she chose to marry an impecunious army officer.'

'He does not act like someone whose heart is broken,' observed Flavia, showing her guest to a seat.

'Good Lord, no,' answered Mrs Retford, laughing. 'That would not be like him at all.'

'I am already acquainted with Mrs Glenn,' Flavia put in. 'She was a pupil at Miss Bredale's.'

'Poor you!' exclaimed her visitor frankly. 'Was she ghastly to teach?'

'She wasn't very easy,' Flavia replied diplomatically.

'To be honest, I was quite relieved when she did marry Sidney Glenn. She would have led Paul a merry dance, and although in some ways that would have been no more than he deserves for being such a flirt, he is my brother after all.' Flavia could not think what reply to make, but luckily, Mrs Retford did not seem to require an answer to this.

Once they were seated in the little sitting-room, and Grace had hurried to make them tea — the notion of her mistress entertaining the gentry being very much to her liking — Mrs Retford said, changing the subject, 'Now tell me the *real* reason for your choosing to bury yourself in the country. I vow it must have been to escape the attentions of some man!'

'No indeed,' laughed Flavia. 'I am sorry to disappoint you, but there is no secret reason at all.'

'That isn't what *I* heard,' said Mrs Retford coyly.

'What you heard?' uttered Flavia blankly.

'Why yes. A little bird told me that you had a secret attachment.'

'I must say, I have no idea from where *that* story originated,' declared Flavia. 'Unless . . .' she went on slowly, suddenly recalling Sir Lewis's insinuations when she had been interviewed by him together with Mr Wheaton and Mr Steeple. What was more likely than that Wheaton had passed this information on to his sister? 'Oh, abominable! I don't believe it!' Mrs Retford looked at her questioningly, and she coloured, then felt annoyed with herself for doing so as it would surely look very suspicious. 'I think that perhaps an erroneous tale has been spread concerning me,' she said eventually. 'There is no secret reason for my presence here at all.'

Mrs Retford made a *moue* of disappointment. 'Oh, sad stuff! You mean that it really is true? That you like to teach?'

'I'm afraid so,' replied Flavia. 'I'm sorry if that makes me rather dull.'

'Well, not dull, precisely,' said Mrs Retford. 'But it is just that so many people go to the country to escape from something in the town — or sometimes, of course, it is the other way round.'

'To escape?' At this point, Grace came in with the tea, and Flavia quite thought that the moment for confidences might be over. But as soon as Grace had left the room, Mrs Retford leaned forward. 'Yes, to escape,' she breathed. 'At least, that was my motive.'

Flavia did not want to indulge in unseemly gossip, but it was quite plain that, for whatever reason, Mrs Retford had chosen her as a confidante, and was undoubtedly going to confide in her, by hook or by crook. She therefore confined herself to saying 'Indeed,' in calm tones, hoping that thereby she was making clear that if her visitor confided in her, it was by no means because any secrets had been wormed out of her.

'After all,' Mrs Retford went on, looking down at her hands, 'a failed romance is enough to make anyone run, is it not?'

Flavia nearly said 'indeed' again, but decided that this would sound as if she did not know what to say, and instead merely raised her brows enquiringly.

'You do not ask me the name of the man whose fate once seemed as if it might be linked to mine,' Mrs Retford went on obligingly. 'It was Lewis, of course.'

Flavia could not stop herself then. 'Sir Lewis Glendenning?' she exclaimed.

'You seem surprised, Miss Montague,' her visitor murmured complacently. 'But after all, his family is the only one of any standing in this immediate vicinity apart from ours. You may be wondering why I am choosing to tell you this,' she went on, 'but when one is new to a district, it is so easy to make insensitive remarks because one does not know the nature of the relationships in the area. People are bound to talk, and forewarned is forearmed, is it not?'

Flavia agreed that indeed that was so, and waited to see if there would be any further disclosures. She was not to be disappointed.

'We were engaged for a time, you know.'

Flavia just stopped herself from exclaiming out loud again. She did not want to appear intolerably naïve. Instead, she merely said, 'When was this?'

'Oh, before I was married to Augustus,' the widow replied. 'It must have been about five years ago now. It all came to nothing, and I insisted that Mama take me right away. We went to Bath and it was there that I met Augustus.'

'So . . . so we must have been in Bath at the same time, and not known it,' remarked Flavia, because she could not think of anything else to say.

'Exactly so,' agreed her visitor. 'Which is why I knew that I would feel a certain empathy with you from the first moment when Paul told me about you. Of course, you will have seen that Lewis and I are still upon good terms. I suspect that he would still like to marry me, but of course it could never be. He was very angry at first, of course, so he went dashing off to London, and it was then that he got that horrid scar in a duel. Doesn't it make him hideous?'

Flavia stared at her for a moment, not knowing what to say. She had noticed that the scar tended to alter the baronet's expression, making it difficult at times to detect his exact feelings, but she had never thought that it had made his face unsightly; on the contrary, it sometimes made her want to look at him more. Naturally she could not disclose this to her visitor who would doubtless assume that she was attracted to Sir Lewis, so she contented herself with saying, 'Was that when he acquired his limp as well?'

'Oh no,' said Mrs Retford calmly. 'That was in a riding accident when he was a boy.' Flavia waited in silence for more disclosures, but before she could speak, Mr Steeple appeared at the cottage door with some minor query about the school, and the time of telling secrets was at an end.

After her visitor had gone, Flavia thought with some puzzlement about the kind of person who could so easily reveal personal details to someone who was after all little more than a stranger. She came to the conclusion that she must be more discreet than most, for she recalled that in Bath, many of the girls at school were ready to be almost unbearably frank to those around them about their most private concerns. Perhaps, though, that had been because it was an all female establishment. Certainly, with boys present in the village school it made for a more boisterous atmosphere.

A little later on that same day, Mrs Steeple made a visit in company with her sister-in-law. Mary Glenn was much as Flavia remembered her from her time at Miss Bredale's; a diminutive, dark person with an excellent figure, a restless manner, and a disconcertingly knowing expression. Mrs Steeple's attitude towards her seemed more like that of a mother towards a slightly wilful child than that of an older sister. The two ladies only stayed for half an hour, as was appropriate for a formal visit, but Mrs Glenn promised to return, and the next afternoon, she came back by herself.

'I wanted to talk to you without Phyllis hanging over us all the time. Isn't she tedious? And don't for goodness sake say that I shouldn't speak about her like that, because I've known her for, oh, fifteen years or so, and it's true. Anyway, I've said the same thing to her face.'

Watching her former charge lounging back in one of her chairs in a far more uninhibited way than she had done the previous day, Flavia decided that she could well believe it. 'Just because we believe that something is true about someone does not mean that we must necessarily feel bound to share it with others,' Flavia remarked calmly.

'You mean, like the fact that you smoke?' suggested Mary, getting up and wandering round the room.

'I beg your pardon?' exclaimed Flavia, honestly startled. She had so seldom indulged that particular habit at Miss Bredale's that she had thought that no one was aware of it. Trust Mary Steeple, as she had been, to find out.

'You smoke,' Mary repeated matter-of-factly. 'I saw you, in the garden one night. I thought it might be a friend of mine, but it turned out to be you.' She paused. 'I wonder what Brian would say if he knew?'

Flavia straightened her spine. Of any of her acquaintance, Mary was probably the one whom she least wanted to know anything to her detriment. But she was determined not to be manipulated by this young woman. 'Perhaps he is just so thankful to have found someone to teach here that he will not be interested in such information,' she said, keeping her demeanour outwardly calm.

'Oh yes, I remember, you have private means, don't you?' said Mary carelessly. 'This job doesn't really matter to you one way or the other. Well, I probably wouldn't tell him anyway. You were always quite reasonable to me. Tell me, what do you think of Paul Wheaton? Don't you think he's handsome?'

'Yes indeed,' responded Flavia, relieved at the change of subject. 'I think I have rarely seen a more handsome man.'

Mary had paused in front of the mirror to examine her reflection, but now by the angle of her gaze, Flavia could see that she was looking at her, her eyes narrowed. 'You don't have an interest there, do you? Because if you do, I think I must warn you that you haven't a prayer. Don't be misled by the fact that he flirts with you. He flirts with any female, but he is only ever seriously attracted to very pretty women.'

Flavia gave way to perfectly genuine laughter. 'Good heavens, no,' she replied.

Mary's expression relaxed. 'I nearly had him myself, you know,' she declared. 'But for all that he likes to flirt, he's rather too much attached to his acres, and his landowner's duties, and that wouldn't suit me at all.

Besides, I think that living so close to Brian and Phyllis would probably drive me to screaming point.'

Thinking that it was about time that she took some initiative in this conversation, Flavia said 'How did you meet Captain Glenn?'

'I had an invitation to go and stay with friends in Norwich, and I met him there,' Mary replied. 'I expect you have heard rumours that he is penniless?'

Flavia, remembering Mrs Retford's description of his being 'impecunious', nodded.

'It isn't true,' Mrs Glenn replied. 'Sidney isn't rich, but he is a captain, and he has an elderly aunt who really can't hang on for much longer, and she is leaving him all her money, so we shall be *rolling* in riches.'

'And is Captain Glenn to join you here?' Flavia asked.

For the first time, her disturbing visitor seemed a little discomfited. 'He is busy,' she replied shortly, and soon afterwards she left.

The last thing Flavia wanted to do was to encourage Mary to come again, but the young woman called round quite regularly. Although Flavia did not care for her very much, she had to acknowledge that her visitor's views on various matters were refreshingly different from those of other people, devoid as they were from any constraint imposed by good manners or discretion. She wondered what she might have to say on the subject of Miss Price and her involvement with Sir Lewis, but she did not know how to approach the subject without appearing to be vulgarly curious — which after all, she had to acknowledge that she was.

In the event, the subject came up without Flavia's having to raise it at all. It happened that when Mrs Glenn came to the school-house for tea one day, she picked up the copy of Wordsworth's poetry that had belonged to Miss Price and looked inside. 'Sylvia Price!' she exclaimed. 'Now there's a name inclined to give rise to strong reactions around here. Perhaps you've already noticed it.'

'I confess that I have,' replied Flavia, 'but the story is apparently much too shocking to be repeated.'

'It was quite a scandal,' agreed Mary. 'Brian and Phyllis know about it of course, but they fondly imagine that they have protected me from it, deeming it to be unsuitable for my chaste ears! How they think I manage to follow the drum with Sidney and not hear some rather warm stories, I cannot imagine! Fortunately Pauline — Phyllis's sister — is a little less mealy-mouthed than they are, and she kept me informed by letter. Tell me, what do you know?'

Flavia looked at her doubtfully. The girls at school had never been encouraged to gossip, and she was very reluctant to admit to this failing herself.

'Oh don't be a hypocrite,' declared Mary. 'I won't tell anyone you asked. And you do want to know, don't you?'

After an inner struggle, which Flavia had to admit, to her shame, was very brief, she said, 'I have heard that she was expecting a child when she left, and that she was engaged to be married to the gentleman who is now her husband. I have also been told' — and here she coloured a little — 'that Sir Lewis was involved in some way.'

'Oh yes, he was having an affair with her! They tried to be discreet and indeed when they met in public places no one would ever have guessed! But his horse was seen tied up outside the cottage, sometimes all night, and she was observed sneaking off to the manor house on other occasions. There could be no doubt. You only have to look at him to see that he's dangerous, don't you?'

'So was she dismissed in the end?' Flavia asked, ignoring the last part of this speech.

Mary shook her head. 'She disappeared one day without any word at all. In fact,

Phyllis had to come and teach in the school for a few days, before they decided to close it. You can imagine how much she loved that!'

Flavia smiled. That might explain Mrs Steeple's hostile attitude to her. She obviously saw schoolteachers as an unreliable breed.

'Sir Lewis had left the neighbourhood, and everyone thought that they must have eloped. Then later, a letter came saying that she was married, and carrying with it a belated apology. And soon after that, Sir Lewis returned, and everything got back to normal; except for the scandal, of course.'

'Of course,' Flavia replied thoughtfully. It only occurred to her much later that she still did not know the name of Miss Price's husband.

★ ★ ★

During the early days of her time in the village school at Brooks, Flavia had to admit to herself that she would, in truth, have been very glad to have an extra pair of adult hands available. With such a large group of children, all of very different ages and abilities, she was sometimes tested to the limits of her energy and patience. There had, indeed, been times when she had been sorely tempted to resort to the use of the cane, but she was determined not to do so unless really desperate. She had seldom travelled on board ship with her father, but she had been present on one occasion when a man had been flogged, and this experience had given her a horror of corporal punishment. Although her father had explained to her that at sea, firm discipline was necessary, she could not help thinking that there must be a better way.

Over the next few days, she kept thinking about Penelope, and wondering what kind of monster could have taken a stick to her. The two children had not come to school that following day, but the day after that, they arrived just as school was beginning and slipped quietly into their places. Beyond greeting them quietly, Flavia did not say any more. She was determined not to let the matter go, but she would not allow her disgust at the way in which Penelope had been treated to tempt her into indiscreet words this time.

Rather to Flavia's surprise, Sara Briggs, the girl who had helped to clear out the schoolroom, also joined the classes from time to time. The day when Penelope and Philip returned was one of the days when Sara came to the school and after lunch, when the sewing class took place, she came back to take part in that also. About ten girls attended the sewing class, some much more adept with a needle than others.

'I thought that your mother was not going to allow you to come to school,' Flavia commented, as they packed the things away at the end of the session.

Sara grinned. 'She found out that there was sewing to be done,' she said, 'and she wants me to be able to do it better. She'll let me learn the other things if I get more handy at my sewing.'

'Forgive my saying so,' said Flavia, as she folded the last of the sewing and put it in the large wicker basket which she had purchased for that very purpose, 'but it seemed to me that you yourself were not very interested in attending the school. What made you change your mind?'

Sara looked a little embarrassed. 'Well, miss, I thought I'd give it another try and . . . well . . . you make it all so much more interesting than Miss Price did.'

Flavia's sense of propriety meant that she could hardly comment on this, but she could not help smiling secretly to herself as she and Sara put the basket into the cupboard.

When they had done so, Sara said, 'Ma says that if you would like to come to the farm, you'll be very welcome, and she'll give you a cup of tea and p'raps a slice of cake.'

Flavia took this as a compliment of no mean order, and as soon as the school was locked up, she walked with Sara down the half-mile of track which led to the farm where she lived with her parents, three brothers and two sisters.

'I'm the youngest, or Ma'd never have let me come to school,' Sara confided, as they went.

Mrs Briggs confirmed this after she had welcomed Flavia with a cup of tea and a piece of cake, served in the best parlour. 'It's not that I don't approve of schooling in its proper place, miss, although I'll be bound to say I'm not sure what good it does. My Fred needs to do a bit of reckoning and reading with going to market, and so do the lads, but as for the girls, well it's not as if it serves any purpose, is it?'

Flavia was not sure how to reply to this without giving offence. 'I have always found it to be quite useful,' she said eventually, a little diffidently.

'Ah well, you're a lady, and that's different,' answered Mrs Briggs. 'And the sewing that you're doing with the girls, well, I can certainly see the use of that. Sara's stitches have improved already, with your help. Now tell me, miss, are you settling in well? If you

137

want anything like eggs or milk or butter, just tell Sara and she'll bring it to the school when she comes.'

Flavia thanked the farmer's wife warmly. 'It is very good of you to be so thoughtful,' she said. 'As I am new to the district, it is not always easy for me to know where things may be obtained.'

'That's very true,' agreed Mrs Briggs nodding sagely. 'Those who've always lived here are apt to forget how difficult it can be to settle into a new place. I was a foreigner myself, when I married Fred and came to live here, so I know what it's like.'

'Indeed? Where did you live before you were married?' Flavia asked her.

'Oh, I'm from Bromham, miss,' she replied, referring to a village which was approximately a mile away.

Flavia had to hide a smile, but she merely said, 'You must be very familiar now with this neighbourhood.'

'Yes, we are. Of course, you know that we're tenants of Mr Wheaton.'

'Yes, he sent Sara to help me clean out the school.' Flavia waited, hoping that Mrs Briggs might say something about her landlord, but when no remark was forthcoming, she went on, 'I have met his sister, Mrs Retford. She seems a very pleasant lady and quite interested in the school.'

'I don't know her very well, since she has been away with being married.' She paused for a moment, then, clearly deciding that Flavia was worthy of further information, she said, 'She was engaged to Sir Lewis Glendenning at one time, you know.'

Flavia was glad that she had already heard that piece of information, for since she was presently taking a sip of tea, she feared that had it come as a surprise to her, she might well have choked. 'Yes, I had heard.' she replied, when she had put her cup down. 'Sir Lewis's wife must have died quite early on in their marriage, then.'

Mrs Briggs nodded. 'The story goes that it wasn't a very happy marriage,' she said, dropping her voice a little. 'She took sick when she was expecting, and died when her baby was born. Sir Lewis and Miss Wheaton, as she then was, got engaged eighteen months later, more or less, but it's said that she broke it off when she discovered that his son was an idiot. Miss Wheaton didn't want any child of hers to be the same, and who's to blame her, when all's said and done?'

It was not long after this that Flavia left the farmhouse. As she walked back she reflected upon what she had heard. She also thought about the dinner party at Mr Wheaton's house when she had seen Mrs Retford with Sir Lewis. Her behaviour towards him had certainly indicated an intimate relationship of some kind; indeed, she had appeared to claim his attention on every possible occasion. Could she be regretting her rejection of him all those years before, or did she hold fast to her original resolution? Most intriguing of all, was Sir Lewis aware of the reasons for her breaking the engagement? If such as Mrs Briggs knew all about the matter then he could hardly remain ignorant of it. If his son was indeed deranged from some hereditary cause, then Mrs Retford's reluctance to marry him was perhaps understandable, but detestable though he was, Flavia could not help feeling a degree of sympathy for Sir Lewis Glendenning.

On the other hand, if her suspicions about him were correct, then there were two women who had taken a romantic interest in him; Mrs Retford (or Miss Wheaton, as she had been) and Miss Price. The latter had even been willing to sacrifice her own reputation for the sake of her relationship with him. In addition, Mrs Glenn had referred to him as dangerous. It all went to show that any man, however detestable, could find a way of ingratiating himself with the opposite sex, so perhaps pity was wasted on him after all.

9

After her clear declaration to Mrs Retford that she would have little time for day-time socializing, Flavia did not expect another invitation to come her way from that quarter. To her surprise, however, both Mr Wheaton and his sister called at the teacher's cottage after school that Friday.

'Now, my dear Paul, you will be able to see how charming Miss Montague has made this room,' declared Mrs Retford.

Flavia looked around the place that she had begun to think of as home. During the short period of her occupancy, she had laid a handsome rug, which had belonged to one of her aunts, on the floor, and had covered the table in the window with an embroidered cloth. A painting of her mother hung over the mantelpiece and the bookshelves were full of her own books. The changes she had made had been few enough, but they had made a difference, and the room looked considerably less spartan.

'You have put your own stamp upon it in a most pleasing way,' said Mr Wheaton, elaborating on his sister's words.

'Thank you; you are very good,' said Flavia. 'May I offer you any refreshment?'

Brother and sister both declined, but told her that they had come with an invitation. 'We are to go to Bedford tomorrow to do some shopping,' explained Mrs Retford. 'Paul will take me, but will desert me as soon as possible — horrid thing! — as he has some business to conduct. There are some purchases which I simply have to make, so take pity on me, I beg of you, Miss Montague!'

Flavia hesitated, so Mrs Retford added hastily, 'Pray, do accompany us. We shall have a delightful time shopping together, then we shall meet Paul at the Swan for lunch when his business is concluded.'

Flavia was on the point of refusing when she remembered that there were one or two books which she would be glad to purchase. She also wanted to make enquiries about the cost of a new globe, and to do so in Mrs Retford's presence and with Mr Wheaton's knowledge would do no harm. It might even prompt one of them into making a contribution towards its purchase. With these considerations in mind, therefore, she agreed to go with them on the following day.

'Oh, excellent,' declared Mrs Retford. 'At what hour shall we collect Miss Montague, Paul?'

'At ten o'clock?' suggested Mr Wheaton. 'That is, if that will be convenient to you of course, ma'am.'

Flavia agreed to this proposal and soon afterwards, her visitors left.

The following day, they arrived as promised, only a little after ten o'clock. The day was a bright and sunny one, and Mrs Retford, clearly in high kick, was full of lively conversation. While glad of her welcome and her positive approach, Flavia found herself watching her prominent teeth as she spoke and wishing that she would just keep quiet for a little, so that she could enjoy the journey. Paul Wheaton smiled sympathetically, and Flavia wondered whether he, too, found his sister's constant chatter annoying.

On their arrival in Bedford, Mr Wheaton left them in order to attend to a small matter of business, promising to meet them for lunch, and Flavia and Mrs Retford set off to do their shopping.

The expedition proved to be much as Flavia had feared it might be. She had asked herself, rather impatiently, why she had been so reluctant to go with Mrs Retford. Now she knew why. She had a sudden feeling of being transported back to Bath, where from time to time she had been pressed into service to accompany one of the young ladies around the shops. At once, she found herself making the same approving and disapproving noises, encouraging any evidence of good taste, and above all wishing for the day to be over so that she would no longer be in the presence of someone whose company she would never normally choose.

'Oh, Miss Montague, pray look at that delightful bonnet!' exclaimed the widow, breaking into her thoughts. 'Do you not think it would suit me? It is quite discreet, after all, and very suitable for half mourning.' Flavia was about to say something along the lines of its not being quite her colour or style in order to discourage her from making such a purchase, when she realized that she bore absolutely no responsibility to anyone with regard to what her companion might buy. It was a very liberating feeling. She took a deep breath.

'I don't know,' she replied. 'Why don't you try it on whilst I go to that bookshop to see if I can find something, and I will come back in a moment to discover how you are getting on?'

Mrs Retford wrinkled her brow. 'Books? Sad stuff! But I suppose you cannot avoid them as a teacher. Very well then, but make sure you come back in time to see how I look in that bonnet.'

Thankfully escaping, Flavia crossed the road, went into the bookshop, and was soon happily absorbed in examining the wares on display. She soon found two that she wanted and, in a moment of inspiration, asked the shopkeeper if he ever had globes available in his shop.

'It does happen from time to time, ma'am,' he admitted. 'If you did not mind its being second hand, I think I might be able to get one for you quite quickly.'

'Second, third or fourth hand, it doesn't worry me as long as it is in good condition,' replied Flavia cheerfully. 'Pray let me know as soon as you have one in and I will come and see it.' She gave the man her address, and he promised to let her know when one became available.

She smiled as she began to cross the street, thinking of the expression that would adorn Mr Steeple's face when he heard that she intended to purchase a globe. She decided that if he refused to pay for it, and if no money was forthcoming from Mr Wheaton or his sister, then she might easily purchase it herself. She would then take it with her when, eventually, she left Brooks.

Thinking about the following incident later, she was bound to admit that she had allowed herself to be distracted from paying proper attention to the road. All she knew at the time, however, was that she was suddenly aware of a horseman checking his mount then calling out in a familiar voice, 'What the deuce do you mean by — ' and then stopping abruptly. With a sinking feeling in the pit of her stomach, she looked up into the face of Sir Lewis Glendenning. His expression of anger changed to that familiar one of malicious amusement. 'Well, well!' he went on. 'Good day — schoolmarm. How fate does seem to throw us together, does it not?'

'Sir Lewis,' she replied, flushing angrily for she knew that she had been at fault.

'Might I suggest a little more care in crossing the road?' he said. 'Such a bad example to set to any of your pupils.'

'None of whom is present, of course,' she snapped back, any impulse to apologize killed at birth by his sarcastic tone. He is enjoying this, she thought to herself.

'Perhaps it's just as well,' he murmured. 'This impulsive nature of yours will be the death of you, ma'am.' So saying, he touched his hat before riding on.

'Insufferable man!' she declared, staring after him. Perhaps fortunately, she had to wait before crossing the road as a slow wagon was coming past, and these few minutes enabled her to regain control of her temper.

She had no desire to reveal to Mrs Retford how much the baronet had annoyed her.

'Ah, there you are,' exclaimed that lady as Flavia entered the milliner's shop. 'I have tried on the first bonnet, but did not care for it so much on my head as I did when it was on the stand. But what about this one? Is it not ravishing?'

The straw bonnet which she was trying on was fastened with broad lilac ribbons and trimmed with tiny flowers of the same shade and it did indeed become her admirably, and Flavia said so. 'But then,' went on Mrs Retford thoughtfully, 'the one with white netting is also delightful, you know. Oh, the choice is so difficult!'

Abandoning the principles acquired over many years, Flavia said recklessly, 'Why not have both?'

Mrs Retford smiled at her, her eyes sparkling. 'Then I shall,' she declared. 'And what is more, you must have a new bonnet as well! Must she not, Mrs Springer?'

Quite understandably, the proprietress was very ready to agree that the wealthy and fashionable Mrs Retford had the right idea. In vain did Flavia protest. In no time, she found herself having all kinds of confections placed upon her head until eventually Mrs Retford declared 'There! That is the one! Just

147

look in the mirror, pray, Miss Montague! You never did see anything so becoming!'

Flavia did as she was bid, and was privately surprised at how well she looked. It occurred to her that although she was not a beauty and never would be one, she might possibly look better than she normally did if she could but have some good advice from someone like Mrs Retford who knew about such things. Because she was not short of money, she agreed to buy the bonnet, and was suddenly conscious of a most unworthy desire to have Sir Lewis see her in it and discover that she need not look like the 'schoolmarm' that he was always declaring her to be.

'Kindly have the bonnets sent round to the Swan,' Mrs Retford said, as she was re-tying the strings of her own bonnet. 'The bill for mine may be sent to Wheaton Place, and for Miss Montague's . . . '

'Oh, there is no need to send a bill,' said Flavia, drawing her purse from her reticule. 'I shall pay for it now and have done.'

'Pay for it now?' exclaimed Mrs Retford. She could hardly have sounded more astonished had Flavia suggested stealing it instead. 'But why do so, when the shopkeeper is perfectly ready to send the bill?'

'Why trouble to have it sent when I have the money to hand?' asked Flavia. She knew that among the rich, the custom was frequently to receive a bill and then make the poor unfortunate tradesman wait for his money for longer than was reasonable. On the other hand, because of her father's profession, she had been used to staying in places for a comparatively short period of time, and for that reason settling accounts quickly. Furthermore, the amount of credit that shopkeepers were ready to extend to Mrs Retford and her kind was not normally available to a sea captain on shore leave and his daughter.

The widow said no more about the subject, but merely shrugged as if at the inexplicable, tucked her hand into Flavia's arm, and said, 'Come, let us go or we shall be late for lunch.'

As they were walking together, Mrs Retford suddenly disconcerted Flavia by saying 'Did I see you speaking to Lewis just now?'

Flavia could feel her face colouring with annoyance at the recollection of the encounter, but fortunately her companion turned away at that moment to look in a shop window.

'Yes,' she said. 'He was riding past as I was about to cross the road.'

'Oh dear,' murmured Mrs Retford, catching something from her tone. 'Was he very rude to you?'

Surprised at the nature of the question, Flavia was caught off guard and she said at once, 'Yes he was. As a matter of fact, I have found that he nearly always is.'

'You must have caught him at a bad moment,' the widow replied. 'Actually, he can be quite fascinating if he tries.'

'So are certain species of snake, I believe,' answered Flavia dispassionately.

The widow giggled. 'Poor Lewis!' she murmured. 'He has upset you, hasn't he? I wonder whether I should insist that he beg your pardon!'

At that point, they arrived at the Swan and the business of locating the private room, which Mr Wheaton had bespoken, prevented Flavia from arguing against Mrs Retford's suggestion as strenuously as she would have liked. But she comforted herself that the widow had probably only made the suggestion in order to be provocative, and had no intention of carrying out such a course of action.

Mr Wheaton appeared within minutes of their arrival, and they all sat down to a well-chosen dinner. His business must have been successful, for he was in high good humour, and kept the ladies very well entertained. Inevitably, the talk turned to the shopping that the ladies had been doing, and

Mrs Retford was delighted to have the chance of describing the beauty of the bonnets which she had purchased. 'And Miss Montague has purchased one as well,' she added after she had extolled the merits of her own headgear, 'and it is quite delightful'.

'I have no doubts at all that she will look absolutely charming in it,' smiled Mr Wheaton.

Repressing the desire to say 'How can you possibly know?' Flavia merely coloured, leaving her shopping companion to describe it in detail. Irritated though she was by the conversation, however, it did give her the chance to reveal that she had gone to other shops, notably the bookshop.

'They have no globe in stock at present, but the man has offered to let me know as soon as one comes into the shop,' she went on. Then, after a pause, she added thoughtfully, 'Of course they are very expensive.'

'And not half so useful as a bonnet,' added Mrs Retford. 'I hated the globe when I was at school. So tiresome! I could never understand it at all.'

'I expect your interest in foreign lands must have been kindled by your father's travels,' remarked Mr Wheaton.

'Yes, that may well have been so,' agreed Flavia.

'Well I think that with *my* papa out of sight, I should have taken every chance to flirt with all the agreeable men!' declared Mrs Retford, tossing her curls.

'I have no doubt that you would,' answered her brother. 'But Miss Montague is obviously far more sensible than you.' Again, he flashed his charming smile at Flavia, and again she did not know how to respond. She managed to say something non-committal, but unfortunately, the subject of the globe had passed and she could not bring it up again without sounding too obvious.

Whilst Mr Wheaton was speaking to the ostler and as the two ladies were about to get into the carriage, they heard voices behind them, and turning, they saw Mr and Mrs Bell and their daughters.

'Mrs Retford! Mr Wheaton! Miss Montague! Never say that we have missed you!' exclaimed Mrs Bell. Her words were for them all, but her eye, not surprisingly, was on Mr Wheaton.

'Very nearly,' replied Mr Wheaton, coming towards them, his business with the ostler finished. 'We have had lunch and must now return home.'

'How disappointing!' replied Mrs Bell. 'But at least I can invite you in person to an alfresco luncheon in the grounds of The

152

Swallows next Saturday. All our friends are coming, and our gardener who is infallible in these matters has assured me of fine weather.'

'Thank you, we should be delighted,' replied Mrs Retford.

'And what of you, Miss Montague?' Mrs Bell asked.

Flavia opened her mouth to refuse, but Mr Wheaton forestalled her. 'Fortuitously, she has bought a new bonnet today,' he put in, 'and will no doubt be delighted to show it off.'

'Then in that case, we look forward to seeing you all at eleven o'clock on Saturday,' declared Mrs Bell. 'Come along, girls.'

As they drove back, Flavia reflected upon one hitherto unforeseen circumstance of living in a village, namely, that she would be included in any social activity that took place. She could not decide whether this circumstance was desirable or otherwise.

10

Flavia had half hoped that rain would prevent the alfresco meal at The Swallows from taking place, but the day dawned bright and clear, and Mr Wheaton and his sister arrived to pick her up as arranged. Grace had approved the new bonnet wholeheartedly, and threw herself into preparing her mistress for this treat with great enthusiasm. 'Now, if some gentleman should seem to take a fancy to you, don't drive him away with your eddicated ways,' she warned.

'Educated ways? Now, what might they be?' asked Flavia, quizzing her.

'You know very well what I mean,' replied the other severely, as she handed her mistress a Norwich shawl. It was one she seldom used, being much too fine for working days, but Flavia did not demur. She was happy to be known as a schoolteacher, but she had no intention of being mistaken for an *indigent* schoolteacher!

The Swallows was a house built in the same style as Mr Wheaton's residence, but it seemed to be a little older, and the creeping plants which had been allowed to gain some hold upon its walls gave the place a pleasantly mellow appearance. Flavia decided that although she did not care very much for Mrs Bell and her daughters, she very much liked their house.

Quite a number of people were already present in the gardens when they arrived, and Lucy and Evelina came at once to greet them. While applauding their courtesy, Flavia wondered whether they would have been quite so punctilious had Mr Wheaton not been with them.

'Upon my soul, I am very fortunate,' he declared. 'I have four beautiful ladies surrounding me! I am spoiled indeed!'

'But one is your sister, so she does not count,' said Mrs Retford spiritedly, 'and I will therefore take myself off.'

'And so will I,' added Flavia, 'for I can see someone beckoning me, and I am wanted elsewhere.' Quickly she made her escape. 'Beautiful indeed!' she muttered out loud. 'For heaven's sake have some sense!'

'My goodness, someone has annoyed you!' exclaimed Mary Glenn, who had approached unseen. She was dressed charmingly, and perhaps a little provocatively in a pale-green gown with a rather low neck and a bonnet with matching ribbons.

'Not really,' replied Flavia, reflecting

irritably that it was just like Mary to be able to spot what she wanted to conceal from those around her.

'Now don't tell stories,' replied Mary provocatively. 'I'm quite sure that you set great store by truthfulness, as did the rest of that pious crew of old Bread 'n' ale's.'

Flavia could not help smiling, but she merely said, 'I simply detest flummery, that's all — especially when I know it isn't true.'

Mary laughed. 'Let me guess — the endlessly charming Mr Wheaton?' Flavia smiled, but said nothing. She was conscious that she had been a little indiscreet, but she did not wish to compound it by naming names. 'I'll allow that much of what he says is flummery, but it is most agreeable flummery, you must admit. As long as you think of it as sport rather than as something serious, no one gets hurt.' She looked about her, then turned back to Flavia with a provocative smile. 'Such a beautiful day, and a perfect setting for sport, I'm sure you'll agree.' Seeing Flavia's disapproving look, she pulled a face in return, then walked off laughing.

Fortunately for Mrs Bell's plans, the day continued fine, and when the time for luncheon arrived, the party were able to eat at tables which had been set partly under the trees in the dappled shade.

'There is no precedence today!' exclaimed Mrs Bell in the carrying tones which Flavia felt would have been easily heard on board one of His Majesty's ships from bows to stern. 'None at all. Pray, everyone, sit where you like. Mr Wheaton, come and sit here! This is a very good place. I am sure that there is none better!'

Flavia smiled when she saw that Mr Wheaton was being directed to a chair which was set between Lucy and Evelina Bell. Everyone except him was to be allowed to choose their place, it seemed. Then Mrs Bell's voice rang out again. 'Sir Lewis! Here is an excellent place for you as well. Do come and sit here.' She was indicating a seat on the other side of Lucy Bell.

Today, dressed in a dark-green coat with buff breeches, the baronet looked every inch the country squire, but as always, that lock of hair was flopping over his forehead. For a moment, Flavia wondered what he would do if she were to get up and brush it back in place, but no sooner had the thought come into her mind than she hastily dismissed it, colouring a little. After all, his appearance was none of her business.

He bowed slightly. 'You are more than kind, ma'am, but I have already promised to give Gunnersbury my company.' With that, he turned away from his hostess, sat down next to an elderly gentleman with rather heavy features, and engaged him in conversation. Whilst this interchange had been taking place, Flavia noticed that a young man, whom she guessed by his dress to be a clergyman, had taken the vacant place next to Lucy, and that Lucy, far from objecting, looked more pleased than otherwise.

'Who is the young man?' she asked Mrs Retford, who came to sit next to her.

'Oh, that is Duncan Leyton,' Mrs Retford replied. 'He's a curate in a neighbouring parish, and very smitten with Lucy Bell as you can see, and she with him.'

'Is it a doomed romance?' Flavia asked, watching them. Even now, although Lucy was responding to anything that Mr Wheaton might say with perfect amiability, there was a warmth in her expression when she spoke to the young curate which was quite absent when she addressed her more exalted neighbour.

'I shouldn't think so,' replied Mrs Retford dispassionately. 'Leyton is the son of a bishop, and his mother has money and a title, and I doubt if he'll remain a lowly curate for long. Mrs Bell might hope for better but she'll have nothing to blush for in that connection.' She dropped her voice. 'One can see where her thoughts are taking her, of course, and I shouldn't be surprised if Paul were to oblige her in the end. Evelina is disposed to admire him, and I'm sure he would be quite prepared to fall in love with her, given the opportunity, and if only Mary Steeple will leave him alone. He is, after all, very susceptible, as I expect you've realized.'

Flavia, observing how readily Mr Wheaton responded to female attention, nodded in reply.

'Lewis, of course, is cut of a very different cloth,' went on the widow, as she tucked into a bowl of strawberries. 'Naturally, one knows that he has his female interests in town, but since our engagement ended, he has never given anyone here grounds for hope as far as I am aware. There was Miss Price of course, but that was all a bit of a mystery. In some ways he is almost a recluse, which is rather provoking of him. But you can't blame him completely, you know. I suppose you must have heard his wife died when Philip was born. And then, of course, the fact that he turned out to be deranged was a severe blow.'

Flavia stopped eating, her spoon halfway to her mouth. 'Sir Lewis's son is called Philip?' she said hollowly.

'Yes, that's right,' agreed her companion. 'What of it?'

'And is he about seven years of age, and silent?'

'He's certainly about seven, but as to his being silent, I don't know,' she replied frankly. 'I've never seen him.'

'Does . . . is there a niece living with Sir Lewis?' Flavia asked faintly.

'I believe so, although I haven't ever seen her,' agreed Mrs Retford. 'Why do you ask?'

'I think they may be coming to the school,' replied Flavia; then she bit her lip at her indiscretion.

'Oh dear,' exclaimed her companion. 'Does Lewis know? No, of course he doesn't,' she went on, answering her own question. 'I'm afraid he won't like that at all.' They sat for a few minutes in silence. 'What is Philip like?' Mrs Retford asked tentatively. 'Does he look very peculiar, or . . . or make funny sounds?'

Flavia felt suddenly repelled by her avid curiosity. 'He doesn't look at all strange,' she said a little more sharply than she had intended. 'And I have already said that he is completely silent.'

'A silent child!' exclaimed Mrs Retford. 'Well, there's something to be said for that, at least.'

By this time, the meal had come to an end, and people were getting up in order to wander about the grounds. Flavia was glad of the opportunity for a little solitude, for at that moment, she could give her mind to nothing but the unwelcome discoveries that she had made.

The first one to address, of course, was the fact that Sir Lewis clearly did not know that his son and niece were attending the school. It was of absolutely no use her upbraiding him concerning his treatment of either child whilst she herself was doing wrong by teaching them without his knowledge. This fact was bad enough, but far worse, in her mind, was the realization that it must have been the baronet who had terrorized Penelope. It was not a comfortable thought. She kept thinking of how big he was and of how he had stood facing her in the schoolroom, slapping his riding crop against his boot. Then she remembered how Penelope had cringed away at the sight of the cane in her hand and her resolve returned. What if he had used that riding crop on her? He must certainly be spoken to, and by her if nobody else would do it. He's a bully, she told herself, and bullies must be confronted. She just wished that she was not the one who would have to do the confronting. Well, he need not think that just because he was a man and a wealthy landowner that she was going to allow him to get away with it. She would find some way of exposing his brutality to those around him, so that he would be forced to change his ways.

She found a path which, to her relief, was deserted, and although she could still hear the sounds of voices nearby, the immediate vicinity afforded her some welcome solitude. Her walk led her beneath leafy trees, to a statue of a faun playing a flute, and upon reaching this statue, she turned left down what appeared to be a tunnel formed out of greenery. Once into it, she saw that the tunnel was in fact made from trellis, over which climbing plants had been trained to grow. Intrigued by this, she began to walk along its length, and indeed, she had almost reached the end of it, when suddenly Sir Lewis Glendenning appeared at its exit in front of her.

He was the very person to whom she knew she must speak, but as she had not yet decided how to deal with a conversation in which she must first apologize to him and then upbraid him, she found herself saying the first thing that came into her head. 'If you dare to call me schoolmarm again, I shall scream,' she declared, then bit her lip.

'You terrify me, ma'am,' he replied. 'I suppose it would not do any good for me to say that I was not going to call you anything of the kind?'

She looked at him doubtfully. 'That has almost invariably been your manner of greeting me,' she said.

He started at her for a moment, then grinned. 'You're right, of course,' he admitted, with a great air of frankness. 'In fact, that was exactly how I was going to greet you. But I don't really understand why you should object to it. After all, we call Steeple 'vicar', don't we? That's what he is. And you are a schoolteacher — or so you're always insisting.'

'Yes, but it is your sneering manner of addressing me that I dislike, and you know it,' she said forthrightly. 'Besides, you make it sound as if that is all that there is to me.'

'And of course, there is a secret side to you, is there not, ma'am? A side that no one knows anything about — apart from me, of course.' His sneer had become very marked, and he had taken a step or two closer to her, so that she was forced to look up at him.

'What on earth are you talking about?' she asked him, honestly bewildered.

'Perhaps it would be as well not to speak about it now. Anyone might be listening to this conversation, and besides, no doubt you have a tryst to keep.' He stepped even closer and took hold of her by her shoulders. 'But I trust you will remember my discretion when the time comes to call in favours.' He bent his head and swiftly kissed her on her lips. 'Schoolmarm!' he added, as he released her, then stepped past her and dealt her a hefty tap on her bottom. 'On your way, then,' he said, a note of rough impatience in his voice. 'You don't want to keep him waiting!' With that, he strode off hastily in the direction from which she had come only minutes before.

Outraged, she stood staring after him, momentarily lost for words. He had now given her yet another reason to confront him, and her first instinct was to follow him and give him a piece of her mind. Unfortunately, she knew that she would not catch him easily, hampered as she was by her skirts, and she had no desire to come face to face with him flustered and out of breath. Furthermore, it had now occurred to her that to confront him concerning Penelope was a matter that needed a degree of delicacy on her part. She had no wish to earn the girl another beating. Eventually, pulling herself together she began to retrace her steps, but when she reached the end of the walk, she was almost knocked over by a figure coming the other way. It was Miss Evelina Bell, and she looked as though she had been crying.

'My dear Miss Evelina!' she exclaimed. 'Pray, calm yourself. Come, let us find a quiet bench on which to sit so that you may become more composed.'

It was not the first time that Flavia had dealt with a distressed young lady of that age, and her sensible, even tones did their work. 'There is a . . . a little summerhouse nearby,' said Miss Evelina between delicate sniffs and sobs. 'We can . . . can go there.'

Once they were sitting down, and Flavia had provided Evelina with another handker-chief (her own having become sadly soggy) she said, 'Would you like me to fetch your mama? Or your sister, perhaps?' Miss Evelina shook her head vigorously, her curls bouncing with the movement.

'If I can just sit with you for a little?'

They sat in silence for a while, then Flavia said tentatively, 'Would you like to tell me what has happened to distress you?'

'Nothing has happened,' declared Miss Evelina defensively.

Flavia thought of how happy the young girl had appeared during the meal, and then remembered how Sir Lewis had disappeared round the corner of the hedge, in the direction from which Evelina had only just come. 'If some gentleman has not behaved as he should, then someone ought to bring him to book,' she hazarded.

Evelina stared at her, her face losing some of her colour. She was, Flavia reflected, one of those fortunate persons who, unlike herself, did not look hideous after a fit of crying. 'I am sure that I am not concerned with the actions of any gentleman,' she said with a pretence at carelessness that might almost have fooled a five-year-old.

No amount of coaxing could elicit any further information from her, and a short time later, she declared that she had a headache and needed to lie down upon her bed.

'Insufferable man!' Flavia said to herself over and over again that evening, in the privacy of her cottage. He had behaved in an outrageous way towards her; he had probably insulted Miss Evelina as well — perhaps in a similar manner — and he had certainly beaten the gentle Penelope. 'What a brute!' she exclaimed. But later, her mind turned to the question of what he could possibly have meant by saying that she had a secret side known only to himself. Could he have been referring to the way in which he had almost kissed her in the schoolroom? This was the only secret that she could think of that they shared; yet this hardly made sense when she also recalled that he had suggested that she might be trysting with someone. She had been warned by more than one person that he was someone of whom she should beware, and now they had been proved to be right. To run after him would have been a mistake, she decided. If she judged him correctly, he would have been quite capable of thinking that she wanted another kiss, which of course, she told herself severely, was certainly not the case!

She would have liked to have gone to Brooks Hall to see him the next day and confront him with some if not all of the matters on her mind, but by chance she had overheard that he was going to London for a few days to attend to some business. Probably enriching himself at someone else's expense, Flavia thought, then inwardly reproved herself. She had no reason to suppose that Sir Lewis's behaviour with regard to financial matters was anything other than above reproach. On the other hand, she reminded herself, a man who could allow one woman to destroy her reputation for his sake, man-handle another, reduce a third to tears and, worst of all, strike a gentle child like Penelope was probably capable of the lowest deed.

11

A few days later after school was over, Grace greeted her return to the cottage with the news that Mr Steeple wanted to speak to her.

'He sounded very excited, Miss Flavia,' she said, 'and he was disappointed that you weren't here.'

'Perhaps I ought to walk round to the vicarage straight away,' said Flavia.

When she arrived, she discovered that Mr Steeple did indeed appear to be in a state of excitement. He came to the door himself, and said, 'Come in, come in, Miss Montague! Such news! Such tremendous news!'

She followed him into his study. 'What is it, Mr Steeple?' she asked him.

He invited her to be seated, and sat down himself, but almost immediately got up again and walked restlessly about the room. 'I knew that he was coming of course; naturally I had been informed, but I never supposed that he would come here! We are such a tiny parish, you see. Of course, I had expected to be invited to Bedford to meet him, but this! Miss

Montague, it is quite beyond my expectations! That he should come here!' He looked at her, beaming.

'Forgive me, Mr Steeple, but you have not yet told me: who is coming?'

He stared at her uncomprehendingly for a moment before exclaiming, 'Oh Miss Montague, I beg your pardon! I am so excited, I don't know whether I am on my head or my heels! It is the bishop who is coming, and he is coming here!'

'You must be very gratified,' responded Flavia dutifully, not quite sure as yet how this prospective visit would concern her. 'When is this visitation to take place?'

'He is coming next Wednesday,' said the vicar.

'Is it not short notice?' Flavia asked, wrinkling her brow.

'Short notice?' exclaimed Mr Steeple. 'Short notice?'

In just the same way, Flavia supposed, he might have protested had she declared that a visit from the Almighty was not well timed. Realizing her mistake, she said quickly, 'Surely a bishop's visitation takes some time to prepare.'

'Oh yes indeed,' agreed Mr Steeple, clearly relieved that her remarks were not intended as any kind of criticism of his lordship. 'Did I not say that I had expected an invitation to meet him in Bedford? But apparently, the bishop wishes to see us. Us!'

'Us meaning . . . ?'

'Meaning you — and me, Miss Montague!'

'Me?' exclaimed Miss Montague, her voice coming out in a most uncharacteristic squeak. Then she cleared her throat and said in her usually low-pitched tone, 'But why should he want to see me?'

'Why, because of the school, Miss Montague! It is a notable success! The bishop is very impressed by what he has heard, and he wants to see the school in action.'

'A notable success?' replied Flavia. 'It's hardly had time to be that, surely.'

'Be that as it may, the bishop has heard about it and now he wants to come and see the school for himself.'

'That is certainly very encouraging,' said Flavia. 'We will, of course, welcome him as we would any other guest.'

'I hope that you will welcome him rather better than that,' said Mr Steeple reprovingly. 'It is not every day that the bishop comes, you know.'

★   ★   ★

The following Sunday, the visit was discussed at church, and in his prayers Mr Steeple

170

referred to the forthcoming occasion in such fervent terms that Flavia began to worry about it as she had not done before.

'I'm keeping well out of the way,' declared Mrs Glenn when they met in the porch after the service. 'Brian is being exceedingly tiresome about the matter, and Phyllis scarcely less so, so I shall go and stay with a friend in Bedford until it is all over.' Paul Wheaton was standing nearby as she spoke, and she glanced at him in such a saucy way, that Flavia wondered whether he would be finding a reason to ride into Bedford very soon.

Monday, Flavia decided, would be best spent in drilling the children into performing some recitations for their august visitor. At least, she reflected, they all knew the Lord's Prayer, and some of the older ones had been learning the twenty-third psalm. On the Tuesday, she decided, she would close the school and spend the day with Grace and perhaps Sara, cleaning and polishing everything in sight.

Mr Steeple arrived on Tuesday morning about half an hour after they had begun their work. 'I have had a short note from the bishop's chaplain this day,' he said. 'The bishop will be arriving to see the school at about one o'clock.'

'That isn't very convenient,' replied Flavia. 'Isn't it possible for him to come any earlier?'

Mr Steeple stared at her as if she had suggested that Christmas might be put forward for her own convenience. 'Come any earlier?' he faltered.

'It is just that the children will all have gone home for their lunch,' she explained. 'If he comes then, he will probably be seeing the school with no children in it.'

'But can they not stay on until he comes?' asked the vicar.

'I'm afraid not,' replied Flavia firmly. 'They are very good, but their ability to concentrate for long periods is limited. I fear that if I made them stay on at school for another full hour, then he would not see them at their best.'

'I see,' sighed the vicar. 'Then what is to be done? I do not want us to waste this valuable opportunity. If he is very pleased with what is being done, then some money from the diocese might come in our direction.'

Flavia thought of the new globe, and suddenly had a bright idea. 'Perhaps some of the children might remain behind; just a handful of the most co-operative ones. I could give them some lunch, and if he arrives early, then they will be there. And although it is not one of the days for the sewing group, I could ask them to come in the afternoon, so that whatever time the bishop comes, he will see something going on.'

Mr Steeple beamed. 'I knew that I might depend upon you, Miss Montague,' he said. 'Kindly see that that is done. Tomorrow will be a proud day, I am sure.'

He lingered for about another half-hour, and wandered about the building, peering out of the windows, and examining the desks and the floor, and making comments like 'Is it possible to get some of the marks off this wood?' or 'There is a cobweb here that someone has missed.'

When eventually he left, Grace said bluntly, 'Well that's a mercy! If he hadn't gone when he did, I'd have been driven to do something very un-Christian with this broom!'

The schoolroom was not dirty in the way that it had been before Flavia had started working there, so three of them worked steadily but calmly through the day until by four o'clock it was as perfect as it could be. The desks had been scrubbed and polished, the blackboard was gleaming darkly, and not a speck of dust could be seen anywhere. It was Grace who put their thoughts into words.

'I reckon that there bishop could eat his

173

dinner off the floor if he'd a mind to,' she said.

The following morning, however, when Flavia unlocked the school, a shocking sight met her eyes. She had left it spotlessly clean; now the school looked as if someone had scattered dirt everywhere. The vase of flowers that she had set upon the table had been overturned, and someone had scribbled all over the blackboard. The furniture was all higgledy-piggledy and some of the desks and benches had been knocked over. Mercifully, she had locked the cupboard and taken the key with her, and so the chalk, slates and all the other equipment that she had bought were unharmed.

She took a deep breath, then stepped back into her cottage and called 'Grace! Jane! Henry!' The three servants came quickly, and Jane and Henry both stood in silence, whilst Grace exclaimed, 'Oh my Lord!'

'Precisely,' replied Flavia.

'There's been mischief at work here and no mistake, ma'am,' said Henry. 'What can we do to help you put it right?'

These words of honest support threatened to bring tears to Flavia's eyes as the damage that had been done had not; but determinedly she pushed up her sleeves. 'We can get started straight away and get this place cleared up,' she said. 'I think it probably looks worse than it is, but if we are to be ready for when the bishop arrives, then there is no time to be lost.'

It was half an hour before the children began to arrive and Flavia sent them away immediately, with instructions that those who were part of the sewing group were to come back at their usual time. Sara and Penelope refused to leave, however.

'Just tell us what to do and we'll help,' Penelope insisted.

Jane found aprons for them all, so that they could keep clean for the bishop, and then they all set to work with a will. Philip remained with Penelope for the most part, not appearing to do anything very much, but when at last the work was finished at about half past twelve, he came in carefully carrying the vase in which he had placed some fresh flowers.

'Oh Philip, you good boy!' Flavia exclaimed. 'Fancy your thinking of that! Grace, take Sara, Penelope and Philip to the cottage so that they can wash their hands, then I will go and tidy myself up. Thanks to all your hard work, we should have a little time to spare before the bishop comes.'

Grace did as she was bid, Jane and Henry both went back to their usual tasks, and

Flavia was left alone in the schoolroom. It was only now that the work had been done and the panic was over that she began to wonder why it had been made necessary in the first place. Why had someone come in and deliberately made a mess in the schoolroom? She could not think of anyone whom she had alienated sufficiently for them to do such a thing.

Just as this thought came into her mind, however, the main door of the school opened with a crash as it flew back against the wall, and Sir Lewis Glendenning strode into the room. His golden eyes glowed, his scar stood out lividly against his complexion, and the usual lock of hair flopped over his brow.

'How dare you!' he spat at her. 'How dare you keep my children in this filthy place without my permission?'

His sudden attack took her breath away, but she could not but be aware that part of his accusation was just.

'I did not know that they were yours . . . ' she began.

He laughed derisively. 'Oh please! A little less ingenuousness would be more convincing.'

'It's true,' she replied, becoming angry herself. 'I had no idea that they were anything to do with you — poor little things — and

I'm not accustomed to being called a liar.'

'Well perhaps you should be,' he retorted. 'Where on earth did you think they had come from, children of that quality? Did you not even make enquiries?'

'I . . . ' she began.

'Why, you could even have asked Penelope herself,' he interrupted. 'But obviously that did not occur to you, madam.'

She was on surer ground now. 'It certainly did occur to me, sir,' she replied, emphasizing the last word to the point where it was almost an insult, 'but the only time when I broached the subject of her home background, she flinched away as if she feared to be struck!'

If she had expected him to be abashed by this thinly veiled accusation, then she was to be sadly disappointed. 'She might well,' he replied.

She was unprepared for the stab of disappointment that she felt at his words. 'You don't deny that she has been ill-treated, then,' she exclaimed.

'No, I don't,' he retorted. 'Although how you think that you are making things any better for her by encouraging her to frequent this mean and filthy place is a mystery to me.'

Flavia straightened her spine, drawing herself up to her full five feet. 'It may be small and simple, but it is not filthy, for we have been cleaning it all morning. I dare say you might eat your dinner off the floor,' she added, echoing Grace's words.

Sir Lewis's eyes narrowed, and, to her discomfiture, he latched on to the one word that aroused his suspicions. 'We?' he said ominously.

'Yes, we: myself and my servants and some others.' Her tone was calm but she could feel her colour rising and she wanted to kick herself.

'Tell me; has my niece been involved in this cleaning?' he asked her. His tone had become even lower and more ominous, and he bent over her threateningly.

'Well, yes, if you must know,' replied Flavia, determined not to be cowed and scorning to tell a lie. 'She wanted to do so. They were both keen to help . . . ' Her voice died away.

'Both? God Almighty, have you had the infernal impudence to have my son sweeping up here as well?'

'No, he has not been sweeping,' replied Flavia hastily. 'But he did bring in the flowers.'

The baronet's face was white with anger and his scar stood out even more lividly against the pallor of his complexion. 'Your effrontery passes all bounds,' he whispered. 'Not content with putting my children to work, you expose my son to public ridicule. Do you not think that it is torture enough for me to know that he is . . . is not as he should be, without having his affliction broadcast to the world? What kind of heartless harridan are you, in God's name?'

'At least I'm not a child beater, a libertine and a vandal,' she threw back at him, so angry that she was quite beyond all discretion. 'I wondered, when I came in this morning, what kind of depraved mind could possibly dream up the idea of strewing filth about my newly cleaned school, and the answer is before me now. It is the mind of a man who would do anything to keep his son and his niece indoors for fear that the world might discover the kind of . . . of unnatural monster that he is!'

'What the deuce are you raving on about now?' he demanded.

'My school was deliberately covered with dirt this morning,' she replied. 'But of course you knew that, did you not? 'This filthy place', you called it, when anyone possessed of the meanest intelligence could see that it is sparkling clean! But you did not expect it to be so, did you?'

They stared at one another in silence, and at that moment, they heard the sound of footsteps outside and voices in the courtyard.

'Oh good heavens, the bishop!' exclaimed Flavia involuntarily.

'Is it indeed?' said Sir Lewis, his expression at its most malicious. 'Then he comes in a good hour. He shall be told exactly what kind of interfering, high-handed, insensitive female has the running of his precious school!'

He turned and stepped down from the teacher's dais, and in that split second, Flavia realized how much she enjoyed teaching here, and how a few words from the baronet would ruin everything, and destroy all that she had managed to achieve. Without thinking for one moment of the consequences, she snatched up the vase of flowers on her desk, and struck him on the head, using all her strength.

He swayed, murmured, 'What the . . . ' then fell heavily to the ground and lay still.

12

Grace, Sara, Penelope and Philip came back in as Flavia was looking down at her work with an expression of horror on her face, the remains of the vase still clutched in her hand.

'Oh no, Miss Flavia, what have you done now?' exclaimed Grace, her expression more one of disgust than of surprise. 'You've killed him, that's what. It'll be Newgate this time, that's for sure.'

'What do you mean, *this time?*' asked Flavia, annoyed. 'You talk as if I am for ever hitting people on the head.'

Henry, who had followed up the rear, knelt beside the baronet and felt his pulse. 'No, he's not dead, nor even anything like it,' he said. 'He's only stunned. The bishop's just outside, miss. What shall I do with Sir Lewis? Put him in the cottage?'

'No, they may want to look in there,' replied Grace, taking the piece of vase from her mistress's hand. Flavia, suddenly and belatedly overcome with the enormity of what she had done, seemed to be temporarily deprived of speech, and could only look down helplessly at the insensible figure lying at her feet.

Taking over leadership of the situation, Grace said 'Put him in the cupboard. No reason why the bishop should want to look in there. Come on, Henry, you take his shoulders and I'll lift his legs. Miss Flavia, take the children outside to meet them and keep them talking until we've got him safely locked away.'

'What?' said Flavia blankly. 'Oh . . . oh yes; of course.'

She moved to the door rather in the manner of a sleep-walker, and was only roused by Penelope's saying to her, 'Miss Montague, why did you hit my uncle over the head?' Flavia looked down at her, but Penelope looked directly back at her with nothing in her expression but curiosity. There was no suggestion in her tone that she might think that her uncle deserved it.

There was no time to say more, however, for they reached the door and found, as Flavia had supposed, that Mr Steeple was there talking to a man in a clerical wig, and the gaiters and apron that declared his calling.

'Ah, our efficient schoolmistress!' exclaimed Mr Steeple, as she emerged. 'My Lord Bishop, may I beg leave to introduce Miss Montague to you?'

'Yes, of course, how do you do, Miss Montague? I have been hearing your praises sung,' the bishop declared in a rich plummy voice, 'and I could not resist coming here to see for myself what you have achieved.'

'That is very kind of you, my lord,' replied Flavia, dropping a curtsy. The fresh air had revived her, and the dreadful scene that had just taken place in the schoolroom, and above all its horrific conclusion, almost seemed to be part of another reality with which she had little or nothing to do. 'I am at a loss to discover, however, from where you have received the glowing reports of my performance, for I have only been here for a matter of days.'

Mr Steeple looked aghast. Clearly it was not the done thing for a mere ordinary mortal to appear to question anything that a bishop might say. The bishop, however, did not appear to be similarly shocked, for he beamed delightedly and said, 'I wondered whether you would realize how I have heard about you so quickly. The truth of the matter, Miss Montague, is that Miss Bredale is my cousin. I have known for some little time that Priscilla had been very sorry to lose her best teacher. She told me that you were to come here, so when I recalled that I was to make a visitation in this area, I made enquiries as to your progress. I must tell you, ma'am, that I have been very impressed by everything that I have heard; very impressed indeed! And so I have come to see your work for myself.'

'You are very welcome, my lord,' replied Flavia. 'May I introduce you to some of my pupils?'

The bishop signified his assent, and Flavia introduced Sara, Penelope and Philip, using their Christian names only, from a sense of discretion.

'Are you attentive for your teacher?' he asked them, his voice become even more plummy as he bent slightly to speak to them.

'Yes we are,' said Penelope. 'Would you like to hear us say the Lord's Prayer?'

The bishop signified his assent to this, and listened carefully until they had finished. Flavia noticed that Penelope, who started them off, was saying the prayer extremely slowly. She's making more time, so that we can be certain that the body is in the cupboard, Flavia thought to herself. Suddenly, she felt rather sick.

When they had finished their recitation, Brian Steeple said, 'Would you like to go in now, my lord?' The bishop agreed, and with that, they all went inside. Flavia's eyes were drawn to the door of the cupboard as to a magnet. It was closed, and the key was in the lock. Everything was quiet.

'This is splendid!' exclaimed the bishop, looking round and beaming. Quite what he found to commend in an admittedly clean but rather bare room filled with utilitarian furniture Flavia found it difficult to understand, but he certainly seemed pleased. 'And where do you usually sit?' he asked the girls and Philip. Penelope went to her usual place and took Philip with her, and Sara did the same. Then he began to ask Flavia about the number of pupils who attended the school, their ages, backgrounds and abilities.

'Well, I am delighted,' declared the bishop. 'Absolutely delighted.'

'Perhaps the bishop would like to see inside the cupboard?' suggested Mr Steeple.

'No, I don't think so,' said Flavia very quickly. She was about to suggest that they might adjourn to the cottage when a faint tapping was heard coming from the direction of the cupboard.

'What might that noise be?' the bishop asked.

'What noise, my lord?' Flavia replied, wrinkling her brow. The tapping gradually increased in force.

'That noise,' replied the bishop.

'Rats,' said Penelope, whilst Sara said 'Woodworm' at the same time.

185

'Rats?' exclaimed the bishop, looking a little alarmed.

'Well there aren't many of them and they're quite small,' said Penelope. 'In fact, they might only be mice; or voles.'

At this point, the hammering on the cupboard door became quite pronounced.

'Miss Montague, do you think it possible that someone might actually have become trapped in there?' the bishop asked.

'Oh, I shouldn't think so,' said Flavia in as casual a tone as she could manage. 'I'll look later. And now, if you would like to come to the cottage . . . '

The hammering became even more vigorous and was now accompanied by a muffled shout.

'Miss Montague, there is indeed someone in there,' declared Mr Steeple, and hurrying over, he unlocked the door, opened it and Sir Lewis staggered out. He was looking very pale.

'Good heavens!' exclaimed the bishop.

'Yes . . . good heavens,' echoed Flavia, suddenly realizing that she ought to be surprised at seeing a somewhat dishevelled baronet emerging from the schoolroom cupboard.

'Sir Lewis!' added the vicar. 'How can this be? Did you become locked in, sir?'

Sir Lewis looked at him for a long moment, then turned his gaze upon Flavia. 'It appears so,' he agreed.

'I suppose that you were . . . were satisfying yourself that the . . . the shelves were properly fitted, Uncle,' Penelope put in quickly.

'That was indeed kind of you,' said the vicar.

'Indeed! And what a sad reward for a selfless gesture, to have become trapped inside the cupboard,' declared the bishop in shocked tones.

'You are very right, my lord,' agreed Mr Steeple. 'In fact, such a striking incident could surely provide an illustration for a sermon. Do you not think that it is striking, Miss Montague?'

'Very striking,' agreed Flavia; even as she spoke, her own words made her think of the vase, and she only just managed to suppress a most unnatural urge to burst into hysterical laughter.

'I wonder whether I might sit down?' said Sir Lewis. 'The blow to my head has made me feel a little giddy.'

'The blow to your head, sir?'

'I expect you stood up suddenly and struck your head on one of the shelves, did you not, sir?' said Flavia hurriedly. 'But pray come into the cottage and sit down, and let me attend to your hurts.'

Sir Lewis stared at her. 'You are very gracious, ma'am,' he said, his voice almost becoming a growl.

'Well, it was in . . . in some sense my fault,' she ventured. 'After all, it was my cupboard that you were . . . were maintaining.'

'Some of what you are saying may be true,' he replied, his lowering gaze leaving her in no doubt as to which part of the sentence he believed to be correct.

She gestured for him to go before her into the cottage, then turned to Penelope and Sarah. 'Would you please show the bishop some of the things that you have been doing whilst I see to Sir Lewis?'

They went into the cottage through the double doors, but as they entered Flavia's sitting-room, the baronet swayed a little, and she caught hold of his arm.

'Oh Sir Lewis,' she exclaimed. 'Are you still feeling giddy?'

'Oh yes, you're all solicitude now, aren't you, ma'am?' he snarled. 'But you don't fool me one whit. Where d'you keep your heavy ornaments? I'd like to sit somewhere where I can keep my eye on 'em — *and* on you.'

Despite his words, he allowed her to lead him to a chair where he sat down heavily with a sigh, closed his eyes, leaned his head back, then winced as the tender part of his head

188

touched the chair back.

Flavia hurried towards the kitchen, but before she could get there, his voice stopped her. 'It was the flower vase, I take it.'

'It was,' she agreed.

'I hope it broke.'

'It did come off worse in the encounter,' she replied. Surprisingly, there was a sound from his direction that might have been a chuckle.

She went into the kitchen but there was no sign of Grace or the other servants. She supposed that they must be keeping an eye on the bishop. She found a bowl and put some water into it from a jug, then went back to the sitting-room. He was still sitting with his eyes closed, but he was leaning his head to the side, so that the back of it did not touch the chair. She soaked a cloth in the water, then probed gently amongst his hair to find the place where she had struck him. He had very plentiful hair, she noted, almost straight, of a dark golden brown, like toffee in colour. He winced as she touched the place.

'Damnation, woman, haven't you hurt me enough already?' he growled.

'It was quite your own fault,' Flavia retorted.

At that moment, the front door opened and Grace came in. 'Beg pardon, Miss Flavia, but the bishop is going soon and he wants to see you before he goes, and also to satisfy himself that the gentleman is all right.'

Flavia opened her mouth to speak, but Sir Lewis beat her to it. 'Go and detain him for a few minutes, then bring him in,' he said. 'See that no one comes in here.'

Grace looked at him for a few moments, then, clearly acknowledging his authority, although possibly against her own better judgement, she dropped a rather reluctant curtsy and withdrew.

As soon as she had gone, Sir Lewis caught hold of Flavia by her wrist with a steely grip. 'My own fault?' he exclaimed incredulously. 'What the deuce do you mean by it?'

'Kindly let go of my wrist,' she said angrily.

'Damned if I will,' he replied. 'How the hell was it my fault?'

'Curb your bad language in my presence, and let go of me,' she said. 'Or, believe me, I shall do something that you will regret.'

'Indeed?' he murmured, grinning malevolently. 'And how do you intend to do that — schoolmarm?'

Saying nothing, she brought her free hand down to join the one that he was holding, and squeezed the cloth hard so that cold water ran down onto the legs of his breeches. He did release her then with an oath, and sprang to his feet to brush the water off, but, as he did so, he swayed again, and was forced to resume his chair. She tried to help him, but this time he shook her arm off and sat down unaided.

'No, I'm not going to be fooled again,' he said, his eyes shut. 'You may choose to put on this face of womanly compassion, but you're a virago, ma'am. I've seen through you, and I could tell the world. And remember, there are other things that I know to your detriment.'

'What other things?' she demanded.

'Such as trysting with men at garden parties. Such as illicit meetings here.'

'What trysting? What illicit meetings? Sir Lewis, you must explain yourself,' she declared, honestly puzzled.

'Not to mention your kissing me in the shrubbery at the Bells',' he went on, as if she had not spoken. 'Your reputation would be destroyed.'

'No it wouldn't. In any case, I did not kiss you, you kissed me,' Flavia replied, but although her tone was confident, she was conscious of a sense of foreboding. After all, she recalled, he had already destroyed one schoolteacher's reputation. Automatically, she began to sponge the bump on his head.

'Ah, that helps,' said the baronet, after an initial wince. 'You think that you can rest on your Bath reputation, I suppose. But recall that I am a powerful man in this district. I could make it impossible for you to stay.'

'You are not the only person of importance in this district,' she replied, but her tone was less confident. True, Miss Bredale was a powerful advocate, and she had the approval of Mr Wheaton and Mrs Retford, and now the bishop, but would all this weigh against the fact that she had struck a local landowner on the head? And although she could explain away the other things of which he accused her, they could certainly put her in an awkward position.

'I could make it impossible for you to stay,' he repeated in dreamy tones. 'Or I could . . . shall we say *withdraw* my opposition? Ouch! Did you do that deliberately?' he exclaimed, in quite a different tone as, in her nervousness, she pressed a little too hard.

'No, I didn't, but it would serve you right if I did,' she said crossly.

'Everything appears to be my fault in your eyes,' he answered. 'I suppose I cracked my own head with that blasted vase, and threw water over my own breeches?'

'No, but you . . . you . . . Oh for goodness sake, you are the most infuriating man that I have ever met,' she finished eventually in exasperated tones.

'Be assured that I feel very much the same about you,' he replied. 'But to return to the subject in hand, how would you like the bishop to hear about your assault upon my person? I know he has a high opinion of you at present, but will that continue when he knows what I know?'

'You wouldn't tell the bishop,' she exclaimed, leaving off from her work and standing up straight in horror.

'I might not, if you agree to my terms.'

At that moment, Grace entered again, and said in tones of ill-concealed impatience, 'Can his whatever-he-is come in and see Sir Lewis now?'

'Five minutes,' replied the baronet. 'Take him round the outside and get him to count all the chimney pots, or something.'

'Chimney pots! My life,' muttered Grace as she withdrew.

'That won't detain him,' observed Flavia. 'He wouldn't have to count very long to come up with a sum total of two.'

'Then you'll have to make up your mind quickly, won't you?'

'Very well, what are your terms?' asked Flavia resignedly.

'Put that cloth down and come back over here,' he said. She did as she was bid, placing the cloth back in the bowl on the table, and then came towards him again. 'Now kiss me.'

She stared at him aghast. 'I beg your pardon?' she breathed, her eyes full of shock.

'You heard. Kiss me, I said.'

'But . . . but that's absurd,' she protested, turning a little pale. 'You don't even like me. You've just said so. Why on earth should you want me to . . . ' — she swallowed — 'to kiss you?'

He opened his eyes and looked up at her. They were gleaming with malice. 'Perhaps just to annoy you,' he suggested. 'Perhaps to remind myself of that charming idyll that we enjoyed together in the shrubbery: perhaps to enjoy what you give so freely elsewhere. The reason is immaterial, surely? Or if you like, we can stay here weighing the merits of your kissing me or not. Then when we've done that, I'll tell the bishop about how you hit me on the head with a vase and locked me in the cupboard, and you can explain to him exactly why you did it. Or had you forgotten that you have been educating my son and my niece without my knowledge and against my wishes?' Flavia stared at him in consternation. 'Well, make up your mind,' he went on. 'It's entirely up to you.'

What could she do? The mere thought of kissing him filled her with panic; yet how could she do anything else? She had no doubt that if she refused to comply, then he would tell the bishop what had happened, just as he threatened, and no doubt he would also throw in the other little bits of tittle-tattle that he had mentioned as well. Although she might tell herself that she could always return to Bath, the likelihood was that any gossip would follow her, especially since the bishop was related to Miss Bredale. She simply could not take the risk.

She glanced anxiously at the front door. There was no sign of anyone coming through it as yet. 'Oh, all right then, if you insist,' she said crossly, and bending down, she kissed him on his tanned cheek, then straightened as quickly as possible. 'Now will you promise not to tell the bishop?' She had no real hope that he would agree, for she was certain that what he had had in mind had been something far more lingering and romantic.

She was right. 'Will I promise?' he asked scornfully. 'After *that*?'

Strangely enough, it was as if his scorn brought back her courage. 'What is the matter with you?' she demanded. 'Do you collect kisses from schoolmistresses?'

For a moment, he stared at her, an incredulous expression on his face. Then with an oath which, with all the ripe language that she had come across as a sea-captain's daughter, she had never heard before, he pulled her down on to his knee and tilted her chin with his right hand, clearly intending to kiss her very thoroughly indeed. For a brief moment, the sneer disappeared from his expression and, as their eyes met, Flavia was conscious that her heart was beating very hard.

Before he could carry out his intention, at that very embarrassing and undesirable moment, the door opened to admit the bishop and Mr Steeple.

'Miss Montague!' exclaimed the bishop, his expression astonished.

'Miss Montague!' echoed Mr Steeple, looking not so much astonished as horrified.

Hastily Flavia scrambled off the baronet's knee, her face aflame. 'I tripped,' she stammered.

Sir Lewis looked at her under his brows for a long moment, and added, 'Or slipped. And I caught her.'

Instantly, the bishop's expression changed to one of approval. 'One good deed deserves another,' he exclaimed. Briefly, Flavia and Sir Lewis exchanged glances of complete bewilderment, but before either of them could work out to which good deeds the bishop was referring, he went on by saying, 'I am very pleased with what I have seen, Miss

Montague. Very pleased indeed.'

'Good chimney pots, are they?' Sir Lewis asked.

'Chimney pots?' echoed the bishop, looking very puzzled. Then, when Flavia surreptitiously indicated the bump on Sir Lewis's head, he nodded paternally, and went on, in much the same tone that might be used to a person of unusually small intellect or perhaps very poor hearing, 'Oh yes, yes indeed. The best I have seen.'

'I am glad that you are satisfied with the school, my lord,' said Flavia hurriedly.

'Oh yes, more than satisfied,' agreed the bishop. 'I also came to . . .' — he cleared his throat — 'to see how Sir Lewis was faring.'

The baronet rose to his feet. He was easily the tallest person in the room. 'I am bruised, but still in one piece,' he replied. He glanced down at Flavia. 'A poor reward for seeking to check the safety of the shelves in the cupboard, would you not say? Knocking myself out as I rose, and then being locked in . . . by mistake.' Flavia's first feeling when she heard his words was one of relief, but when she looked at his face, this feeling was replaced by one of deep foreboding.

'Indeed, indeed,' answered the bishop, his rubicund face wearing a solicitous expression. 'A most unfair reward for virtue. How are you to travel home, Sir Lewis? May I take you up in my carriage?'

The baronet made a dismissive gesture with his hand. 'I thank you, sir, but I am feeling very much better, and shall ride home. The fresh air will do me good.' He turned to Flavia. 'Miss Montague, will you have the goodness to send my children home?' His tone was bland, cordial even, but she could not mistake the expression in his eyes. He had not finished with her by any means.

'Of course,' she replied, her tone and her expression calm.

After they had all gone, the bishop with further words of congratulation, and the vicar, with an expression of approval, Flavia would have appreciated the opportunity to sit down in order to think about what had happened, but it seemed that no sooner had the visitors all gone than the sewing group arrived. In the excitement, she had forgotten that they had been given instructions to come that day, and her first instinct was to send them away again. Reluctantly, she came to the conclusion that she had been doing quite enough of that recently. Furthermore, after what almost everyone else in the community would have seen as a triumph, but which in her mind had been the most disastrous morning of her entire life, she should welcome the girls with enthusiasm.

She did her best. The gentle nature of the activity should have been calming to her nerves, but the conversation of the girls on this occasion drove her to screaming point, and she was heartily glad when, at the end of the hour, Grace came and shooed her into the cottage, declaring that she would supervise the putting away of the sewing basket.

★　★　★

It seemed as if that day, peace was determined to elude her, for no sooner had she sat down on the sofa in her little sitting-room, than there was a knock on the cottage door. Jane had gone out again, this time into the village to procure something for dinner, and Henry had not yet returned from escorting Philip and Penelope to their home, so Flavia was obliged to get up and answer her own front door. She could not think of anything she wanted to do less than entertain a visitor at that moment, so flinging the door back in a manner which would have shocked Miss Bredale to the core, and which was, in fact, very reminiscent of Sir Lewis Glendenning in high force, she barked out, 'Yes? What is it?'

Standing on the threshold was Mr Wheaton, his hat in his hand, and at her tone, he stepped back in comical dismay. 'Oh Lord!' he declared. 'I take it the visit didn't go well?'

'What? Oh no, no, it went very well,' replied Flavia, sounding distracted. 'I am just a little tired, that's all.'

'And not surprisingly in my opinion,' replied Mr Wheaton. 'I do not know anybody who works as hard as you, Miss Montague. And for so little reward.'

'No, that's not true,' she replied swiftly. 'My work is my reward, and the children are so responsive . . . ' She stopped. With a few brief words, drawn from her by this man, she had reminded herself of how rewarding her work really was. She smiled, a sunny smile that lit up her face, and for an instant made her almost pretty. 'Thank you, Mr Wheaton. You have shaken me out of my tiredness, and reminded me of how fortunate I am.'

'Blessed if I know how I've done it, but you certainly look better than you did when I arrived,' he replied. 'Thinking what a busy morning you will have had, I've come to take you for a drive. Would you like that? We could go to Turvey and have a bite to eat at The Three Fyshes. I'll swear you haven't stopped to eat yet.'

She looked at him and suddenly realized that he was right. She was hungry and ready for a change of scene. 'Thank you,' she replied decisively. 'A ride in the fresh air will do me all the good in the world.'

She was about to go upstairs when Grace came in from the schoolroom, and apprised of the nature of the outing to come, declared her intention of helping her mistress to get ready. She insisted on Flavia's changing her gown, despite her protests.

'Now, Miss Flavia, I know what's what and you can't go driving with a gentleman in that gown. That's what I call a work gown, and it's not proper and nor is your hair, done in that severe style.'

'Oh, Grace, for goodness sake, it's only a drive,' protested Flavia, but she submitted to her ministrations none the less, because experience had long since told her that this was the wisest course.

'Maybe, and maybe not,' replied the other. 'But there's no telling where it may lead after all. I must say, I never thought that coming to the country would work out well, but I may have been mistaken: I think he'll do very nicely.'

'Really, you make him sound like a length of ribbon or a pound of . . . of scrag end,' replied Flavia crossly, as she left the room to go downstairs. Then as she saw Mr Wheaton smiling up at her, she remembered with horror what a small house it was, and wondered how much he had heard.

As he handed her up into his carriage, he murmured, 'I must say, I've never been compared to a pound of scrag end before.'

'Grace is an old servant,' replied Flavia, colouring hotly. 'She talks a lot of nonsense.' The next time she spoke, it was to refer to the countryside through which they were to travel, and Flavia was very thankful that he seemed content to have dropped the subject. It was only much later that she remembered that it was she herself who had referred to the handsome landowner as a pound of scrag end.

As they continued in this gentle and undemanding way, she felt the tension inside her gradually unwind, so that when eventually he said to her, 'So tell me about the bishop's visit,' she suddenly saw the funny side of it, and in the middle of explaining how pleased the bishop had been she began to laugh, and the whole story came out. By the time she had finished, Mr Wheaton was laughing so much as well that he was obliged to bring his gig to a halt as he faced losing control of his horses.

'Do you really mean to tell me that you

locked poor old Lewis in the cupboard!' he exclaimed at last, as soon as he was able.

'Well . . . yes,' replied Flavia. She had told him something of the argument that she and Lewis had had, but she had said nothing about Philip's disability or about her suspicions concerning Sir Lewis's ill-treatment of Penelope, or of his vandalizing the school. She allowed Mr Wheaton to believe that the baronet's anger had stemmed partly from his disapproval of the school in general and partly from his annoyance at her having Penelope and Philip in the school without his permission. 'I was going to let him out later,' she added defensively.

'I'm sure you were,' he laughed. 'But did *he* know that? Lord, I'd give anything to have seen the bishop's face when he emerged!'

'It was rather a picture,' agreed Flavia. It was odd, but the more Mr Wheaton laughed about Sir Lewis's discomfiture, the less she felt she wanted to do so.

Mr Wheaton picked up the reins and drove on. 'What intrigues me is how you managed to persuade Lewis not to tell the bishop about what you did?'

Foolishly, it was not a question that she had anticipated, and she certainly did not want to tell him about Sir Lewis's demand that she kiss him in exchange for his silence.

Fortunately, Mr Wheaton was now giving his attention to his horses, and he did not see her colour up at the question.

'It wasn't difficult,' she said at last. 'He came to the cottage to have his head bathed, and the bishop left very soon after that.' It was true enough, she reflected. And after all, it was not likely that anyone else would tell Mr Wheaton that Sir Lewis and the bishop had had the chance to share a conversation.

'Well, to do him justice, Lewis might well not have told him anyway,' her escort remarked. 'With all his faults, he was never a sneak.'

'You have known him for a long time then,' Flavia observed, a little surprised to hear this word of praise for one whom she had previously thought of as being beyond the pale.

'Lord, yes. His family have been in this area for five ... six, generations? I don't remember. He'd be able to tell you better than I. And Wheatons have been farming around here for nearly as long. Lewis and I were at school together.'

'Oh!' exclaimed Flavia in surprise. 'I thought that he was older than you — by quite some years, actually.'

Mr Wheaton laughed merrily, and Flavia was conscious of finding the sound a little irritating. 'Yes he is, but only by about three years. I'm thirty, so Lewis must be around thirty-three, I suppose. He kept an eye on me at school — and I was devilish glad of it.'

Flavia was by now beginning to feel a little confused. 'Forgive me, Mr Wheaton,' she said, 'but you told me that he was an ugly customer. Now, you tell me that he is discreet and loyal. In short, you seem to portray him as being admirable.'

'Lord no, he's not that,' replied her companion. 'He can be an ugly customer if you cross him. That's true enough. It was one of the reasons I was so glad to have him looking out for me at school. And there's no denying he can be devilish prickly about that idiot son of his. I suppose anyone would be.'

As always, Flavia could feel her hackles rise at this insensitive description of Philip, but she hid her feelings, and simply made assenting noises. Obviously Mr Wheaton took this as sufficient encouragement to continue, for he went on, 'D'you know, I wonder if that was partly why he was so angry with you; because you encouraged other people to see him? Still, that's enough about poor old Lewis for now. Let's talk about something more agreeable — like how charming you look in that bonnet, for example.'

Flavia bit her tongue just in time to prevent

herself from commenting waspishly on Mr Wheaton's predilection for using the epithet 'old' to describe someone scarcely older than himself. In fact, there was much more that she would have liked to have asked Mr Wheaton about Sir Lewis, but she did not want to arouse his suspicions by seeming to be unduly interested in the baronet; instead she allowed him to move the conversation on to other subjects.

The Three Fyshes was an old, interesting inn by the side of the river Ouse, and in asking him about its history, she managed to prevent him from talking about her looks in a manner which, although clearly pleasing to most women, was not welcome to her.

It was only as they were travelling home after a very pleasant light luncheon of bread and cheese that Flavia ventured to mention the vandalism to the school.

Mr Wheaton looked serious. 'Have you any idea who might be responsible?' he asked her.

'I was hoping that with your local knowledge you might have some idea,' she replied. 'Are there any troublemakers who might take pleasure from perpetrating that kind of mischief?'

With uncanny insight, he said, 'If you're thinking about our friend Lewis, then I feel bound to tell you that you are probably mistaken. That kind of sneaking, conniving behaviour is not his way at all.'

'No, I had almost come to that conclusion myself,' Flavia agreed. She could not help feeling relieved that her companion was of the same opinion. She told herself that her relief was perfectly natural. It would be very unnerving to have a man as powerful locally as the baronet engaged in active sabotage of her little school.

'Would you like me to make some enquiries?' he asked her. 'One of my people might know something.'

'Oh, would you?' she exclaimed. 'I would be most grateful.' When they next spoke, it was of other subjects, and before long, they arrived back at the school.

After Mr Wheaton had driven off, she stood outside for a while, looking at the front door of the school. Who had been responsible for that morning's vandalism? Sir Lewis was the first suspect, and despite what Mr Wheaton had said, she could not rule him out completely. After all, he had not betrayed any surprise when she had accused him of vandalizing the school. Nor had he denied doing it, for that matter. Furthermore, he was furious about the fact that Penelope and Philip were attending the school, and he had made no secret of the fact that he had never approved of the school in the first place.

But taking revenge in this kind of surreptitious way did not really seem to be in keeping with the rest of his behaviour. It had not needed Paul Wheaton to tell her that. Storming into the school, throwing back the door so that it made the very rafters vibrate, shouting at her, glowering at her under his brows, those kinds of activities were Sir Lewis's way; not creeping into the school and scattering soil about in the middle of the night. Nevertheless, she resolved to find another opportunity to challenge him about it. He might not have done it himself, but perhaps he had employed others to do his dirty work. There was, after all, a hint of ruthlessness about him that seemed to indicate that he would be prepared to do anything in order to achieve his ends.

The thought of his creeping into the school under cover of darkness reminded her that Mrs Glenn had said that he had visited Miss Price secretly in the cottage. This did not really seem to be in accord with what she knew of his character either; although such secrecy would obviously have been necessary to save the lady's reputation.

The other thing that came to her mind was that he had not denied ill-treating Penelope. In fact, he had confirmed that such ill-treatment had taken place. But Penelope had seemed honestly bemused at the fact that she, Flavia, had struck Sir Lewis. What was the answer to the problem?

In thinking about the question of Penelope, another thought occurred to her: the baronet had referred to his son and his niece as 'my children'. What did that betray about his attitude to Philip and Penelope?

She went inside, and stood looking at the little clock on the mantelpiece as she untied the strings of her bonnet. The day had been an exhausting one. It was still only part way through the afternoon, and yet it seemed to her to be at least a week since she had opened the school doors that morning and seen the mess that had been made. Even the drive with Mr Wheaton, although pleasantly diverting, had also been tiring in its way, because of the topics which had been raised.

'You look worn out,' observed Grace, as she took the bonnet from her.

'Well, it's been a long day,' Flavia replied, giving voice to some of her most recent thoughts.

'Likely to be longer, too,' observed Grace dispassionately. 'You've a visitor coming.'

'Oh no!' sighed Flavia, her heart sinking right down into the toes of her shoes.

At that moment, there was a knock on the

cottage front door. 'That'll be her,' said Grace.

Bracing herself to confront Mrs Retford or even the vicar's wife, Flavia was surprised to see Penelope being admitted.

'If you please, Miss Montague, may I speak with you? I promise I won't stay long.'

Realizing that her weariness must have shown on her face, Flavia exclaimed, 'Of course you may. Grace, pray make some tea. Penelope, would you like tea, or would you prefer a glass of milk?'

'Milk, if you please,' replied Penelope.

When Grace had gone into the kitchen and closed the door, Flavia said 'Penelope, my dear, what has happened to distress you?' The thought went through her mind that she might have received another beating. 'Is it something at home?' she ventured.

'Not really,' Penelope replied in a small voice.

'Well, what is it, then?' Flavia asked, inviting Penelope to be seated, then sitting down next to her. The girl continued to sit with her head bent. 'We're friends, aren't we?' Flavia went on coaxingly. 'You can tell me all about it — whatever it is.'

Penelope thought for a little longer, then said all of a rush, 'It's just that I don't think that we — Philip and I — will be allowed to come to school again.'

Knowing that now was not the moment to utter optimistic lies, Flavia said as gently as she could, 'No, I think that probably you won't. But your uncle is right,' she went on, determined to give the devil his due. 'This is only a village school, and here I would not able to teach you all the things that you need to learn in order to take your place in society, which is no doubt what Sir Lewis wishes you to do one day. No doubt he will employ a governess for you very soon.'

'But I *like* coming here,' replied Penelope. 'Do you think that he might let me come to the sewing group even if I'm not allowed to come to school?'

'You could ask him,' replied Flavia. Then she almost kicked herself because, of course, Penelope would probably be too afraid to do any such thing.

'I was hoping that perhaps you might ask him for me,' said Penelope tentatively. 'He would listen to you. Miss Montague, are you quite well?'

Suddenly conscious that she had been goggling at Penelope like a goldfish, Flavia closed her mouth and said 'Oh yes, yes. Look, here is Grace with our drinks.'

After Grace had put down the tray, made sure that they had all they wanted, and disappeared back into the kitchen, Flavia had had a chance to pull herself together. 'And what makes you think that he would listen to a woman who had cracked him over the head with a vase only this morning?' she asked, with a hint of irony. 'He would be far more likely to show me the door.'

'No he wouldn't,' replied Penelope positively. 'In fact, I think he likes you.'

'Likes me? He can't possibly,' replied Flavia in positive tones, trying to ignore the completely unexpected shaft of pleasure that had run through her at Penelope's words.

'I think he does,' insisted Penelope.

'Well, I'll see what I can do, but I make no promises,' Flavia temporized. Almost immediately she had spoken, she began to regret making even such a feeble promise as that.

Before she could take back her words, or qualify them in any way however, Penelope said, 'I hardly like to ask him for any more, because he has been so kind to me already.'

'*Kind* to you?' exclaimed Flavia involuntarily.

'Yes. Then of course, I don't know him very well,' went on Penelope confidingly.

'You . . . you don't?' murmured Flavia.

'No; I have only been living with him for two months now,' replied Penelope. 'He brought me here from . . . from where I was living before.'

The thoughts to which Penelope's words had given rise had the effect of leaving Flavia almost speechless. Fortunately, her young visitor seemed to feel that her errand had now been satisfactorily discharged, and left soon afterwards.

It was now five o'clock, and if by lunch-time it had seemed that at least a week had gone by since the morning, it now occurred to Flavia that it felt as if a month had elapsed. Clearly there was much more to be unravelled here, but although she would have liked to question Penelope about where she had been living before she came to Brooks, she could see the impropriety of doing such a thing. One thing was perfectly clear: since Penelope had only been living with her uncle for a matter of weeks, whoever had been beating Penelope, it was almost certainly not Sir Lewis. She was unprepared for the sensation of relief which she felt as that knowledge dawned fully upon her.

But she was also conscious of a feeling of guilt, for she had accused him of that vile crime only that morning. There was a slim possibility that he had missed what she had said, or had forgotten it when he was struck over the head, but her hopes were not high.

Even if he had not heard or grasped a word, there was no excuse for her behaviour. She had accused him of a loathsome abuse of his power; she must apologize for it, and as soon as possible.

* * *

It was much later, when she was tossing and turning, trying to get to sleep that night that she got round to asking herself why on earth he had asked her to kiss him. He did not like her; she was sure of that, despite what Penelope had said. She did not like him; of course she did not. What could be his reason? Today had been the third occasion on which he had attempted to kiss her, and twice he had been interrupted. Would he try again? And why had he intimated that she had been bestowing kisses on someone else?

That night she slept fitfully, her slumbers punctuated by dreams in which the bishop locked her in the cupboard, insisting that she mend the shelves, whilst Sir Lewis Glendenning, rather oddly but not unbecomingly attired as a clergyman, cornered her in the vicarage, saying that if she did not kiss him, he would break a vase over her head! Ironically enough, just as in life the bishop had entered in the nick of time, so she woke up, just as Sir Lewis was on the point of pressing his lips to hers. 'Thank goodness!' she exclaimed, getting out of bed and preparing to rise. But she could not deceive herself: in the corner of her mind there lurked a feeling that was very like disappointment.

13

The following day should have been one filled with triumph as far as Flavia was concerned. The bishop had been, he had inspected the school and he had clearly been thoroughly delighted with all that he had seen. But the other events that had taken place had cast a cloud over everything else, and she found it impossible to enjoy her achievement. For the first time that she could remember since she had begun teaching, her only sensation when the children left at midday was one of relief, but this feeling was quickly succeeded by one of creeping guilt.

After the lessons were over for the morning, Flavia knew that the first thing that she ought to do was to seek out Sir Lewis and beg his pardon for her groundless accusations, but much to her shame, she found herself putting it off. She told herself that she needed time to think about what to say to him, but deep down inside, she knew that she was just being a coward. She wanted something to happen that would postpone what she knew to be her plain duty, and so when Mrs Retford appeared at the schoolroom door, she was more relieved than she would have believed possible.

'Miss Montague, have you finished for the day? I was wondering whether you would care to come and have a little light luncheon with me? Paul has gone to Bedford on business, so we can have a nice prose without his getting in the way.'

Flavia agreed to come, and invited Mrs Retford to go through into the cottage whilst she locked up the schoolroom, then put on her bonnet. As she was tying the strings, she remembered that Mrs Glenn was still in Bedford visiting friends. Was that the 'business' which had taken Mr Wheaton there?

Mrs Retford had come to the cottage driving herself in a little gig pulled by a handsome chestnut mare, and whilst she was inside, Henry took charge of her equipage. On the short journey to the house, the ladies talked of indifferent subjects. Predictably, Mrs Retford took the lion's share of the conversation, but it seemed to Flavia as if some of her remarks were uttered rather at random, and her conversation in general appeared to have a rather brittle quality. The reason for this became clear when they arrived at Wheaton House.

On their arrival, Mrs Retford led her visitor to the saloon to which Flavia remembered being taken after she had dined there as Mr Wheaton's guest. As soon as the door had closed behind them, Mrs Retford turned impulsively towards her guest. On her face was an expression of acute anxiety which she did nothing to disguise.

'We'll have luncheon shortly, but Miss Montague, I must say something to you for which I have been summoning up all my courage.' Flavia waited patiently, and was rewarded when her hostess said, 'I'm afraid that it was I who told Lewis about Philip and Penelope. I am terribly sorry.' Flavia was quite taken aback, and seeing her nonplussed expression, Mrs Retford went on quickly, 'I know that you did not expressly forbid me to do so, but I might have known that you would not want me to say anything. I did not intend to tell him, but it just sort of slipped out.'

By now, Flavia had had the chance to pull herself together. 'It doesn't matter,' she replied. 'I had no idea until I spoke to you at the Swallows that Philip and Penelope were even related to Sir Lewis. Penelope introduced herself by the name of Lynton, you see, and I thought that Philip must be her brother. But having discovered it, I certainly knew that it was my duty to disclose the matter to him. It was only the bishop's visit and all the preparations that went with it that prevented me from doing so.'

Mrs Retford looked relieved. 'I was sure that you would be dreadfully angry with me,' she confessed. Looking at her, Flavia was reminded of nothing so much as one of the girls at Miss Bredale's academy when she had been caught in mischief. Briefly, the memory amused her, but that amusement was soon superseded by a feeling of rather unwelcome surprise that an adult woman such as Mrs Retford should regard her in the same way as she would a teacher of whom she should be wary. 'When he stormed off, I knew that he would do something dreadful, but I could not guess what it might be.'

'I'm afraid that I was the one who did something dreadful,' said Flavia ruefully, and once more she recounted the story of how she had hit him over the head with the vase.

Mrs Retford did not laugh immoderately as her brother had done, but she did give a tiny gasp, and her hand flew to her mouth. 'Miss Montague, you are quite redoubtable!' she exclaimed. 'I should never dare do anything like that! No wonder you are a teacher.'

Flavia was on the point of saying that hitting people over the head had never before played even the tiniest part in her teaching career when the butler came in to announce that the table was now laid for luncheon.

Once in the dining-room, Mrs Retford announced that they would serve themselves from the cold collation which had been prepared for them. When the servants had gone, she said, 'Now we can talk. Do tell me more, Miss Montague. Did Lewis tell the bishop about what you had done?'

This time, Flavia was prepared for such a question and she said calmly 'There was hardly any opportunity. The bishop left soon after the incident took place.'

'You were lucky,' replied Mrs Retford, passing Flavia a plate with some slices of ham on it, then taking some for herself. 'Do you think that Lewis will make another opportunity to tell the bishop?'

'I don't think so,' stated Flavia firmly. She realized the mistake she had made by speaking so positively when her hostess asked, with narrowed eyes,

'What makes you think so? Did he say that he would not?'

Thankfully, before Mrs Retford could worm the story of the kiss out of her, Flavia remembered something that Mr Wheaton had said. 'Your brother told me that he is not given to telling tales,' she explained.

Mrs Retford wrinkled her nose. 'Oh, masculine honour and all that,' she said.

Flavia was struck by a sudden thought. 'I

suppose that Sir Lewis will be more against the school than ever now,' she exclaimed.

Her hostess thought for a moment. 'In all honesty, whatever happened, Lewis would have been against the school for a number of reasons, but mostly because of what happened in the past — with Miss Price, you know.'

With all that had happened, Flavia had forgotten about the mystery surrounding Miss Price. Now, the mention of her name acted as a very welcome diversion. 'Many people have mentioned Miss Price's name to me, but no one has told me very much about her,' replied Flavia. Of course this was not true, strictly speaking, for Mrs Glenn had been quite forthcoming on the subject; she was interested to know, however, what contribution Mrs Retford might make.

'Miss Price came here about twelve months ago but only stayed for six. She was in her early twenties and quite lovely.'

'Why did she decide to become a village schoolteacher?' Flavia asked.

'Why does any woman become a teacher? Because of lack of money,' replied Mrs Retford. Then, realizing the infelicitous nature of what she had just said, she apologized, colouring.

'Not all women,' Flavia corrected, smiling.

'I suppose there must be many who, unlike myself, are forced to become teachers because there is no alternative. But go on. Why did Miss Price become a village schoolteacher and not a governess within a wealthy family?'

'Ah well, that is where Lewis comes in,' said Mrs Retford in confidential tones. 'It seemed that the post had been procured for her by him, and it was widely suspected that she was his mistress. But there was a disagreement between them and she left under something of a cloud. Lewis was very angry, I believe.'

'Did he not want the school to close then?'

'He has never approved of the school, but I've no doubt that having it associated with a failed romance probably gave him an added distaste for the place,' said Mrs Retford dispassionately.

'Miss Price is now married, I believe,' remarked Flavia.

'Yes, she is,' answered Mrs Retford. 'How did you know?'

'I think Mrs Glenn may have mentioned it.'

Mrs Retford snorted. 'That doesn't surprise me. Yes, Miss Price married soon after she left Brooks.'

'I don't suppose you know her married name?' asked Flavia. 'I have a book of hers which I need to return but do not know to whom I must send it.'

'You could try asking Lewis,' said Mrs Retford impishly. Then she laughed, shaking her head. 'Poor Lewis! He doesn't seem to have very much luck with women.'

'You remain upon good terms with him even though you were once engaged to him,' speculated Flavia. Then she bit her lip. 'I beg your pardon; you will tell me, quite rightly, that I am being vulgarly intrusive.'

Mrs Retford laughed merrily. 'No, not at all,' she replied. 'Our engagement was over a long time ago and his entanglement with another is of no concern to me. Now, we flirt very agreeably and exist as neighbours without the least difficulty, but it could never go any further than that. I could never take the slightest risk that any child of mine might turn out to be an idiot like Philip.'

Flavia could feel her hackles rising at this slighting reference to Philip, but Mrs Retford, failing to realize the infelicity of what she had just said, began to speak about London, and soon it was time for the visit to come to an end. Mrs Retford offered to drive Flavia back, but this offer was politely refused.

'The day is fine, and the walk will do me good,' she explained. In fact, she had decided that instead of walking straight back to the school, she would go to Brooks Hall and speak to Sir Lewis in person. Up until now, she had had legitimate reasons for not going, but these were now exhausted. The deed had to be done.

She was halfway down the drive when she met Mr Wheaton riding back home, and he dismounted civilly in order to greet her. He did not look to be in very good spirits.

'Have you been with my sister?' he asked her.

'Yes, she was kind enough to entertain me to luncheon,' replied Flavia.

'But she has allowed you to walk home unescorted,' he replied. 'Now that I cannot permit.' He turned in order to accompany her.

'No really, there is no need,' replied Flavia. 'Your sister offered to take me home, but I refused her offer, and am quite content. And besides, you will be wanting your luncheon, I'm sure.'

He smiled ruefully. 'I am ready for a bite to eat, I'll confess. But let me walk with you to the end of the drive, at any rate.'

To this Flavia gave her consent, reflecting that she could turn to walk in the direction of Brooks Hall after he was out of sight. 'Did your business in Bedford prosper, Mr Wheaton?'

'It was very tiresome,' he replied, in tones that were just the polite side of irritable. 'In fact, had I realized how tiresome it would be, I would not have gone; especially if I had known that my sister would be entertaining a charming guest in my absence.'

'Mr Wheaton, you are being absurd,' replied Flavia.

She meant it in all honesty; he took it as a contribution to a flirtatious conversation, and said, 'Come come, Miss Montague! Now it is you who is being absurd. Or am I the only man who has ever had the sense to tell you how charming you are?' By now, they had reached the entrance to the drive, and Mr Wheaton took hold of her hand. 'Such a dainty member,' he commented. 'It is difficult to believe that such a hand could ever have wielded a cane.'

'Believe it, Mr Wheaton,' she said decisively. She tried to pull her hand away, but Mr Wheaton was holding it a little more firmly than she had supposed and she did not want to take part in an unseemly scuffle in the gateway.

'Well, if you tell me that it is so, of course I must believe it,' he replied.

Another little tentative tug revealed that her hand was held as firmly as before. Any of the senior girls at Miss Bredale's, with that instinct for flirtation which for some of them seemed to be inborn, would have known how to make him let go, she thought crossly. The only phrase that came to her mind was 'unhand me sir', and to use it would have seemed to make too much of the matter. At that moment, there was a sound of horse's hooves, and Sir Lewis came trotting by. He looked down at them, a quizzical look on his face.

'You do well to keep that hand of hers imprisoned,' said the baronet sardonically. 'She can do a good deal of damage with it, as I know to my cost.'

Mr Wheaton released her then, and sketched a bow. 'As indeed we all know,' he replied, his eyes sparkling. 'How is your head, Lewis? Still smarting?'

The baronet stared down at Flavia, his expression far from friendly. 'If it isn't, then it's no thanks to Miss Montague. I see I don't need to tell you anything about it: she has clearly spread the story far and wide.'

'Well, she's such a tiny thing to fell a great fellow like you! You must admit, Lewis, it was far too amusing to keep to herself,' answered Mr Wheaton, beginning to laugh as he spoke.

'Very amusing,' snapped the baronet. 'I suppose, Miss Montague, it must be very pleasing to think that you have managed to keep the neighbourhood so well entertained. Good day to you!' So saying, he rode away in the opposite direction to Brooks Hall before either of the two on foot could speak another word.

'Poor old Lewis!' exclaimed Mr Wheaton, laughing again. 'He can't bear to be laughed at.'

'Well, of course he can't,' retorted Flavia angrily. 'Mr Wheaton, how could you?'

'What's the matter?' he asked her, much surprised. 'You laughed as heartily as I when you told me about it yesterday.'

'Yes, and I wish I'd never done so,' she replied wretchedly. Then she repeated 'Oh Mr Wheaton, how could you?' The horse, a little disturbed by her raised voice, moved restlessly.

'Are you worried about hurting Lewis's feelings?' Wheaton asked her, keeping a firm hold of the reins and giving the horse a reassuring pat. 'He hasn't got any, you know. Don't worry, he'll soon forget about it.'

'Oh will he?' said Flavia in an ironic tone which had brought many a recalcitrant senior pupil back into line. 'Mr Wheaton, you made much of his sense of play which would prevent him from 'sneaking' about me as you put it. What will his reaction be now that he has discovered that I cannot keep his humiliation to myself? In short, why should he play fair if I do not?'

Mr Wheaton's face fell ludicrously. 'Oh Lord, I hadn't thought of that,' he said. 'Had I better ride after him, do you think?' He made as if to mount his horse, but Flavia spoke before he could do so.

'No, no, I don't want you to say another word to him about me unless I am present to hear it,' she said decidedly. 'Go and have your luncheon. I will speak to him later.'

Mr Wheaton, responding to the note of authority in her voice which had inspired obedience in so many, got back on his horse. 'I'll bid you good day, then, and . . . er . . . I do apologize for . . . for . . . '

'Think no more of it,' replied Flavia, more because she felt that she ought than because she really meant it. 'I'll speak to him myself later.' But it would have to be much later, for he had not ridden back home, and she had no notion of when he might choose to return.

Oh dear, she thought to herself as she walked away. *The list of things for which I need to apologize to that wretched man is getting longer and longer!*

14

For the second day running, Flavia awoke with dread in her heart, and for a few moments she could not recall why. Then she remembered that the encounter with Sir Lewis could not be avoided any longer. As soon as school was over, she decided, she would go over to Brooks Hall and request an interview with Sir Lewis. If he was not there, then she would request — politely — that he should call upon her at his earliest convenience. And when she did meet him she would have to grovel. There was no other word for it.

She got up, began to descend the stairs, then paused halfway down. The baronet's tendency to manhandle her was already proven, and on both occasions that had been on her own ground. Would it really be wise, she wondered, to confront him on his own territory? After all, she thought indignantly, he had just as much to apologize for as had she, though doubtless he would not admit it. Clearly he thought of unprotected schoolmistresses as fair game. Crossly she resumed her journey down the stairs and ate her breakfast with none of her usual relish. How she wished that it could be just twenty-four hours later, and the job done!

As the time for lessons drew near, she could hear the children assembling noisily in the yard, and when the moment came for school to start, she went outside with the bell — yet another item acquired during her shopping expedition to Bedford. It was as she was ringing it that she saw the two people she least expected to see — Penelope and Philip. She had not thought it possible for her heart to sink any lower, but it certainly seemed to do so. Sir Lewis had made his wishes clear. The children must be sent home. Her first instinct was to send them immediately, but she did not want to single them out in front of the others, as if they had done wrong. Furthermore, she felt quite powerless before the appeal of those two solemn up-turned faces.

She had written some letters on the blackboard for the class to copy, so she decided to allow that work to proceed whilst she talked to Penelope, then dismiss the whole class and take the two children back to Brooks and see Sir Lewis at the same time.

After the children were all settled down with their slates and their chalk, Flavia beckoned Penelope over to her desk.

'Does your uncle know that you are here?' she asked, her voice lowered. Penelope stood looking down at her feet. Flavia sighed. 'I thought as much. You told me only yesterday that he would not let you come to the school. Why have you disobeyed him?'

'I like it here,' replied Penelope, also in a low tone. 'I like the other people in the school and I like you, Miss Montague.'

Flavia could not help being touched at these words, but she knew her duty. 'My dear, I cannot possibly go against his wishes and you know it.'

'I was hoping we wouldn't have to tell him,' said Penelope.

'There is nothing I would like better than to teach you, but it would be very improper of us to deceive him, wouldn't it?'

'I suppose so,' answered Penelope in a downcast voice. 'Can I just stay and copy my letters, though?'

'Very well,' answered Flavia with another sigh. 'But then I really must take you home.'

As Penelope stepped down from the platform, she brushed against the blackboard and, before either Flavia or Penelope could do anything to stop it, it fell down on to the floor with an enormous crash. Fortunately, it did not fall on to anybody, but every head tilted up, and Flavia was aware of every face staring in surprise; every face except one. Philip had taken no notice of what had happened and was carefully drawing on his slate. Flavia stared at him, a sudden, breathtaking notion entering her mind.

Immediately absolving Penelope from blame, Flavia replaced the blackboard on the easel so that the children could continue their work. Then she walked around the classroom until she was standing immediately behind Philip, and firmly, she clapped her hands. The other children, interrupted once more, but by a noise that was familiar to them, looked up to see what she wanted. Philip ignored her completely.

Of course he did not respond when people spoke to him. Of course he was not able to talk. It seemed perfectly obvious now: he was deaf.

Knowing that after her momentous discovery she would not be able to give her mind to anything else that morning, Flavia quickly inspected the children's work, then gave instructions for the equipment to be put away and dismissed the class. The bishop would probably have been less impressed with her performance, she decided, had he realized that she had recently developed a regrettable habit of teaching for approximately ten minutes a day.

She instructed Penelope and Philip to wait whilst she put her things away and she hurried as she did so. It occurred to her that Sir Lewis might well suspect her of luring his son and his niece away and that he could easily be distrustful of her motives. It was with a sinking heart, therefore, that she heard the sound of firm footsteps outside, and when the door opened, she looked up and saw with a horrible feeling of inevitability that it was Sir Lewis himself.

Aware of tension in the little figure of Penelope, Flavia said, 'Don't worry, it will be all right.'

Sir Lewis walked purposefully towards her. 'Perhaps I did not make myself sufficiently clear to you,' he said in a soft tone which did not deceive her at all. He was furiously angry, but did not want to reveal this in front of the children. 'The day before yesterday, you told me that you did not know that these children were mine and that, if true, did at least amount to some kind of excuse for your conduct. But today, you cannot even offer that sop to your conscience. You knew that they were mine, you knew that they were here against my will, yet still you lured them here.'

'Lured!' she exclaimed contemptuously, quite forgetting that she had used that very word in her own imaginings. 'What kind of

literature do you read, Sir Lewis? If I have
lured them, as you express it, then it was
quite unconsciously. Their arrival here this
morning was unbidden and a complete
surprise to me. I have now closed the school
for the day so that I might bring them back.'

He gave a crack of laughter. 'Easy to say,'
he sneered.

'It also happens to be true,' she flashed
back at him. 'Why else do you think I have
dismissed the other children?'

'How should I know?' he asked incredulously. 'Why should I have the slightest idea
what goes on or what hours you keep in this
squalid hovel? What kind of teacher are you,
anyway? Lacking in respect for those upon
whose good will you depend; callously
unconcerned for those who suffer; by God,
madam, I'll have you hounded from this
place for what you have done.'

Silence fell between them, and then they
heard a small cry. Penelope was standing,
white-faced, her hands to her mouth. 'Please
don't be angry,' she whimpered. 'I'm sorry,
it's all my fault. I should never have come.
But, Uncle, I like Miss Montague and I did
so want to learn.'

To Flavia's amazement, the baronet's face
softened. 'It's all right,' he said gently, putting
out his hand to stroke his niece's hair. 'It's

not your fault, sweetheart.' Then he turned once more to Flavia, all softness gone from his face. 'You're the one I blame,' he said.

'I?' she exclaimed. 'How can I be to blame? It is not my responsibility to hire a governess for the children in your care.'

He flushed. 'I grant you that that is my responsibility with regard to Penelope, but how can you speak so concerning Philip?'

'Oh for goodness sake,' Flavia declared exasperatedly. 'Philip only needs — '

'How dare you lecture me on what Philip needs?' he stormed. 'I am his father.'

'Then take some notice of him,' she shouted. 'Can you not see, you stupid man, that there is nothing whatsoever the matter with Philip, save that he is deaf?'

The silence that fell then was palpable in its intensity. 'Deaf?' breathed the baronet, in the tone of one who was unsure as to the meaning of the word.

Philip was standing in his usual place, looking out of the window. Flavia came up behind him and sharply clapped her hands. He did not react by as much as the twitch of a muscle. Then she touched his arm, he turned and she led him to one of the desks. Philip looked at her solemnly, then got up, and went to sit elsewhere.

Flavia looked at the baronet. 'That is his

usual place,' she said. 'Penelope, fetch me a slate and chalk please.' The girl did as she was bid. Making sure that the boy was looking at her, Flavia said to him, 'Philip, I want you to write '4' on your slate. She held up four fingers in front of him. He looked carefully, then drew four marks on his slate, and painstakingly wrote the figure 4 next to them. 'You see?' she said to Sir Lewis, her voice not as steady as she would have liked. The baronet bent down to examine the writing on the slate, then looked wonderingly at his son. It seemed to Flavia as if he was trying to discern what it was that he had failed to understand all these years.

'When did you discover this?' he asked, a hint of sharpness in his voice.

'Only just now,' she replied. 'Do you really think that I would have kept such tidings from you?' At that moment, Philip looked up into his father's face, and quite involuntarily, Flavia found herself adding, 'He's so much like you.'

Sir Lewis looked straight at her. 'But whereas one of us is deaf, the other is blind, eh? Miss Montague, I have a feeling that there are things that I need to say to you, and, possibly, things to unsay, but at the moment, my mind's in a turmoil and I don't have the words. You'll forgive me, I hope, if I take these children home.'

He took Philip by the hand, and gestured to Penelope to go with him. Then, when he had reached the door, he turned round and, with something like the usual gleam in his eye, he said, 'Good day to you . . . school-marm.'

15

After the rather painful and exciting scene involving Sir Lewis, his son and his niece, Flavia felt very much in need of a period of quiet reflection, in order to think about what had taken place. The occurrence seemed to have taken her appetite away so after telling Jane that she would not be requiring any lunch, she put on her bonnet and set out for a walk. She took the path that led behind the church and the vicarage, then turned left in the direction of Stagsden. Neither Brooks Hall nor Wheaton House overlooked this road; and since it was in the opposite direction to Bedford, where Mrs Retford seemed to spend an inordinate amount of time, Flavia judged that the chances of meeting with any of the local gentry would be comparatively small. The last thing that she wanted was for the dashing widow to whisk her away for another of those intimate little chats of which she seemed to be so fond.

At last free of the village, she felt that she could think about the scene that had just been acted out in the schoolroom. It was, of course, a shocking thing that a child should attain the age of seven without his father's realizing that he was deaf. And yet, at the same time, she was forced to acknowledge that it was not entirely surprising. People of Sir Lewis's degree did not commonly have a great deal to do with their children in infancy; even later, parents tended to be distant beings. Boys were generally sent away to school in their early teens, or even before, only returning for holidays. Before that happened, they would spend most of their time with tutors or governesses, only being brought down to the drawing-room at certain times of day, providing, of course, that it was convenient for Mama and Papa.

Nor was it surprising that Sir Lewis, losing his wife at the birth of his child, should initially refuse to have anything to do with him. Someone with very little understanding of deafness and its effects had obviously made the judgement that there was something wrong with Philip's mind, and had allowed this information to be spread about the neighbourhood. Slashing fiercely across some nettles with a stick that she had found, Flavia decided that she would like to have words with that person. Immediately, a memory of Sir Lewis slapping his riding crop against his boot came into her mind and she hurriedly dropped the stick. Good grief, she thought, I'm turning into the wicked squire!

To distract her mind from that very disturbing thought, she looked around her at the growing crops. She was not a country-woman, but it seemed to her that the corn was now looking golden and very well grown. Surely it would be harvest time soon. She was just thinking that it was about time for her to turn back, when she saw a smart little gig coming towards her pulled by a neat bay horse, and in the driving seat was Miss Evelina Bell. 'Miss Montague!' the younger woman exclaimed. 'What a lovely day it is!'

'It is indeed,' replied Flavia, thinking that Miss Evelina was looking much more cheerful on this occasion than when she had last seen her.

'May I take you up? You can drink tea with us. Mama and Lucy will be glad to see you, and we will make sure that you are taken home again afterwards.'

'Thank you,' replied Flavia. 'I should very much like to do so.' The groom got down to help her up, and was about to scramble up behind them, when Evelina said, 'Would you mind walking back, Duncombe? I want to talk confidentially with Miss Montague.'

'Very good, miss.'

'It isn't far,' said Evelina. 'He won't mind, and his daughter's cottage is on the way. He'll be glad of the chance to pop in and see her.'

Evelina turned the gig very competently, and they were soon trotting smartly towards The Swallows. 'I think Mama would call it The Belfry if she thought she could get away with it,' said Mama's younger daughter. 'I love her dearly, but honestly, I think sometimes that if she tells anybody else about that Stagsden Belles thing, I shall scream.'

Flavia laughed. 'Parents do not always understand how their children feel, I think,' she said, remembering how careful she had had to be when telling her father that she wanted to teach.

They drove on a little further in silence, then Evelina said carefully, 'Perhaps you will recall, Miss Montague, that when we last met, I was a little less cheerful than I am today.'

'Yes, I do recall,' Flavia replied. 'I am glad to see that you are so much recovered.'

'I have been wanting to thank you for your discretion. I did not want anyone to know about my . . . my distress.'

'I have certainly not mentioned the matter to anybody,' Flavia reassured her.

'There is a . . . a gentleman in whom I have an interest,' she went on, 'and I had been given to understand that that interest was a mutual one.' She paused. 'Something happened . . . ' She fell silent again.

'Pray do not feel obliged to tell me anything, Miss Evelina,' said Flavia reassuringly.

Evelina smiled. 'You are very kind, but I want to tell you about it. You seem to understand young people.' She paused again. 'Something happened which made his protestations seem false, and I felt betrayed.'

'But you are now feeling better about the matter?'

'Yes,' said Evelina, as they turned into the gateway. 'I have decided that I may have been mistaken about the . . . the incident which I saw, and that I would be very foolish to take an irrevocable step on such slim evidence.'

As they entered the drive, Mr Bell rode up, calling a greeting, and the time for confidences was therefore at an end.

As Evelina had predicted, the whole of the Bell family were pleased to see her. Mr Leyton the curate was present, and from the affable way in which he was being included in the family gathering, Flavia gathered that he had been fully accepted as Lucy's suitor. Mrs Bell seemed less strident on her own home ground, with only her family about her, and Flavia spent a much happier hour there than she would have supposed possible after her first meeting with them. When Mr Bell drove her home afterwards, she felt that she had made some agreeable new friends.

On her arrival back at the cottage, she did not go straight in, but wandered down to sit on the grass at the place where the two brooks intersected. She had not had time to think about what Miss Evelina had said to her before their arrival at The Swallows, and she wanted to go over the conversation again in her mind. When she had encountered Evelina in great distress, that day at the Swallows she had assumed that the girl had been man-handled by Sir Lewis in some way. At worst, she had reckoned that he might have insulted Evelina in a similar manner to the way in which he had insulted her. She had no doubt that he was something of a rake; the scandal concerning Miss Price was evidence enough of that. But even the most confirmed rake would hardly kiss one woman at a garden party, then, only moments later, risk further discovery by kissing another.

At best, she had wondered if he had simply brushed the younger woman aside in an unmannerly way, perhaps causing her to fall. Of course it was quite possible that he had jostled Miss Evelina rudely, but such an incident would hardly have reduced a healthy young countrywoman to tears. And from what Evelina had said, she now perceived that neither of these explanations would do. 'The incident which I saw', she had said, not 'the behaviour to which I was subjected'.

For one horrible moment, it seemed possible that the incident to which Evelina had referred had been the moment when Sir Lewis had kissed her, Flavia. But, just as quickly, she realized that this could hardly have been the case, or why would Evelina have come to her for comfort? She could not forget either, that since the garden party, she had been given a glimpse of a different Sir Lewis; a man who had certainly not beaten Penelope; a man who *could* show restraint, despite appearances; a man with a sense of humour. But if the man who had upset Evelina was not Sir Lewis, then who could it have been? A memory, too fleeting to be captured, lingered at the back of her mind, and she resolved to think no more of the matter at present but to come back to it later, when the elusive thought returned.

As she sat looking down into the water, she was struck with a sudden brilliant idea, and she hurried inside to speak to Grace. 'The children deserve a reward to celebrate the successful visit made by the bishop,' she said as she took off her bonnet, 'and I've decided what it shall be. Will you please ask Jane to come in here? I shall need her help as well.' When Jane had come through from the kitchen, Flavia went on, 'I have decided that we shall have a picnic to celebrate our success with the bishop.'

'A picnic, ma'am?' questioned Jane.

'Certainly. What could be better?'

'Well I don't know, I'm sure,' said Jane doubtfully. 'Do you think that they'll be allowed?'

'Why not?' replied Flavia, ideas now coming to match with her enthusiasm. 'It need not be a big picnic or a fancy affair. We could have a short lesson in the schoolroom, then go out and play some games by the brook. If we have the picnic on Monday, we can spread the word today so that all the parents know what is happening.

'Henry could go round the village and let the families know about it,' suggested Grace.

'That's a good idea,' replied Flavia. 'Jane, I shall want your help. Do you think you might be able to make each of them a little cake and perhaps some lemonade? Am I giving you enough time?'

'I reckon I can manage the cakes,' replied Jane, 'and we may be lucky with the lemons. The carter hasn't yet come through today, and he may have some, but if not, it'll have to be milk.'

'Bless you, Jane,' declared Flavia.

After all that had been decided upon, she went in search of Henry, who was replacing part of one of the wooden window frames in the schoolroom. At her arrival, he paused in his work, and she explained the idea of the picnic, together with the need to let the families know what was happening.

'I'll do that for you, miss,' he replied. 'Pardon me for asking, but what was you going to put the lemonade in, for the children to drink it?'

'That's a good thought,' replied Flavia, suddenly struck. 'When you go, can you ask all the children to bring a cup for their drink?'

'Aye, I'll do that, miss.'

Flavia thanked him and was about to leave, when she suddenly remembered something. 'It occurs to me, Henry, that I did not thank you for what you did on the day when the bishop came,' she said.

'Oh, 'twas nothing at all, miss,' he replied, grinning.

'I assure you it was a great deal, and far beyond the call of duty,' she answered.

'Reckon it made the day more exciting,' he said laconically.

Again, she turned to go, but turned back after a moment's hesitation. 'Will you have time to go to Brooks Hall?' she asked him, her colour a little high. 'I would like to invite Philip and Penelope to the picnic, but must have Sir Lewis's permission, now that he knows about their coming to the school.'

Flavia prided herself on her fluency of thought in letter-writing, but it took her at least three attempts before she came up with a simple note which eventually went to Brooks Hall addressed to Miss Lynton.

Dear Penelope

We are having a picnic to celebrate the success of the bishop's visit, and I wondered whether you would like to attend. I expect it to begin with games at about ten o'clock, and school will finish at half past twelve as usual. Pray bring Philip if possible, and do not forget to ask your uncle.

Your friend,
Flavia Montague

Well, she thought, at least he cannot say this time that I did not ask his permission.

⋆　⋆　⋆

By the time Sunday arrived, Flavia felt that she had planned the picnic for the following day as well as possible. Henry had gone round with all the messages, including the one to Brooks Hall. Flavia had half-braced herself for a rude answer from Sir Lewis, or even for an angry visit. Henry's return, with the simple news that the note would be passed on, came as something of an anti-climax.

Shortly before the service, Flavia took her place in a pew about halfway back on the left-hand side. Mrs Glenn had returned from visiting her friends in Bedford, and she smiled at Flavia before taking her place next to her sister-in-law in the vicarage pew. The church was well attended as ever. Flavia had discovered that whatever might be her personal differences with Mr Steeple, he seemed to be a good pastor, and people appreciated his faithful visiting.

Just after her own appearance, Mr Wheaton and Mrs Retford entered and took their places in the Wheaton family pew. Mr Wheaton inclined his head gravely when he saw her, and Mrs Retford smiled in a friendly fashion. There seemed to be no sign of Sir Lewis. Then, just as Mr Steeple came in from the vestry and crossed to the centre of the chancel, there was the sound of another arrival, and a murmur of interest proceeding from the back caused all those with more curiosity than manners to turn and see what was happening. Walking up the aisle, his limp rather less pronounced than usual, was Sir Lewis Glendenning, accompanied by his son and his niece. Flavia could not help smiling. The devil! She thought to herself. Of course he would not arrive at the same time as everyone else! As the little family group passed the end of her pew, Sir Lewis glanced in her direction, caught the shadow of her smile just as it died away, and returned it with a slightly sardonic one of his own.

By his expression, Mr Steeple was clearly as astonished as anyone else present, but he soon collected himself, announcing the first hymn, and the service proceeded without incident.

During the sermon, Flavia found herself speculating about Sir Lewis's motives for bringing his son to church. Was it in order to show the world that he was proud of his son, regardless of his disability? Or, less commendably, did he want to shock his neighbours who, after all, seemed to regard him as one who could be depended upon to enliven the community by behaving in an eccentric manner?

What of the neighbours themselves? After their initial reaction, how would they behave? Would they give him a chance to explain himself, or would they make their own judgements without being properly informed — as, perhaps, they had always done?

With a shock, Flavia realized that the sermon was over, and she had not heard one word of it. Was everyone present in a similar case? Had Mr Steeple spent the best part of Saturday toiling over a sermon which nobody had heard? She smiled inwardly at the thought.

At the end of the service, Sir Lewis, with his family, was the first to leave, and as she watched them Flavia felt a tug of sympathy. That was what it must be, she told herself, for what else should cause her heart to skip a beat and her insides to feel suddenly as if they had been turned upside down?

Outside the door, Sir Lewis had stopped to speak to Mr Wheaton and his sister. 'So this is the child,' said Mrs Retford, looking curiously at Philip, and obviously taking care not to step too close. 'He looks quite normal, does he not?'

Flavia took a quick breath, horrified at her insensitivity, and looked at the baronet to see how he would react. She saw him glance briefly at her, then look back at Mrs Retford. 'There is a good reason for that, ma'am,' he replied. 'There is nothing the matter with him, save for his hearing.'

'His hearing!' exclaimed Mrs Retford. 'You

mean that he is deaf?'

Sir Lewis inclined his head. 'It has just been discovered, thanks to Miss Montague.'

'Indeed,' murmured Mrs Retford. 'Only deaf, you say. What a relief that must be, although it is still a terrible affliction. How grateful you must be.'

'My gratitude knows no bounds,' Sir Lewis replied, turning to look down at the schoolteacher. She felt a hand tugging at hers and looking down, she saw Philip gazing up at her solemnly.

'Hello, Philip. How are you?' she said to him.

There was a brief silence, then Mrs Retford laughed merrily. 'Oh, Miss Montague!' she exclaimed. 'How droll to speak to someone who is deaf! But tell me, Lewis,' she went on, tucking her hand into the baronet's arm, 'when are you coming to see us again?'

Flavia would have liked to hear Sir Lewis's response to this question, but at this point, Penelope began to speak to her and so she did not hear what he said. But later, she remembered that Mrs Retford had declared that her decision not to marry the baronet had been made because, she had explained insensitively, she did not want any child of hers to be an idiot. Would that decision change now that Philip was shown to be merely deaf?

At that moment, she looked up and saw Mr Wheaton and Mrs Glenn conversing together. She could not tell for how long they had been talking, but they appeared to be keeping one another very well amused. If they had met in Bedford, and she had done something to annoy him, as Flavia had surmised, they had obviously made up their differences. Suddenly, seeing Mr Wheaton's smiling face, she was reminded of the day of Mrs Bell's garden party, and the attentive way in which he had behaved towards Miss Evelina. Could he be the man for whom the younger Miss Bell had formed an attachment; had she discovered him at that garden party engaged in desperate flirtation with Mrs Glenn?

That afternoon, Mary Glenn came round to the school cottage and invited Flavia to go for a walk. They wandered by the stream behind the vicarage and into the countryside. 'So how have you been amusing yourself whilst I have been away?' Mary asked. 'I've been hearing all kinds of interesting things.'

'Such as?' prompted Flavia.

'Such as the rumour that you actually hit Sir Lewis over the head and put him in the cupboard,' replied Mary. 'Lord, I'd give anything to see old Bread 'n' ale's face if she knew!'

'I suppose you got that from Mr Wheaton,' remarked Flavia, desperately searching for something to say which did not involve commenting in any way upon Sir Lewis. As soon as the words were out of her mouth, however, she knew that she had made a mistake.

Mary Glenn's eyes narrowed. 'So the schoolteacher is not as naive as everyone would like to think,' she remarked. 'How did you guess that I met Paul in Bedford?'

'It wasn't so hard,' Flavia replied. 'I knew that you were in Bedford, and then I heard that he had gone there on business. And at church you seemed . . . close.'

'Observant of you,' acknowledged the younger woman, idly dragging the ferrule of her parasol through some long grasses to the side of the track along which they were walking. 'I was very annoyed at having to come back home, but I had forgotten how very amusing Paul can be. His presence has been a delightful compensation.'

If Mrs Glenn was quick of apprehension, Flavia was no less so. 'You were annoyed at having to come back home? Someone compelled you, then?'

Mary darted a quick look at her then she

looked away, assuming an air of carelessness. 'By no means,' she replied. 'It is simply that duty is such a tiresome thing.' Flavia made no reply, but simply looked at her steadily, and at length the other exclaimed, as if the words had been forced out of her, 'Oh, all right then. There's no fooling you, is there? I should have remembered that from school. I never knew whether to like you the best out of all the teachers there, or to detest you the most.' She paused briefly. 'There was a bit of a scandal,' she said at last. 'One of the officers didn't understand the difference between a game and something serious, so before there was any trouble, the colonel had a word with Sidney and told him that I ought to visit my relations. So tiresome, to be packed off home like a child, as if I had been expelled.' Again, Flavia said nothing. 'I expect you think I've behaved childishly,' Mary said shortly. 'But Sidney was so selfish, never paying any attention to anything I did. And all the other officers' wives are stupid, and I get so bored.'

'Have you tried telling Captain Glenn about how you feel?' Flavia asked.

'He ought to know without my telling him,' replied Mary, in a voice which sounded distinctly sulky.

'There is no reason why Captain Glenn should know how you feel if you have not told him.' She paused briefly, then went on, 'It has always seemed to me that men can sometimes be very unobservant, especially about women's feelings.'

Mary smiled wryly. 'Fancy my needing you to remind me of that,' she said.

'Well, it did surprise me that one of the most intelligent girls I ever taught would fail to think of something so obvious.'

Mary looked at her curiously. 'Do you really mean that?' she asked. 'About my being intelligent? You never said anything about it before.'

'Your problem was always application,' replied Flavia. 'When you applied yourself to something, you nearly always managed to achieve it. Which is why I think you should make it your business to ensure that Captain Glenn understands how you feel. I am sure there are all kinds of ways in which someone with your quickness of mind could help him further his career, instead of hampering it, as you are doing now.'

'I'm not hampering it,' Mary declared; then she coloured.

'Precisely,' replied Flavia. She knew that she did not have to spell out to the younger woman how having a wife with a reputation for being flighty might be detrimental to an officer's career. She had

255

already worked that out for herself.

'Well, perhaps I shall write to him,' Mary said eventually, as they turned round to go back. 'But meantime, there is no reason why I should not have a little fun whilst I am here. Which reminds me, you still haven't told me about all the fun and games you had with Sir Lewis. Did you really put him in the cupboard?' From then on, Flavia's mind was so absorbed with making sure that Mary's sharp wits got no inkling of the fact that Sir Lewis had kissed her in the shrubbery and attempted to kiss her again in the cottage, that there was no possibility of thinking of anything else until they parted.

★ ★ ★

The children were delighted with the news that there was to be a picnic, and on the Monday morning, they applied themselves to their work with great enthusiasm so that they could get outside all the sooner. On the stroke of ten by the church clock, therefore, Flavia declared lessons finished for the day, and all the children trooped outside. She had planned to give them some tasks to perform within the immediate vicinity, such as finding a red flower, or a shiny stone, or a nut which a squirrel had started to eat. After they had done that for a while, they would gather together to sing some songs and she would tell them a story. Then they would have their bun and lemonade, play informally for a time, perhaps, and have a penny each before they went home. The penny she would hold back to the end in order to encourage good behaviour. She had been very lucky in that Grace had acquired the habit of collecting pennies in a jar, and was perfectly happy for Flavia to change them for a larger coin.

She was just ushering the last of the children to the pleasantly grassy area at the junction of the two brooks behind the school, when she became aware that others were approaching, and saw Sir Lewis, Penelope and Philip coming towards them.

'Sir Lewis!' she exclaimed, so astonished that she almost forgot to curtsy.

'Miss Montague,' he replied, with an inclination of the head. 'I'm fascinated. You close the school when the bishop's coming, you close it when he's here and now you close it when he's been. Tell me, have you ever considered the novel idea of teaching a full day?' The familiar gleam was there in his eyes, but for the first time, Flavia wondered whether it might be indicative of mischief rather than malice.

She opened her mouth to speak, but before

she could say anything, he went on, 'We were delighted to receive your invitation and are very glad to join your party.' Flavia stared at him in consternation. 'You did intend to invite us all, didn't you? I brought the invitation with me just to be sure.' He drew a folded paper from inside his coat. ' 'Do not forget to ask your uncle', you put.'

Flavia looked up into his face. 'Are you telling me seriously, Sir Lewis, that you wish to join a village school picnic?' She was unaware that as she spoke, the mischievous gleam in his eye was now echoed by a similar expression in her own.

'I assure you, Miss Montague, that nothing would give me greater pleasure,' he replied.

'Then by all means join us. We were just about to begin the morning's activities.' She put the children into pairs, in order to conduct what she called her treasure hunt, with older ones helping younger ones. As might have been expected, Penelope took Philip for her partner. Flavia was just realizing that it would be difficult for Philip to take part when he could not be told in the same way as the others what needed to be looked for, when one of the older boys, who had returned to the schoolroom unseen, came running up to her with a slate and some chalk.

'That's for Philip — so you can draw what

258

he's got to find,' he said.

Flavia looked down at him. It was difficult for her to hold back the tears. 'Thank you, Robert,' she said. 'That was very thoughtful.'

'Aren't you Bradshaw's son?' Sir Lewis asked from behind her.

'Yes sir — the third oldest.'

'You're a good lad,' replied the baronet, handing him a coin. The boy thanked him, round eyed, and hurried back to his friends to show them what he had received.

There was no time to say more, for the children were waiting eagerly for the treasure hunt to begin, and Flavia was kept busy with telling them about each item and drawing them in turn for Philip, as Robert had suggested.

After he had spoken to Robert Bradshaw, Sir Lewis settled himself down on the grass, leaning up against the broad trunk of a tree. Flavia had not really believed that he would stay. She had been quite sure that he had said that he would do so only to annoy her. But he was now watching the proceedings with an unreadable expression; most of his attention was given to Philip.

No one watching the class would have been able to guess that he was very different from those around him. He ran and hunted with just as much eagerness as any other child.

Only, perhaps in his slight air of detachment could any contrast to the others be detected.

The children thoroughly enjoyed the treasure hunt and when it was over, they were eager to consume the buns and the lemonade which Grace and Jane carried to them on trays across the grass. When Jane saw that Sir Lewis was present, she managed a very creditable curtsy with her laden tray, and announced her intention of fetching him a glass of wine.

The baronet watched the children, who, under Flavia's supervision, were lining up ready to have their mugs filled. 'By no means,' he replied, standing up. 'If this lemonade is of your making, then I'll gladly have a glass of that, if you can spare some. I can think of nothing more refreshing.' This was a side of Sir Lewis that she had never seen before.

Whilst the picnic was being enjoyed, Flavia told the children a story, and then announced that they might play another game before receiving their final surprise. One of the boys produced a ball that he had brought, and organised an impromptu game of cricket with a broad flat piece of wood for a bat, and a couple of pieces of an old branch for the wicket. After watching to make sure that they were all settled and no one was left out,

Flavia, making up her mind that there would be no better time, went to sit next to the baronet.

She was just screwing up her courage to make her apology for misjudging him so badly and was wondering how best to begin when he took the words out of her mouth by saying, 'I feel I must apologize to you, Miss Montague.'

'Apologize? To me?' She felt as if they were in a play and had inadvertently picked up each other's marked scripts.

'Why certainly. I have had chance to observe you this morning and I take back some of the things that I said to you in the heat of my anger. We live in an age when indigent women of a certain class find themselves teaching because there is nothing else for them to do. Some are ignorant; some have no aptitude; neither of those things applies to you. You are clearly a gifted teacher.'

'You . . . you are very kind,' she replied, astonished at his words. 'It's a kindness I don't deserve, especially after having . . . having . . .'

'Assaulted me?'

'Hit you over the head — for which I in my turn need to apologize,' she said fervently.

'You astonish me!' he exclaimed. 'I received

the distinct impression that it was all my fault in the first place.'

'It was very wrong of me,' Flavia went on, ignoring this remark. 'But you see, I thought that you might tell the bishop, and he would then close the school.'

'And the school is very important to you. I see that.'

'It's important to the children who go as well,' Flavia added swiftly. 'To *all* the children.'

He looked directly at her, his gaze narrowed. 'I take your point, Miss Montague,' he said. 'Had I been a better father, I would have discovered Philip's disability long since. You do not need to point out to me how much he benefits from the company of other children.' They both sat for a moment, watching Philip playing his part in the cricket game. There was still an air of detachment about him, but he was taking in the nature of the proceedings with unmistakable interest. 'Penelope too,' the baronet went on eventually. 'She looks more animated than I have seen her since she came to live with me. In fact, it is in connection with Penelope that I wish to speak with you on another matter.'

'And I with you,' she replied. Then before

she could lose her courage, she said, 'If you felt that you needed to apologize to me, surely my need to apologize to you is by far the greater, sir. I accused you of ill-treating Penelope, quite wrongly as I now understand, and I am deeply regretful for my mistake.' She paused.

'Go on, Miss Montague,' he said amiably. 'You interest me vastly.'

She glanced at his face, and took in the expression in his eye. 'You're enjoying this,' she said incredulously.

'Yes I am, exceedingly,' he replied. 'But considering the violence you inflicted upon my person, I think I'm entitled to some slight enjoyment at your discomfiture, don't you?'

'I will concede that your attitude is understandable up to a point,' replied Flavia carefully. 'But you must realize that I was angry because I had very good reason to believe that Penelope had suffered ill-treatment, and — '

'And I appeared to be the obvious suspect? Well that's understandable, I suppose.'

'Understandable?' Again he had surprised her.

'You discovered that she was my niece. Something about her behaviour revealed to you that she had been ill-treated. If no one told you how long she had been with me, then of course you would think I was the one.'

'Especially when you stood slapping your whip against your boot on the day when you first came to the school.'

'Did I do that? How shocking! And you are right. Of course there is more to Penelope's story.' He paused briefly then went on, in a deliberately even tone. 'She is the daughter of my sister, who died when she was born. Tom, my brother-in-law, remarried when Penelope was seven and I am afraid that my little niece acquired the proverbial wicked stepmother. I had no notion of how she was being treated until I visited the North of England on a matter of business. As I was up there anyway, I decided to look in on my own flesh and blood. Not before time, you might say, and rightly.'

He was silent, staring into the middle distance. 'Tom and his wife have two children of their own, but I am afraid that Tom had descended into what I can only describe as a permanent drunken stupor. His wife had completely taken over the running of the house and Penelope had been turned into a kind of slave, at everyone's beck and call, sworn at by her father, teased and pinched by her stepbrothers and beaten by her step-mother and, in sum, frightened out of her wits.'

'Oh poor child!' exclaimed Flavia. 'And she is such a good girl.'

'Just so,' Sir Lewis agreed. 'I . . . persuaded the she-dragon to release Penelope into my care, pointing out that she would thus be relieved of the expense and responsibility of housing and feeding her. Having taken care to get this agreement down in writing — for I don't trust the pair of them an inch — I brought Penelope away with me.'

'That was well done,' murmured Flavia.

'I'll admit that I had an ulterior motive,' he confessed. 'I wondered whether she might perhaps do Philip some good.'

'She certainly seems very attached to him,' Flavia answered. 'I think that having him to look after has probably done her good as well.'

'I shan't forget that it was because of her that he came to the school,' said the baronet.

'I've already told you that I had no idea that they were your children,' she said defensively.

'I wasn't criticizing. If he hadn't come to the school his deafness might not have been discovered. I have you to thank that it was.'

'Oh,' responded Flavia blushing. Then

suddenly remembering her hasty words on one occasion she said quickly, 'You are more generous than I deserve. I have said some dreadful things to you, sir.'

He looked at her quizzically. 'Be sure I won't forget that you did. But there was another matter concerning Penelope that I wanted to raise with you, and here I need to summon up all the tact at my disposal.'

'That shouldn't take too long,' Flavia observed tartly, then wondered whether she ought to beg his pardon until he gave a crack of laughter.

'You've got my measure, haven't you?' he said. 'Well to be blunt with you, I don't want to seem over critical of your school, but you and I both know that in order to take her place in society — which I fully intend that she shall do — Penelope needs to learn more than the things that you teach the children there. In fact, I believe that it was you who told me quite rightly that she should have a governess, and I believe I've found the very one.'

'Miss Price?' questioned Flavia, her heart sinking although she could not imagine why.

'Sylvia?' he asked, his brows closing together. 'Good God, no. I've found someone much more suitable.'

He continued to stare at her, until at length

she understood what he was talking about and said at once, 'Oh no.'

'Now listen,' he went on. 'I don't know what you're paid here, but I'm prepared to double it. Just think; twice the salary, a pupil who already adores you, a congenial situation — '

'An even-tempered employer,' Flavia concluded for him. 'Sir Lewis, kindly remember that I left a genteel situation behind in order to take up my present position. Furthermore, please remember that I have never been a governess, nor have I ever wanted to be one.'

'It's my temper that puts you off, isn't it?' he asked her, his eyes narrowing.

'No, it isn't,' she replied. 'I wish you would listen to what I am saying.'

'I'm trying, believe me,' he said. 'But what you are saying does not appear to me to make any sense at all. How can you possibly prefer to teach in this scruffy little school to — '

'To taking up employment in your house? I should have thought that was abundantly clear.'

By this time, the games were over, and after a last, fulminating glance at the baronet, Flavia stood up and called the children to order, lining them up in order to receive their pennies. Philip and Penelope both lined up with the others.

'Look at them,' Sir Lewis said from behind her, as the two children came forward. 'Can you not reconsider, for their sake, if not for mine?'

'That was unworthy, Sir Lewis,' replied Flavia.

'Come,' he said shortly, as soon as his niece and son had their pennies. Then he strode off, his coat tails swinging, Penelope and Philip fairly running at his heels in order to catch up.

Thinking later about their conversation, Flavia could not help feeling regretful that it had ended in such a way. They had each begun ready to make peace with the other, but by the close of the conversation, hostilities had been resumed. But he simply could not expect to have everything his own way, she told herself. Just because he believed that she would be a good governess for Penelope, it did not mean that she should just fall in line.

Privately, she had to admit that there were certain advantages to the situation. He was right about Penelope; she would prove to be an obedient and amiable pupil, and there would be no doubt that anything that was needed for the schoolroom at Brooks Hall would be instantly provided; no more tussles with Mr Steeple and his like over the purchasing of new equipment! But a governess would of necessity take her place amid the hierarchy of a great house, whereas here at the little school, Flavia was her own mistress, and in all honesty, Mr Steeple never really interfered. She could imagine that living with Sir Lewis might be very different.

Living with him; for some reason, the very thought made her blush. To divert her mind, she thought back to the moment when he had appeared in the church with Penelope and Philip. It would have been quite easy to dismiss his actions as being simply a means of shocking his neighbours, had he not appeared again with Philip at the picnic. Now, however, it seemed more clear than ever that the baronet intended Philip to take his rightful place as his son and heir. How he meant to further this aim remained to be seen.

16

The encounter with Sir Lewis Glendenning had rather unsettled Flavia, and she found herself thinking about it several times over the next few days. If she was completely honest with herself, she had to admit that encounters with him always had that effect upon her. Every time the schoolroom door opened unexpectedly, she glanced up quickly, wondering whether it might be the baronet coming to see her, for she was not foolish enough to imagine that she had heard the last of his plans for Penelope. Then, of course, she became annoyed with herself for thinking about him so much, and for feeling a sharp stab of disappointment when it was never he who came. In an effort to divert her mind, she left the school one day at the end of the morning to pay a long promised visit to Mrs Briggs, Sara's mother.

For goodness sake, why are you being so silly about him? she asked herself severely, as she locked up the school. He's only a man, after all. It was true that she was not very much accustomed to associating with men. Miss Bredale had employed a visiting dancing master and a drawing master, and both of these men had had to be chaperoned on their weekly visits. This task had not always fallen to her lot, but whether it had or had not had never concerned her at all. She had never found either fussy M. Gonville or serious Mr Parsons in the slightest bit disturbing. Nor was she remotely nervous of Mr Wheaton or of Mr Steeple.

Here she checked her pace and thought for a moment, for she was obliged to own that she was not at all nervous of Sir Lewis either. True, she had been at her first encounter with him, and even probably at her second. After that, she had to admit that sparring with him had been stimulating rather than frightening, and had news come that Sir Lewis had decided to remove permanently from the neighbourhood, the prospect of his disappearance would certainly threaten to leave a yawning gap.

Not that there was not plenty to interest her amongst the other inhabitants of Brooks. Whilst in Bath, gossip amongst the girls about whose brother was the most handsome, and which girl's sister was likely to marry a fortune had interested her not at all. Now, however, she found the behaviour of those around her quite fascinating. On the one hand, there was Mrs Glenn and Mr Wheaton.

The match that had seemed desirable to certain parties when they were young had not come off, but obviously they were both very happy to flirt with one another. But the pastime that was so agreeable to the pair of them might easily be causing others pain. Flavia had seen Mr Wheaton out driving with Miss Evelina Bell, and both seemed very happy to be in one another's company, but Mr Wheaton always gravitated towards Mrs Glenn if Evelina was not present — after church, for example. And Mary had freely admitted that she found flirting with Paul Wheaton excellent sport.

At least Flavia was now saved from attaching any significance to Mr Wheaton's charm of manner when it was directed towards herself. She had certainly enjoyed the novelty of having a handsome man pay her some attention, but it would be disastrous if she were to regard it seriously, when he was obviously so susceptible to almost any female.

So deep in thought had she been, that Flavia was quite surprised to discover that she had reached her destination and was walking through the gateway of the Brigg's farm. She was given a very warm welcome, and this gave her a much needed reminder of why she had chosen to live in the countryside, rather than remain in the town.

'No doubt you'll want to make the most of the days left to you,' said Mrs Briggs comfortably, when they were enjoying a glass of her home-made cowslip wine and a piece of her excellent fruit cake.

'The days left to me?' queried Flavia. The phrase had an ominous ring to it, quite out of keeping with the pleasant sunny farmhouse and Mrs Briggs's rosy, smiling face.

'Before the harvest,' Mrs Briggs explained. 'When it's harvest time, everybody helps to get the harvest in. Everyone's needed, including the children. So there'll be no school for a while once that happens. That'll mean a holiday for you, Miss Montague.'

'But if everyone helps, can I not do so as well?' Flavia asked.

Mrs Briggs looked at her doubtfully. 'Well, if you really think you'd like to, then I can't see why not,' she replied. 'You can come here and help get the food and drink ready to take out to the hands in the fields at midday, if you want.'

Flavia smiled a little diffidently. 'I should like that very much,' she said. 'But I would not want anyone to think that perhaps I was interfering in something that did not concern me.'

'Why bless you, miss, but nobody would be thinking that. They'd be very pleased to see you wanted to help, I know. It's just that no one would imagine another teacher — like Miss Price, for instance — soiling her hands in that way. Not but what we can all see that you can work with the best of us, after you cleaned that school from top to bottom.'

After the visit was over, Flavia wandered back to school in a very thoughtful frame of mind. It had occurred to her that even if she did give some help with the refreshments for the field workers, she might still have some time to spare. Although she would not consider a permanent position as Penelope's governess, she could offer to spend a little time with her and enquire a little more closely into the education that she had received. She might even be able to help Sir Lewis as he interviewed suitable candidates for the post. She had, after all, done similar work for Miss Bredale at times. Then of course, it was not inconceivable that Penelope would one day attend Miss Bredale's academy in Bath. Clearly incidents that had happened in the girl's past had made her nervous, but once these were put behind her, the company of other girls of her own age might do her all the good in the world.

It pleased her to think that she had come up with this partial solution to the problem of Penelope's education and, as she drew near to the village, she walked with an increased spring in her step. As she walked down the single street that virtually made up the village, she contrasted this visit with the first one that she had made. Then, she had been greeted with not unfriendly but largely indifferent stares. Today, she received cheerful greetings. She was becoming part of the community. Hopefully, if she helped with the harvest, her acceptance would be assured.

When she got back to the cottage, Grace greeted her at the door. 'You shouldn't go walking about so much in this heat,' she scolded. 'Go upstairs and put off your bonnet, and I'll pour a glass of wine for you to have when you come down.'

Flavia did as she was bid, suddenly aware, now that she had come into the house, of how hot it was outside. She was just coming down the stairs when there was a knock at the door, and Grace, who had come into the sitting-room with Flavia's wine on a tray, opened it to admit Mr Wheaton.

'Miss Montague, forgive me if I intrude, but may I have a few words with you? I need to consult you upon a certain matter.' His tone was polite, his expression charming, and for all that the day was one of the hottest that the year had yet seen, he still looked cooler in his blue coat and breeches than she felt in her cotton print gown.

'Please come in, Mr Wheaton,' said Flavia. 'I was about to have a glass of wine. Would you like to join me?'

He raised his brows. 'Thank you,' he replied. 'Is this not a little unusual?'

'For someone to enjoy a glass of wine after a busy day? I should have thought that it was entirely predictable,' she answered.

'But surely . . . not the whole bottle?' he ventured, looking a little alarmed.

Flavia laughed. 'I should hope not,' she chuckled. 'I should be on the floor! No, Grace replaces the cork very carefully, and I find that a bottle lasts me several days.'

'Now that, Miss Montague, is undoubtedly sacrilege,' he said frankly, making her laugh again. 'And certainly with wine of this quality,' he went on appreciatively, after he had tasted it.

'I buy from the same wine merchant that my father used and I have never been disappointed,' she replied smoothly.

'I see that you are an independent woman, ma'am,' remarked Mr Wheaton, looking at her as with new eyes.

'Circumstances have made me so, but I will admit that I value my independence,' she responded. She was sorely tempted to offer him a cigar, but decided against it. She would save that pleasure until after he had gone. His supposed admiration of her independence might not survive such a shock.

They chatted idly for a little longer before Mr Wheaton said 'I told you earlier that there was a matter on which I wished to consult you. In fact it is a commission from my sister.'

'I thought that your sister was away from home?' said Flavia. Mrs Steeple had informed her several days before that Mrs Retford had gone to stay with friends in Brighton.

'Yes, that is so,' replied Mr Wheaton. 'My sister is in Brighton, and intends to be there for the next few weeks.'

'Then I am puzzled as to how I might be able to serve Mrs Retford,' she commented.

'On the contrary, it is my sister who thinks that she may be able to be of service to you,' smiled her visitor. 'You see, it has occurred to her that because of the harvest, you will be obliged to close the school for a little while,' he said. 'She wondered whether you might like to go and bear her company? Do say you will. It would give her a great deal of pleasure, and as you have been working so hard, she is convinced that a holiday by the sea would do you a great deal of good. I would be able to escort you there and bring you back as soon as you chose.'

'Does not your sister already have company in Brighton?' Flavia asked. 'I should have thought that there would be plenty of people about to entertain her.'

'Yes indeed there are, but she values you very highly,' Mr Wheaton responded. 'And besides, the lady who was to reside with her there is ill, and Mr Retford's family have insisted that she must have a responsible lady to stay.'

'Ah,' declared Flavia in accents of comprehension. 'Now I understand. I am to lend your sister countenance.'

Her visitor looked embarrassed. 'No indeed,' he protested, not very convincingly. 'My sister thinks very highly of you, as I have said. She undoubtedly needs someone to live with her, but she wants it to be someone of her choice.' He paused, then went on, turning the full force of his charm in her direction. 'You cannot imagine how much pleasure it would give me to be the one to escort you there.'

Flavia set down her glass, thought for a moment, then looked straight at him. 'Mr Wheaton, I have spent the last eight years lending countenance to young ladies who need someone responsible. I have quite given up that kind of activity. And the fashionable whirl does not attract me at all, I am afraid.'

He looked at her as if she was speaking in another language. 'But this would be different. You would not be a teacher but a companion and a friend. My sister values your friendship greatly. You cannot possibly hurt her by rejecting this offer.'

'Mr Wheaton, that was unworthy and unfair,' she replied. She could also have retorted that the lady who valued her friends highly did not depart from the district without saying goodbye to them, leaving them to find out about her departure at second hand, but she refrained. His colour rose a little.

'I beg your pardon,' he said. 'You see how anxious I am to gain your consent. I will use almost any means.'

She had to smile, then. 'Believe me, Mr Wheaton, I am very grateful to your sister for her invitation. Please convey my sense of obligation to her, but she must understand that I wish to remain in the village which I have chosen to make my home. Perhaps another year, when I am more settled, I will come.'

'So how do you plan to spend the time whilst the children are helping with the harvest?' he asked her. 'Will you also go away to the sea, perhaps? Or have you friends to visit?'

Flavia shook her head. 'No, I have promised Mrs Briggs that I will help with the provisions for the workers.' Seeing him grinning, she added a little defensively, 'Have you any objections, Mr Wheaton? There is nothing wrong with that, surely?'

'No indeed; nothing at all,' he replied. 'It is simply that I cannot imagine any of the teachers of the past doing such a thing.'

'Not even Miss Price?' ventured Flavia, feeling rather daring.

He burst into laughter. 'Certainly not Miss Price,' he replied. 'Why do you ask?'

It was Flavia's turn to colour. 'Oh, just because I heard that she was young and good-humoured,' she said a little lamely. She would have liked to have found out more about the relationship which had, and possibly still did, exist between Sir Lewis and Miss Price. Mr Wheaton, a near contemporary of the baronet, and a life-long neighbour, might conceivably know something, but her sense of delicacy shrank from even attempting to gossip with him. For one thing, there stood between them the gentleman's code, which ensured that secrets whispered between men of honour remained private. For another, Mr Wheaton might misunderstand her motives; might even suppose that she was personally interested in the baronet.

'Oh no!' she exclaimed involuntarily at the very idea. Fortunately, Grace came in at that moment to bring some little cakes to go with the wine, and after she had gone, when Mr Wheaton asked Flavia the reason for her sudden exclamation, she quickly gave an excuse of having forgotten someone's birthday.

Not long after this, Mr Wheaton took his leave. 'Make sure you wear your oldest clothes when you go out to the fields, ma'am,' he advised her. 'It can be a dusty business, or so I'm told.'

'So you're told?' she echoed with a quizzical look.

'You don't suppose I go myself, do you?' was his reply.

After a brief silence, Flavia asked, 'When will it be necessary for me to close the school? I would rather announce its closure myself than find myself all alone in the schoolroom one day.'

'I will make enquiries of my home-farm manager,' he replied. 'He knows about such things better than I.'

Flavia said goodbye and watched him go without regret. No doubt many of her female acquaintances would have thought her mad, she reflected. Not only had she turned down the chance of a stay in Brighton, with all that

that would involve; she had also rejected the chance of a tête-à-tête on the way with a very handsome single gentleman. But such a tête-à-tête would be of very limited value when one was now convinced that the said gentleman would be prepared to flirt with almost anyone in a skirt.

Suddenly the thought popped into her mind; what if Sir Lewis had been the one to invite her to Brighton? Would she have felt tempted then? She thought about the interview to which he had subjected her, along with Mr Wheaton and Mr Steeple. She remembered how he had accused her of being impulsive, even passionate. No one who had encountered her at Miss Bredale's academy would ever have thought of describing her in such terms. It seemed to be only in the baronet's presence that those traits revealed themselves. So what did that say about her relationship with him; her feelings for him?

Glancing into the mirror, she caught herself smiling sentimentally, and gave herself a shake. Why on earth was she indulging in this kind of day-dreaming? It must be something to do with the village air, and village life, she concluded. She sighed. Mr Wheaton was right in describing her as independent, she reflected. So independent was she that she would be very reluctant to surrender her freedom for anything less than a grand passion. And where in Brooks would she find that? Before Sir Lewis's face could come into her mind once more, she snatched up some books and began to prepare a lesson for the next day.

It was no good, however. Although she continued to occupy her mind and her hands until late in the evening, and even after Grace had gone to bed, as soon as she set her books down, the baronet's face came into her mind. Abandoning her efforts to banish him from her thoughts, therefore, she wandered into the garden, sat down, lit a cigar, and allowed her mind to roam where it would.

She found herself remembering their first encounter in the lane, when he had shouted at her for mishandling the reins. Then, just a short time afterwards, he had trapped her in the cupboard, and tried to kiss her. She had wondered later what it would have been like had he succeeded. Well, shortly afterwards, at The Swallows, he *had* succeeded; but the embrace had been a perfunctory one, which had not made a lasting impression upon her. Later, of course, he had demanded that she kiss him when the bishop had visited. She had done so; but the salute to his cheek had not satisfied him. He had pulled her on to his lap in order to obtain the kind of kiss he had wanted, but they had been interrupted.

All at once, Flavia pulled herself up sharp. She had encountered Sir Lewis on several occasions, some more agreeable than others. Why, then, were the times when he had embraced her the ones that stuck in her mind? And why was the most potent memory of all, the one when, in her own cottage, she had lain across his lap, waiting for his mouth to descend upon hers? There was only one explanation, she realized with dismay: she had fallen in love with him. She, who had always regarded her pupils' sighing and day-dreaming over men with a degree of contempt, was herself remembering his voice, his faintly malicious grin, the feel of him, even the way that lock of hair persistently fell over his forehead. What on earth was she to do?

The sound of voices outside the back gate suddenly brought her back to her senses. She could not detect what was being said, but one was undoubtedly a man's voice. She remembered how her school had been vandalized by night, and wondered whether someone might be coming in order to make a second assault. She put out her cigar, and quietly lifted the latch of the back gate, mentally uttering a word of thanks to Henry, who had oiled the hinges so efficiently. Gently she closed the gate, and tiptoed to where she had heard the voices coming from, at the edge of the graveyard, underneath the trees. Belatedly, she wondered whether coming out into the dark to confront malicious and possibly violent individuals was very wise, and she paused in indecision. They were not speaking now and, as the moon came from behind the clouds to give a little more light, she realized that it was a man and a woman in close embrace. They drew apart, becoming aware of her almost at that same moment; it was Paul Wheaton and Mary Glenn.

'Miss Montague!' exclaimed the gentleman. By his voice, she could tell that he was extremely discomfited. 'I had not expected . . . '

'So I see,' replied Flavia.

'We were just . . . ' he began again, then fell silent, unable to think of a way of finishing his sentence that would not make him sound either guilty or absurd.

'It's all right,' said Mary. 'She won't say anything. I'll go back to the vicarage now.'

'Wait,' said Mr Wheaton urgently, 'I'll escort you.'

'No you won't,' replied Mary. 'I'll be safe enough.' She turned to Flavia. 'I'll come and see you tomorrow — to explain,' she said. Then before either Flavia or Wheaton could say any more, she flitted away across the churchyard.

After a long silence, Mr Wheaton said, 'Miss Montague, I am aware that I owe you an explanation.'

'Mr Wheaton, you are of age, as is the lady in question,' answered Flavia. 'Neither of you owes me anything, but you do, perhaps, owe something to the honour of Captain Glenn and to the honour of your own name.'

He was silent again. 'You are right,' he said. 'I have been thoughtless indeed. I have put one lady's reputation at risk, and now by talking with you here, I am compounding my error. I will leave now, but you must allow me to call tomorrow and apologize.'

'There is no need,' answered Flavia, foreseeing that the next day her little cottage would be full of people coming to explain themselves. 'Just go, Mr Wheaton, and resolve to be a little less . . . less gallant in future.'

'Then I will bid you good night,' he said, taking her hand and kissing it. 'You are more gracious towards me than I deserve, ma'am.'

'Yes, yes,' she said impatiently, reflecting that even in these circumstances, he did not know how to refrain from flirtation. 'Just go, Mr Wheaton.' He turned and hurried into the shadows and, after looking for a time towards the darkness into which he had disappeared,

Flavia turned back towards the gate, and lifted the latch. The gate would not move. She tried it again, thinking that it must have caught on something, but it was shut fast. She hesitated to rattle it hard, for Grace was sleeping in the back bedroom, and the noise would wake her. But if she could not get in, then she would have to wake Grace anyway. She was just hesitating, trying to decide what to do, when she heard the faint sound of the bolt on the inside of the gate being drawn. Then the gate opened, and Sir Lewis Glendenning stood inside the garden, blocking the entrance. For a moment, her heart skipped a beat and she was conscious of a sense of elation. Then he spoke, breaking the spell.

'Finished trysting?' he asked her nastily.

'I haven't been trysting,' she replied. Still he stood in her way.

'Oh really? Then kindly explain to me why you were meeting Paul Wheaton in the lane by moonlight.'

'I wasn't meeting him,' said Flavia.

'Oh really,' said the baronet again. 'You happened upon him by chance, I suppose.'

'Yes I did, as a matter of fact. I heard . . . ' — she was going to say voices, but she decided that this would be to incriminate Mrs Glenn, so instead she finished, 'someone in the lane, and came out to investigate.'

'How very intrepid,' said Sir Lewis. 'And why do you suppose, ma'am, he was in the lane at this hour?'

'How should I know?' she asked him crossly. 'Perhaps he was meeting someone.'

'Exactly my thoughts,' he purred.

'Well it wasn't me,' she said. 'Sir Lewis, are you going to keep me standing in this lane all night, or are you going to allow me into my own back garden?'

He stared at her for a long moment, before stepping back and allowing her in. 'Do you swear to me that you weren't meeting Paul Wheaton?' he demanded.

'It is none of your business whom I may or may not be meeting,' she declared.

'It is very much my business; or had you forgotten that this school is built upon my land? I assure you, schoolmarm, that if I have the slightest suspicion that your morals are not as they should be, then I will go immediately to Steeple and demand your dismissal.'

Part of her — the reckless part — wanted to tell him to go and do what he liked, if he did not believe her, but her sensible side said, 'I give you my word that I wasn't meeting Paul Wheaton, or any other man. Satisfied?'

'Not quite,' he answered, bending to pick

something up. 'If you have not been entertaining male companions in your garden, then what is the explanation of this?' In his hand, he held the remains of her cigar.

'Oh, damn,' she exclaimed, before she could stop herself. Then 'I beg your pardon,' she whispered. 'Someone must have . . . have thrown it over the wall,' she said eventually.

'Paul Wheaton, perhaps?' he suggested.

'Yes, perhaps,' she answered, trying to sound nonchalant.

'Indeed,' purred the baronet. 'But what of the occasion shortly after your arrival when I rode past and saw the glow of a burning cigar in this very garden, and smelled the smoke? Was *that* Paul Wheaton?'

Flavia sighed. Whatever she did or said now, her reputation would suffer. The truth seemed to be the most harmless option. She shook her head. 'Wait here,' she said. She went into the cottage, picked up the box of cigars and the tinder box, and came out again. 'Do you smoke, Sir Lewis?' she asked him, offering him the box, her calm tone concealing an inner turmoil.

'On occasions,' he replied, looking at her watchfully as he took one.

'So do I,' she remarked, taking one herself, and closing the box.

His eyes gleamed. 'Allow me,' he said, taking the tinder box from her. She permitted him to light her cigar for her, then sat down and watched while he lit his. He sat down next to her on the bench. 'You're a remarkable woman,' he said.

'These were my father's choice,' she told him.

'And did he educate your palate in any other way?' the baronet asked.

'I enjoy good wine of all kinds,' she answered, 'but my preference is for claret.'

'It makes me wonder what you do when you go to Steeple's for dinner,' the baronet remarked. 'I think he must have the worst palate in the world.'

She smiled. 'Mr Steeple thinks me very abstemious,' she replied. 'I take only one glass, and allow myself something drinkable when I get home.' He gave a bark of laughter. Then, encouraged by his understanding, she found herself telling him about her father, about his visits home, her occasional opportunities to go to sea, and some of the officers she had known. 'My own dear Grace is the sister of a sailor,' she concluded, 'so I cannot escape my heritage.' To her astonishment, she realized that they had both finished their cigars, for so long had she talked.

The baronet stood up. 'I had better go,' he

said, walking to the gate. Before he left, he turned and for the first time, he took her hand and raised it to his lips. 'My compliments, schoolmarm. I can't remember ever enjoying talking with a woman more.' For a long time after he had gone, she stood holding to her cheek the hand that he had kissed.

17

When Flavia woke the following morning, she was conscious of a feeling of contentment. She lay for a while thinking about the companionable atmosphere that had filled the garden the previous evening when she and the baronet had talked together. Had he been conscious of the same feelings? She thought about how he had looked, the things that he had said, most of all about the very small distance that there had been between them as they sat on the bench, and once more, she lifted the hand that he had kissed to her cheek. Before she had her breakfast, she went into the garden and allowed her hand to smooth the place where he had sat. 'For goodness sake, pull yourself together,' she said. 'You're besotted with the man!' But as she said it, she was smiling.

She conducted her lessons in a happy haze, and when lunch-time came, she went to the main door of the school to watch the last child leave. She was about to go back inside when a gig drew up in front of her. The groom went to the horses' heads, and an enchantingly pretty young woman climbed down gracefully from the driving seat. Sitting in the next seat was another woman, holding a baby.

'Good afternoon,' said Flavia, smiling in welcome. 'Can I be of assistance? I'm afraid,' she added with a twinkle, 'that I don't accept children quite as young as yours at this school, but if I can help you in any way, I should be glad to do so.'

The other laughed merrily, and the sparkle in her eyes made her look even prettier. 'No indeed, my little girl is far too young to be thinking of school. Forgive me, but am I addressing Miss Montague?'

'Yes, I am Flavia Montague,' replied Flavia.

'And how are you enjoying being the village schoolmistress? I wasn't very much good at it, I'm afraid.'

'Oh? So you were schoolmistress here?'

'Yes, just before you. Well, six months ago.'

'So you must be Miss Price!' exclaimed Flavia.

The young woman laughed again. 'How clever of you!' she exclaimed. 'In fact — '

She was interrupted by the sudden cry from the baby. 'Ma'am, I think she needs to be out of the sun,' said the nurse.

'May we come in?' asked Miss Price. 'Just for a few minutes? Baby needs to be in the shade, and I confess that I am very curious to see what you have done with the cottage.'

'Yes of course,' responded Flavia, her mind in a whirl. From whence had Miss Price suddenly sprung, and where was she staying? Was this child the baby whom she had been rumoured to have been expecting when she had been a teacher here? No doubt she would find out the answers to all of these questions, she thought, as she ushered her unexpected guest into the cottage.

'Oh, this is lovely!' exclaimed the former schoolmistress as she stood upon the threshold. 'You have made far more of it than I ever managed to do. But perhaps that is because you feel at ease in your role here. I never did, you know.'

'The isolation of the position here is not to everyone's taste,' replied Flavia diplomatically.

'You are very kind, but I must confess that I only came here because it suited my purpose. In many ways, the isolation here was an advantage to me.'

At that moment, Grace emerged from the kitchen and offered to make tea for them all, the nurse having now entered with the baby in her arms. 'She's fallen asleep, ma'am,' said the nurse. 'I'll just sit away from you a little in the window, while she settles down.'

'Yes, all right,' replied Miss Price. 'She has

been a little fretful recently, Miss Montague. I think that perhaps a tooth may be coming through.'

'I sometimes think it a great blessing that we cannot remember gaining our teeth,' replied Flavia. 'It is obviously a very painful process.'

'So tell me how you are settling in,' said Miss Price, when they were all sitting down. 'What do you think to your handsome neighbour? Have you had a great deal to do with him?'

'Only when he comes rampaging into the school to tell me my business,' Flavia replied.

Miss Price raised her brows. 'You do surprise me,' she remarked. 'I always found Mr Wheaton to be very courteous. Now, if you had said the same thing about Lewis . . .'

She paused and at that moment, Grace came in with the tea tray. Flavia was profoundly thankful for the interruption. Why had she thought that her visitor was referring to the baronet? She could feel herself blushing, but whether this was because she had spoken so immoderately before a stranger, or because of her mistake, or, even more disturbingly, because her visitor would have supposed that the current schoolmistress found Sir Lewis attractive, and with good reason, it would have been hard to say.

'Are you making a visit in the area?' asked Flavia, when they were all settled with their tea.

'Not really a visit,' replied her visitor, holding her cup with delicately gloved hands. 'We are staying with Lewis. As I expect you know, he is a very dear friend. We are living in Buckinghamshire at present, but we are going to the sea. My physician thinks that the sea air will be good for baby Louise and me.'

'Is . . . is Louise named after her father, ma'am?' asked Flavia tentatively.

'Yes, of course,' answered the other. Then she gave a delighted cry, laid down her cup, rose gracefully and walked over to the bookcase, on the top of which Flavia had placed the books that she had discovered in the schoolroom cupboard. 'You have found my book!' she declared. 'I could not remember where I had put it. Do you mind . . . is it all right if I take it?'

'Of course you must take it,' replied Flavia a little stiffly, feeling awkward and rather sick. 'It is yours after all. I was intending to send it on to you as soon as I found a forwarding address.'

'Thank you,' said Miss Price. She opened the book and looked inside at the inscription. 'Darling Louis,' she murmured, pronouncing the name in the French manner. 'Such precious memories.'

The baby stirred, and not long after this, Flavia's disturbing visitor took her leave. 'What a pity I do not live nearer,' she said, as she got back into the gig. 'I think that otherwise we might have been very good friends. In fact,' she added with a twinkle, 'in honour of that thought, I might even resist the temptation of telling Lewis that you think him handsome!'

Flavia found herself blushing again, and before she could regain her composure, the gig drove off in the direction of the manor. She stood for a while watching it disappear. So she had met Miss Price at last. She had still not discovered her married name, but whatever it might be, there seemed to be little doubt as to the identity of the child's father. Living alone in the schoolhouse, she must have been an easy target for the philandering baronet. He himself, his suit unwelcome to Mrs Retford because of the rumours of Philip, must have been glad of a chance of a romantic adventure.

Clearly whatever had transpired during the course of their affair, they had parted good friends, despite the fact that Sir Lewis had not married her. Perhaps her family had not been good enough for the baronet, although

Flavia would have thought him to be the last person to take any notice of society's opinions.

When the gig was out of sight, she went indoors and climbed the stairs. Suddenly, she felt very tired. Once inside her room, she closed the door and sat down on the bed. With everything that had happened, she had forgotten about Miss Price, and the rumours that surrounded her. She had allowed herself to dwell upon the easy companionship at the picnic, the conversation that they had shared in the garden, and the kiss that he had placed upon her hand. In short, she had been so wrapped up with her dreams about Sir Lewis and her love for him, that she had not allowed herself to think about anything else.

Now, reality had come crashing in. He might not have been the man who had ill-treated Penelope, but he had had an affair with Miss Price, got her with child and then failed to marry her. How could she have allowed herself to have become infatuated with such a man as that? She had proof that he had been lingering around the school, maybe hoping to take advantage of her in a similar way. And she, foolish woman that she was, might easily have been fool enough to let him, because she loved him so.

There was only one sensible course of

action that she could take, and that must be to leave Brooks as soon as possible. 'But I like it here,' she protested; 'I have made a home here, and made friends.' In her heart, she knew that that was not the real reason. She wanted to stay because she wanted to be with Lewis Glendenning. But he had said nothing, done nothing that might indicate that he felt the same way about her. Oh, he had tried to kiss her, but he had admitted that that had been as much to annoy her as for any other reason. He had also said that he had enjoyed her company, but that did not mean that he was in love with her. The likelihood was that if she stayed, she would one day see him united to Mrs Retford. With Philip's deafness now revealed, there was nothing keeping them from marrying; and why upon earth should he choose a plain schoolteacher when a dashing widow was ready and willing to take him? For the first time that she could remember in all her adult life, Flavia threw herself face down on to her bed and wept bitterly.

18

The night brought Flavia neither counsel nor rest, and she would have welcomed the news that because of an epidemic of measles, there would be no children in school that day. When she opened the front door, however, she was astonished to see that standing behind the usual line of girls was another line of girls and women dressed identically; and behind the boys, a line of boys and men.

Too puzzled to think what else to do, she stepped aside as usual and told them all to come in. The regular pupils went to their usual places, and with a little squeezing, there was just enough space to fit everyone else in.

She called the names of all the pupils who were on her register, noting any absences, then said, 'Forgive me, but I am a little puzzled. From where have you all come and for what purpose?'

After a little glancing around and some whispering, one of the men stood up slowly. 'Please, miss, we're from Brooks Hall,' he said. 'And as for purpose, we'd like to learn, if you please.'

'I see,' said Flavia slowly. 'Brooks Hall

— the residence of Sir Lewis Glendenning.'

'That's right, miss,' replied the man eagerly.

'And is he aware that you are all absent from the Hall at this time?' she asked gently, more than half guessing the answer.

'Oh yes,' replied the man, obviously pleased at being in school and at being able to answer yet another question in the affirmative. 'It was Sir Lewis who told us to come.'

'Today?'

'Yes, miss.'

'All of you?'

'Why . . . why yes, miss, if it's not inconvenient.' For the first time, the man looked a little uncertain.

Flavia took a deep breath. 'Well, let's make a start.'

There were not quite enough slates to go round, and Flavia felt that the regular pupils ought to come first, but those from Brooks Hall were very willing to share. Ideally, she would have liked to divide the class up into groups, with one capable pupil in charge of each one. She would then have been able to set appropriate work for each group, and move about between them as needed. The crowded nature of the room made this well nigh impossible, however, and the fact that she had had no warning of this sudden influx meant that she did not have nearly enough work prepared. By the end of the morning, she was feeling tired, incompetent, and thoroughly annoyed with Sir Lewis Glendenning.

She had no doubt as to why he had done this. He had shown her a more amiable side of his nature in recent times, but no doubt this amiability had all been designed to lull her into thinking that he had withdrawn his opposition to her appointment. He had never disguised his contempt for her 'scruffy little school', as he termed it. It would suit him very well if for whatever reason the school were to close. He was probably hoping that with its closure, Flavia would come to Brooks Hall to be Penelope's governess. He would soon discover his mistake! She had needed a good reason to be angry with him, so that she need not think about Miss Price and the baby and her own broken dreams. As soon as her augmented class had left, she would go to Brooks Hall and give him a piece of her mind.

Her errand was to prove unnecessary. She was just tidying up her desk when the door of the schoolroom opened, and she saw entering the very object of her wrath. He was looking rather pleased with himself, a fact which did nothing to ameliorate her anger, even whilst the sight of him made her heart beat faster.

'How dare you?' she exclaimed, before he had a chance to speak.

'How dare I what?' he asked her.

'How dare you put me in such an awkward position today? I had twenty extra pupils today! Twenty!'

'I should have thought that that would please you,' he remarked, strolling up the aisle between the desks. 'All the more people to whom you can impart learning, surely.'

'Yes, but not when they are crammed together as they were today. Do you know how many pupils I had today?'

'No, but I feel sure that you will tell me.'

'I certainly will. There were fifty! Fifty pupils, Sir Lewis, in a room this size, with one teacher.'

'Well surely you could find something for them to get on with,' he replied, halting as he reached the teacher's dais.

'Yes, I could, but I would have appreciated a little notice. I almost said that I should have appreciated a little more consideration, but the last thing that you want to do is to be considerate to me! Don't think that I am ignorant of why you did what you did, Sir Lewis. You don't deceive me for a moment.'

'And what exactly is that supposed to

mean?' the baronet asked, his brows drawing together.

'I would have thought that that was perfectly obvious,' she retorted. 'You want to make it impossible for me to carry on with the school, so that I will be obliged to come and be Penelope's governess.'

'Don't be so absurd!' he exclaimed.

'It isn't absurd at all,' she retorted. 'You've been against me from the very beginning. I think you must be the most irritating man that I've ever met.' She stood staring at him, breathing rather faster than usual.

'Well, there at least we have reached some measure of agreement,' he replied, stepping up on to the dais. 'I cannot recall a woman who has ever annoyed me as much as you have done, schoolmarm,' he went on fiercely, towering over her. 'You are opinionated, interfering, aggressive, self-willed; damn it all, you aren't even pretty — '

'Thank you!' she said ironically. 'In fact, in every way, I do not measure up to what you, in your arrogance, expect a woman to be. Well let me tell you — '

'No, damn it, no more,' he roared, exasperated beyond measure. 'You don't have the smallest notion of my motives and, in *your* arrogance, you haven't bothered to ask! You put me completely out of patience with you. So why the *deuce* should it be that every time I see you lately, I want to do this?'

So saying, he picked her up bodily and laid her on the teacher's desk. He bent over her, quite clearly intending to kiss her, but stopped short and looked down into her eyes, that familiar gleam in his own. 'I've been a long time collecting this, but you owe it me, schoolmarm.' Then, while she was still paralysed with astonishment, he lowered his mouth to hers and kissed her long and hard.

It was the first such kiss that Miss Flavia Montague had ever received, and she was completely unprepared for the onslaught to her senses that would result from the baronet's salute. Just as he had been a long time collecting what he declared she owed him, so too the response of every part of her being expressed that this was something for which she had been waiting as well. Her hands, which had initially grasped at his shoulders in order to push him away, acquired a will of their own, and crept around the back of his neck instead, so that soon she was embracing him and returning his kisses every bit as fervently as he was bestowing them. Miss Price, her daughter, Mrs Retford, in fact everything else went completely out of her head, as she surrendered to the thrill of the moment.

There was no telling for how long their mutual passion might have lasted, or to what it might have led, but they were interrupted by a sound, which brought Flavia to her senses. From holding on to him for dear life, she began to push against him with all her might, whereupon he stood up straight, breathing hard. She got to her feet, and stared at him, similarly out of breath. She opened her mouth to speak, but her feelings were far too confused for her to be able to put them into words.

He looked down at her. He, too, seemed similarly deprived of speech. It was then that they both realized what the sound had been that had aroused them from their preoccupation with each other. Mrs Glenn had opened the door and was standing on the threshold.

'Good day, Miss Montague, Sir Lewis,' she murmured, her eyes gleaming with amusement. 'I must say, school's changed a little from how I remember it.'

'My God!' exclaimed the baronet.

Flavia stood staring at her visitor, her face flaming. Mrs Glenn walked inside and closed the door behind her. 'I think it's your turn to speak,' she said, looking at Flavia.

Flavia opened her mouth, stammered 'I . . . I . . . ' then fell silent.

'What *is* it about this schoolroom?' mused

the newcomer, strolling towards them between the lines of desks, and looking round the while. 'I should never have thought of it as the setting for tales of high romance, and yet clearly I am mistaken, am I not, Sir Lewis? First Miss Price, now Miss Montague. Do schoolteachers have some irresistible fascination for you?'

'Damnation, woman, this is none of your concern,' declared the baronet angrily, his colour high.

'I should have thought it could be the concern of any person who happened to look through the window of a public building,' Mrs Glenn replied. 'You should be thankful that it was only I, and not my brother. After all, I do have some understanding of these little affairs. But you really should practise more discretion, you know.'

'Now look here,' the baronet began, stepping down from the dais and walking towards her.

'Oh, good heavens!' exclaimed Mrs Glenn, her eyes sparkling, her hand going to her throat. 'Do not lay hands on *me*, I beg you. I am not quite so resilient as Miss Montague!'

Flavia stood staring down at them from the dais. Her mind was in a complete turmoil, and she had no idea how this matter was to be resolved, but clearly while both her visitors were there, no rational discussion could possibly take place. 'Sir Lewis, please go,' she said. 'I will talk about this matter with Mrs Glenn.'

He turned to look at her. 'Flavia,' he said. It was the first time that he had called her by her Christian name, but she could not allow herself to think about that for now.

'Just go,' she said, more harshly than she had intended. 'Now, please.'

He stared at her for a long minute then nodded curtly, murmured 'Ladies,' and left, without looking back.

'Well, here's a turn up for the books,' Mary murmured. 'And to think I came here to explain *my* conduct. Shall we go into the cottage and ask your maid to make us a cup of tea?'

Flavia felt as if a cigar and a glass of her father's good red wine would do her far more good, but she followed her visitor obediently into the cottage. What could she say? What reasons could she offer? There was nothing, she knew, that would excuse her conduct. Mary Glenn was the last person whom she would have wanted to witness the scene which had just taken place. By a strange irony, she was probably also the only person in Brooks who would not be shocked. There was no guarantee, however, that Mary would not use her knowledge to obtain Flavia's dismissal; whilst Flavia knew that she must leave Brooks, she had no desire to leave with the slur of dismissal upon her name.

'Phyllis was going to come with me — just for the walk, you know, and to take a look at the school. Aren't you glad that I persuaded her to stay at home?'

'You mean . . . you won't tell?' ventured Flavia.

'Probably not; that's only part of the problem, isn't it? Sit down,' Mary went on. 'I'll go and tell the maid to make us some tea.'

Flavia did as she was bid, but almost immediately, found herself getting up, and walking restlessly about the room. All she could think of was the look on Sir Lewis's face before he had kissed her and the intoxicating feel of his mouth on hers. So absorbed was she with her own thoughts that it was a surprise to her when the clink of crockery told her that Mrs Glenn was already pouring out.

'I don't suppose you'd be so obliging as to tell me what kind of incident I have just witnessed,' said Mrs Glenn conversationally, as she passed Flavia her cup. 'Was it an assault or a love scene?'

'Forgive my bluntness,' Flavia said after a

short silence, 'but would you mind telling me why it is any business of yours?'

'Oh, none at all,' replied her visitor. 'But you have interested yourself in my business to quite a degree, haven't you?' Flavia looked at her. She could not deny it. 'Well then, let us continue. After all, if it was an assault, then he should be taken to task, probably by my brother. If it was not, although it pains me to do so, I must say to you, in my capacity as an experienced married woman, that there are times and places for that sort of thing and frankly, the schoolroom is not one of them.' For someone whose need to speak was causing her pain, she looked quite amazingly smug.

'And what makes you think that I had any choice in the matter?' retorted Flavia swiftly.

'So it *was* an assault?'

'Yes! No! I . . . ' After these disjointed contradictory remarks, Flavia fell silent. It would be so easy to get out of this, she reflected. All she had to do was to say that Sir Lewis had assaulted her. She had no doubt that Mr Steeple could be convinced of it. But the fact of the matter was that she couldn't say it, for she could not forget how he had released her at the very moment when she had started to struggle. Nor could she forget the fact that she had kissed him back. 'It wasn't an assault,' she said eventually in a low tone.

'No, well, I must admit I didn't think so,' replied Mrs Glenn thoughtfully, as she poured herself a second cup of tea. 'Not with your arms entwined around his neck.'

'Oh no, not entwined!' protested Flavia, blushing.

'Entwined,' insisted Mary firmly. Then, after a moment, she went on in a tone that was surprisingly gentle for her, 'Are you in love with him?'

Flavia got up again and walked to the window. 'I certainly don't feel all silly and giggly about him the way the young ladies at Miss Bredale's seemed to become when they had decided that they were in love with someone quite unsuitable,' she confessed. 'But . . .'

'Well?' prompted Mrs Glenn.

'I can't stop thinking about him,' Flavia admitted. 'And thinking of him makes me . . . happy.'

'Oh dear,' said Mary.

'Is that bad?' asked Flavia anxiously.

'Very bad, I'm afraid,' replied the other, shaking her head.

'What do you think I should do?'

'You want me to be honest?'

'Yes, please.'

311

'I'm sorry if you find me brutal, but I think you need to remember Miss Price, and tell yourself that you are probably not the only woman he has made love to in that schoolroom.'

'Oh no!' exclaimed Flavia. Suddenly, she felt rather sick.

'Well he didn't deny it when I brought the subject up, did he? For all that Paul Wheaton is a terrible flirt, I've always thought that Sir Lewis could be just as dangerous in his own way. It seems to me that you have been a bit of a thorn in his side ever since you came here, and he has been looking for a way to punish you. Unless, of course, you have any idea that your affections are returned?'

'How could they be?' replied Flavia wretchedly. 'Look at the women with whom he has been associated — Miss Price, and Mrs Retford. Both of them are far more beautiful than I. And you are right. I have been an annoyance to him.' She walked back towards the window. She was remembering how Sir Lewis had never wanted the school to reopen and how he had consistently condemned and criticized it, throwing obstacles in her way even that very day, to the extent of sending extra pupils just in order to make life difficult for her. 'There is only one thing for me to do,' she said, voicing for the first time what she had known in her heart ever since Miss Price's visit. 'I must go.'

'Go? But why?' Mary asked. Flavia looked at her questioningly. Mary sighed. 'Whatever his motives, he is plainly attracted to you,' she said. 'Why not stay and enjoy what he has to offer?'

Flavia shook her head. 'I couldn't do that,' she said.

Mary smiled wryly. 'No, you're not like me, are you? Mind you,' she went on, 'perhaps we're more alike than I thought, after all. You see, I've also decided to leave very soon. Meeting you last night in the lane made me see things differently — made it all seem grubby somehow, rather than exciting. I had a letter from Sidney, saying he misses me, and I'll try to talk to him as you suggested.'

'I'm sure you're right,' Flavia answered.

'What about you? Where will you go?' Mary asked.

Flavia smiled humourlessly. 'Back to Miss Bredale's — where you would say I belonged I suppose,' she said.

'Funnily enough, I wouldn't say that,' replied the other, surprising her. 'From what I've heard said around here, you've made a success of this school. Who knows, you might be able to find another place similar to this?'

'Perhaps,' replied Flavia. At the moment,

she could not bear the thought of going to another village that was not Brooks, where she would never see Sir Lewis.

'Well, it's time I was going,' said Mrs Glenn, getting up. To Flavia's surprise, the younger woman took hold of her hand. 'I'll miss you when I come back and you're not here,' she said. 'You're the only one around this place with more than half a brain.'

Flavia had forgotten that Mr Wheaton had promised to call, but shortly after Mary had left, he appeared at the front door of the cottage. She could not think of anything she wanted to do less than receive more visitors, but she welcomed him politely and offered him tea.

'No thank you,' he replied, taking the seat that she indicated. 'I must not stay for long, but I wanted to apologize to you for my conduct last night.'

'Really, there is no need,' replied Flavia. 'I am sure that there is no more to be said.'

'You are too gracious,' he answered, taking her hand. 'I suppose the truth is, Miss Montague, that I am just too susceptible! I am fond of female company; I always have been. Let a lady but show an interest in me and I have to respond. Not to do so would seem so, well, ungrateful and unkind.'

Flavia could not help smiling, but she said, 'Many ladies appreciate your attentions, I am sure. But you will wish to marry one day soon, I should think. Any lady who might be drawn to you would want to feel that she could trust you. If you show yourself to be unreliable now in matters of the heart, how will any young lady who knows you be able to accept your suit with any confidence? Or is it your intention to marry some young lady whom you have never met?'

He looked at her, an arrested expression on his face. 'I believe you may be right, ma'am,' he said. 'Well, if you have forgiven me, I shall take my leave. There are one or two calls that I must make quite urgently.' He stood up. 'By the way, I have just received a letter from my sister and she asked me to send you her compliments.'

'That is kind of her,' said Flavia. 'Pray return mine to her when you next write.'

'I certainly will, but I'm not sure that she will remain in Brighton for long.'

'You surprise me. I thought that she was fixed there for the summer.'

'That was certainly her intention; at least, it was until she found out about Lewis's son,' replied Mr Wheaton grinning. 'She always declared that she wouldn't marry him, because of Philip, but now I think she may be having second thoughts. You had better order a new gown or two, Miss Montague. There may be more than one wedding in our family before the year is out.' He bowed and was about to go, when remembering something else, he turned. 'By the way, we'll be making a start on the harvest in the next few days. I believe you wanted to know.'

Flavia thanked him, and bade him a courteous, if somewhat absent-minded farewell. With one part of her mind, she decided that she could close the school for harvest from the following day. She would inform Mr Steeple that she would not be returning when the harvest was over. That would give him a little time in which to look for another teacher. She would send a message round to the vicarage, asking the vicar to call at the school at his earliest convenience. She really did not want to conduct that interview in front of Mrs Steeple, who, she was convinced, had never liked her.

Slowly, she wandered into the school and looked around her, smoothing her hand over the surface of a desk here, picking up an odd pencil that had somehow been overlooked there. With what high hopes she had begun her work here! She started to think about looking for another job as village school-teacher, but rejected it almost as quickly. The similarity between any new post and the one she was now leaving would be too painful, and the contrast between them would be, if anything, more painful still.

She walked into the cupboard to put the pencil away, and as she did so, she suddenly thought of the moment when she had turned and found Sir Lewis Glendenning standing in the doorway, blocking her way out. From the very beginning he had been bent on thwarting her. Well, now he had succeeded.

From feeling disappointed, dejected and lovelorn, she now started to feel very angry. How dared he treat her in such a way? She emerged from the cupboard, and the first thing that she saw was the teacher's desk, on to which the baronet had thrown her, just a short time before. Resolutely she slapped down the treacherous feelings and desires which threatened to undo her completely. What a fool she would be to harbour daydreams about something which clearly he had only done to punish her for defying him! Particularly now she had discovered that he might soon be announcing his engagement to Mrs Retford. Well, she would leave; honour demanded it, his proximity made it advisable, and these ridiculous feelings of hers made it

317

essential to her peace of mind. But she would not slink off silently as if she had done wrong; and what was more, she was determined not to go until she had told him exactly what she thought of him!

19

Before she could lose her courage, she hurried back into the house to get her bonnet. Grace was upstairs putting away some of Flavia's things that had been washed. 'There's no need to do that,' said Flavia as she tied the strings of her bonnet. 'You might as well just pack everything in the trunk. We're not staying.'

Grace stood staring at her, her hands on her hips. 'You have run mad,' she declared. 'First you drag us over here far from anything that's civilized, then you go round hitting people on the head, and then you insist that we leave.' Her eyes narrowed. 'Is that it? Are you having to leave because of him? For if that's so, then I'm going to give him a piece of my mind, baronet or no.'

'I'll do it for you,' replied Flavia as she walked to the door. 'I'm going to see him now.'

The day was not as hot as some of the previous ones had been, so she was able to set a good pace which enabled her to keep her anger on the boil, and did not permit her to spend too much time thinking about other matters.

As she walked, she made a list of the things that he had done which had infuriated her. Firstly, he had nearly ridden her down in the lane. Then he had cornered her in the cupboard, calling her 'schoolmarm' in that odiously superior way of his. Then he had pretended that she was not suitable, and prolonged the suspense of that wretched interview for as long as possible. He had shouted at her and threatened her, sent large numbers of his servants to prevent her from teaching, and finally he had publicly humiliated her in front of the vicar's sister. 'In fact,' she muttered to herself as she marched up the drive, 'I wouldn't put it past him to make sure that someone was watching before he did it — just to get rid of me!'

The drive was lined with trees and wound round gently, so it was not until she was close to the house that she got a clear view of it. It was an ancient, gracious house built in the traditional Elizabethan 'E' shape, with deep gables, its windows glinting in the sunshine, and Flavia halted involuntarily, struck with its beauty. However careless Sir Lewis might be about his own appearance, he clearly made sure that his home was maintained immaculately. She hesitated, the wind taken out of her sails; even then, she might have drawn back, but for the fact that at that moment, two male servants came around from the side of the house, and approached her. As they did so, she recognized them as being two of the number who had attended the school that day.

One looked nervously at the other, then said, 'Pardon us, miss, but we want to . . . to say we're sorry for the trick we played on you.'

Her eyes widened. 'So it was a trick!' she exclaimed. 'I thought so!'

'It was very wrong of us, but — '

'It was more wrong of the one who thought up the idea,' she interrupted.

'Yes, well . . . ' he fell silent.

'You don't need to say any more,' she said swiftly, recalling just in time that it would be unfair to encourage him to speak against his employer. 'I do not blame you, rest assured.'

The two men looked very relieved. 'Thank you, miss,' said the other man. 'We all liked it this morning.' They touched their forelocks, and went about their business.

Flavia marched up to the front door and rang the bell vigorously. *Trick, indeed!* she said to herself. *Now we'll see!*

'Is Sir Lewis within?' she asked the butler more imperiously than she had intended.

'Yes indeed, miss,' replied the butler. 'If you will come this way.'

The butler led her to one of the heavy oak doors which led off the entrance hall. Before he could open it, however, Flavia said, 'Wait, please. Is he in that room?'

'Yes, miss,' answered the butler. 'If you will but allow me — '

'By no means,' answered Flavia, a sparkle in her eye. 'I know just how to announce myself.' Walking past the astonished butler, she took hold of the door handle and, opening the door, threw it back with all her strength, so that it crashed against the cupboard which stood behind, making it rattle in an ominous way which seemed to hint of breaking china inside.

This sound inevitably gave Flavia something of a pause. Sir Lewis, who was indeed within, whirled round, and stood looking at her, but with his back to the window, it was impossible to read his expression. He soon recovered from any surprise he might have felt, however, for before she could say anything, he remarked 'My dear Miss Montague, the door seems to have flown out of your hand! Simpkins, see that something is done about these doors,' said the baronet.

'Certainly, sir,' said Simpkins, his expression impassive even while he wondered what on earth he was expected to do to remedy the supposed defect. He glanced towards the cupboard from whence the ominous sounds had come. 'Would you like me to . . . ?'

'No, no, it will keep. That will be all.'

'I was only giving you your own again,' she said spiritedly. She glanced at the cupboard door. She was determined not to apologize, but she could not help wondering what valuable articles had been ruined beyond repair.

'Oh, was that what it was?' he answered as he closed the door. Then, seeing the direction of her gaze, he murmured 'Priceless, I should imagine. Shall we have a look?' Hastily, she bit back a refusal. She did not want him to think that she was afraid. 'Well well,' he murmured, pausing as he bent to open the cupboard door. He straightened, holding some broken china in his hand. 'It was a vase,' he said, his eyes glinting. 'No doubt you would say that that makes us even, but the cases are hardly equal, are they?'

'Meaning that my little school doesn't matter, I suppose,' she retorted. She took a deep breath. 'I am sorry if something valuable has been broken, but you have been trying to destroy something which to my mind is of far greater value, and that is my school. Of course you made your contempt for it perfectly clear from the very beginning, so I should not be surprised that you will go to any lengths to have it closed.'

'And to what lengths am I supposed to have gone now?' he asked her, putting the broken china down on top of the cupboard and closing the door. 'I would have thought that anyone of the meanest intelligence would have gathered today that I hold your school in the highest esteem.'

She stared at him. 'Esteem? Do not insult me, sir. Can you deny that you deliberately sent half your staff to my school today as a shameless attempt to sabotage my lessons?'

'Yes I can, and I do,' he replied. 'Why on earth would I want to drag my staff away from their work for such a paltry reason?'

'You're a liar, sir,' she declared. By the lowering of his brows she could see that now she had really nettled him. 'I met two of your servants outside just now and they admitted to taking part in the trick.'

The baronet uttered an extremely rude expletive which Flavia had not heard since she had accidentally overheard an able-seaman giving a raw recruit a dressing-down. 'Call me a liar again, schoolmarm, and I'll put you over my knee! If they confessed to something, I'll warrant you got them so confused with your endless brangling that they didn't know what they were confessing to. If you'd got any sense at all, you'd realize

324

that I sent them to you because of Philip.'

'Philip? Your son?' she said hollowly.

'Of course, Philip my son. Whom did you think I meant — Philip the Second of Spain?' he asked her with heavy sarcasm. 'I would have thought you would have guessed immediately. After all, it was something you did that gave me the idea.'

'Something I did?' she echoed.

'Really, for an educated female you are showing a remarkable degree of obtuseness,' he said in long-suffering tones. 'You communicated with Philip by means of slate and chalk. If Philip is to take his place as my heir, he will need to manage this house and this estate, and to do that he will have to be able to communicate with all the staff.'

'So all the staff must be taught to read,' she said slowly. 'Of course.'

'It wasn't a trick,' he said seriously. 'You've said that I hold your school in contempt, but you're wrong. If you would but recall, I told you that you were a gifted teacher. Who better to teach my staff?'

She turned away, at a loss for words. She had come prepared to do battle with him, but he had completely taken the wind out of her sails. After a moment or two, she turned back towards him. 'I am astonished,' she said at last. 'You leave me speechless.'

He grinned. 'I thought there was only one way of silencing you,' he remarked, coming towards her.

'No!' she exclaimed, darting behind the desk. 'You may have explained yourself in one respect, but that does not mean that you are entitled to . . . to — '

'To kiss you?' he asked, closing the gap between them. She remained behind the desk, poised, ready to take evasive action, should he try to come at her from either direction.

'I was going to say, to assault me,' she answered. 'I admit that I may have misjudged you with regard to Philip, but you still have much to answer for. You have tried to intimidate me, put me through an absurd farce of an interview, vandalized the school, shouted at me, sneered at me, blackmailed me, overcrowded my school, and finally — '

He halted, leaning across the desk, his hands flat upon it. 'Vandalized the school? When upon earth did I do that?'

'You made my classroom dirty before the bishop's visit,' she told him, wishing that the accusation did not sound so absurd now that it was out in the open.

'I did no such thing,' he said forthrightly. She opened her mouth to speak but he went on. 'Nor did I pay any of my people to do it. But I think you might find that one or two of them did do it, possibly out of jealousy of the ones who were learning.'

Suddenly, a look of comprehension crossed her features. 'Oh,' she whispered.

'Precisely,' he grinned. 'Find those servants you met outside and I'll warrant that that was what they were confessing to. But to move on, I'll be obliged if you would tell me when I blackmailed you.'

She eyed him warily. 'When you insisted that I . . . I kiss you, to prevent you from telling the bishop about what I had done.'

'Ah, yes. How convenient that you have remembered that little incident, and accused me of assaulting you, but made nothing at all of *your* assault upon *my* person. But that incident is easily explained.' She stared at him uncomprehendingly. 'I wanted to kiss you very much indeed, schoolmarm, and so I seized my advantage.'

'And later on, assaulted me in my very own classroom! What more could you have done?'

He made a move to catch her, but she darted away from him around to the other side of the desk. 'Wait a minute,' he began, but she did not allow him to finish.

'I suppose I am a fool to be surprised,' she declared. 'Everyone warned me about your reputation, almost from the moment of my arrival.'

'Now listen, schoolmarm,' he said, moving towards her again, but again, she evaded him.

'Kindly do not use that odious, sneering expression when you speak of my profession,' she stormed. 'Perhaps I should have guessed when I heard about Miss Price what my fate would be! Clearly you will not stop even at the seduction of the schoolteacher if it suits you!'

'God in Heaven, woman, there *is* clearly only one way of silencing you,' he declared, moving again. This time he was too quick for her, and he caught her about the waist, pulling her against him.

At once, she remembered something else that he had said. 'Why did you want to kiss me?' she asked him in bewildered tones.

'Why?'

'You . . . you said that you wanted to . . . to kiss me very much. Why?' she whispered. But before he could either answer her or kiss her, as he clearly intended to do, the door opened to admit the lady whom Flavia knew as Miss Price, and an extremely handsome tall dark gentleman.

'*Sacre bleu!*' the gentleman exclaimed with a twinkle in his eye. '*Are we de trop?*'

At once the baronet released Flavia. 'I do not think, ma'am, that you have been properly introduced to my guests,' he said, straightening his cuffs, his colour a little high. 'Louis, Sylvia, this is Miss Montague, our esteemed schoolmistress. Miss Montague, these are my guests, the Comte and Comtesse de Lengalle.'

Flavia made her curtsy, conscious the while that her face was as red as Sir Lewis's and that her hair was somewhat dishevelled. I shall be lucky if I ever teach again, she reflected. No doubt the news of her damaged reputation would be around the district, if not the entire country, like wildfire.

'We have already met informally, when I was out with Louise for a drive,' said the comtesse, smiling. She turned to her husband. 'It was Miss Montague who returned to me that precious book that you gave me.' She smiled at Flavia, then. 'It was Louis' first gift to me, and I was devastated to have lost it. You can imagine how happy I was to have it returned.'

'Yes, of course,' replied Flavia hollowly.

'But I have heard much of the talents of the esteemed Mam'selle Montague,' said the comte, bowing over Flavia's hand in a practised manner. 'You are fortunate indeed to have gained the services of so able a person!'

'Undoubtedly,' agreed Sir Lewis.

The comte turned to his wife. 'My dear, it

seems to me that Lewis and Miss Montague are consulting on a matter of the most grave and important, so I think that we should absent ourselves.' He opened the door for his wife, then turned and said with a twinkle, 'The library is no doubt the best place for such weighty matters.'

Barely had the door closed behind them than Sir Lewis said, 'Now, where were we?' before pulling her into his arms and kissing her soundly. For a brief moment or two, she surrendered to the power of his kiss; then, remembering something else that she had heard, she struggled free and, as soon as she was able, slapped him across the face.

'What the deuce was that for?' he exclaimed incredulously.

'I will not be kissed by another woman's fiancé,' she declared, her voice not quite steady.

'God in Heaven, to whom am I supposed to be engaged *now*?' he asked her, completely bewildered.

'To Mrs Retford,' she answered in a small voice.

He burst out laughing. She stared at him for a moment, then turned, and made as if to hurry to the door. He caught her before she could reach it, and pulled her into his arms. 'I don't know from whom you had that, but it isn't true,' he told her, 'and this is the reason.' Then he kissed her again. This time, quite independent of her will it seemed, her arms crept around his neck. Eventually, after quite a long interval, he said, 'I am going to carry on doing that until you stop making foolish assumptions and listen to me. In fact,' he went on, punctuating his words with kisses, 'I might just do so anyway.' He drew back again, then said masterfully, 'Will you listen to me now? Well?'

Flavia nodded meekly.

'Then first of all I shall tell you about Sylvia. The neighbourhood in general believes that I had an affair with her, but I never did. She was secretly married to Louis, who has been a friend of mine for many years. He was involved with some vitally important business in connection with the attempts to rescue the French king and queen. He came to visit her here but it was essential that no one should discover his movements. Of course, the wise thing would have been to defer their marriage and cut off all communication, but who is wise when it comes to matters of the heart? Inevitably, the comings and goings between this house and the school were noted, and people came to the obvious conclusion. And it was better that they should think ill of me than that Louis' work should be jeopardized.'

Flavia felt a weight fall from around her heart. 'You were never in love with her at all?' she said wonderingly.

'No, never. Nor was I ever in love with Celia. We were engaged once, and she threw me over. Philip was the reason she gave, but I think that we had both come to realize that we wouldn't suit. She likes to think that I went off to London heart-broken, and fought a duel to forget my woes; hence the scar. The truth is far more prosaic. I acquired it when I was set upon by footpads.'

'You did not love either of them?'

He shook his head. 'Instead, I fell in love with a strong-minded, opinionated school-teacher with a taste for fine wine and good cigars, who persistently thinks the worst of me.'

'But ... you can't have done,' she murmured, looking up into his face. He certainly looked sincere. 'I'm not pretty; you said so yourself. I'm not wealthy or accomplished or anything. And I might always think the worst of you,' she went on more spiritedly, 'but that is probably because there is always a worst to think.'

'I don't deny it,' he replied, unabashed. 'You mentioned that I tried to intimidate you. I think you must mean when I trapped you in the cupboard. Well yes, I suppose I did, remember that I was rather drunk at the time. But you see, you reminded me of an indignant little bird with your feathers all fluffed up, and you intrigued me no end. Yes, I did say that I didn't think you pretty, but I lied. You aren't conventionally pretty, but there's something about the way your eyes light up when you are animated, as, for instance, when you are talking about the school, that compels a man's attention.' He leaned forward and lightly kissed her brow. 'You're a woman of passion, my dear. I told you so at that farce of an interview, but I don't think you believed that I meant it. And you can be quite formidable, you know. I might have tried to intimidate you, but I didn't succeed, did I? The interview wasn't my idea; it is laid down in the foundation documents of the school, that Wheaton and I and the present incumbent should all approve of you. But, well, I — '

'You wanted to ruffle my feathers again, I suppose,' she declared indignantly, pulling herself out of his arms. He allowed her to do so, but then he caught hold of her hands, rubbing his thumbs gently across their backs in a way which made shivers run up and down her spine in the most delightful fashion.

'Exactly so,' he agreed. 'But you did some ruffling of your own, you know.'

'But how?' she asked him.

'You wouldn't be the first woman to be enslaved by the charms of Paul Wheaton. I knew for a fact that he had taken you driving, and I was certain that you were allowing him to smoke cigars in your garden.'

Flavia coloured. 'He is very handsome,' she conceded. 'But it wasn't long before I realized that I wasn't the only recipient of his charm.' At that moment she remembered something. 'I am hoping that he may have put all that behind him now, for I have a suspicion that he will soon be proposing to Miss Evelina Bell.'

'About time too. If Evelina thinks that marriage will stop him flirting, though, I'm afraid she is in for a rude awakening. Paul Wheaton will be flirting with pretty women to the day of his death. I only forgive him,' he went on, pulling her close to him again, 'because Sylvia could not resist telling me that you think me more handsome than he is. Which lack of judgement proves,' he added, punctuating his words with kisses, 'that you must be as much in love with me as I am with you.'

'Such conceit,' she said with a chuckle, as soon as he had released her.

He paused for a long time. 'You really made me angry over the matter of Philip and

Penelope, you know.'

'Yes, I know I did, and I'm truly sorry.'

He laid a finger on her lips. 'We'll put that behind us, now. I can never forget that it was because of you that Philip's deafness was discovered. Thanks to you he has a future.'

'Life will never be easy for him,' Flavia reminded him.

'Life hasn't exactly been a ride in the park since I met you,' he answered. 'But then,' he went on, raising her hand to his lips whilst not for a moment taking his eyes off her face, 'I always found riding in the park rather dull.'

At that moment, they heard the sound of the door opening, and they moved a little apart. Philip and Penelope stood hand in hand on the threshold. 'Mme. de Lengalle said that you had come, Miss Montague,' said Penelope in her usual quiet way. 'Have you . . . did you come to ask my uncle if I might come back to school?'

'Not exactly,' said Sir Lewis. 'In fact, I am hoping that Miss Montague will come to live with us here.'

'As our governess?' asked Penelope, her thin little face lighting up.

The baronet walked over to her and placed a hand gently on her shoulder. 'No, we'll have to get someone else as a governess,' he said. 'I am hoping that she might consent to be your aunt, and Philip's mama.'

For a moment, Penelope stared at them uncomprehendingly. Then a change came over her expression. If her face had lit up before, now it fairly glowed. 'My aunt,' she breathed. Then she knelt down in front of Philip. 'Philip, Miss Montague is to be your mama,' she told him. He looked carefully at her face, and although he could not hear what she said, he obviously realized that something very special had happened, for the corners of his mouth turned up in a rare smile. Then Penelope stood up and hugged her uncle very tightly, and Flavia could barely hold back her tears.

'You must leave us now,' Sir Lewis said gently. 'You see, I haven't had the chance to ask her yet.'

'Oh yes,' answered Penelope. 'I'm sorry we interrupted you, but we did want to see Miss Montague. Come Philip.' The two children walked to the door, but before they went out, Penelope turned and spoke. 'Please say yes,' she said, 'for I don't think I would like anyone else half as well.'

Sir Lewis chuckled as the door closed behind them. 'You'll have to say yes now,' he laughed. Then he turned and saw that Flavia's eyes were bright with unshed tears.

'Why, sweetheart, what is it?' he asked, going to her.

'I accused you of ill-treating Penelope,' she whispered.

'You did,' he agreed. 'As a matter of fact, my darling, that was when I think I really fell in love with you.'

'Oh, why?' she asked him, completely mystified.

'You are half my size and weight, and the merest fraction of my strength, but without hesitation, you were prepared to put yourself between me and her.' He pulled her into his arms again. 'In short, you have completely captivated me — schoolmarm.'

'I wish you would not call me that,' she said, intending to sound cross but not quite managing it.

'I will call you that until you tell me that I may soon call you by another name.'

'Another name?'

'Lady Glendenning, of course,' he answered. 'You will be my wife, won't you? I'm afraid that I'm not nearly so exciting as local rumour and your vivid imagination makes me out to be, but I do love you very much.'

'Are you sure you want to marry me?' she said wonderingly.

'You seem surprised.'

'Well, no one has ever wanted to marry me before.'

'Lucky me, then, to be the only man with any discernment. Now, tell me that you love me.'

'Of course I do,' she replied, smiling up at him and, for the first time but certainly not for the last, brushing back that errant lock of hair. 'And I will marry you, for it seems to me that thanks to you I have very little reputation left; but you don't deserve it, Lewis.'

'No more I do,' he replied, and bent his head to receive his completely unmerited reward.

We do hope that you have enjoyed reading this large print book.

Did you know that all of our titles are available for purchase?

We publish a wide range of high quality large print books including:
Romances, Mysteries, Classics
General Fiction
Non Fiction and Westerns

Special interest titles available in large print are:
The Little Oxford Dictionary
Music Book
Song Book
Hymn Book
Service Book

Also available from us courtesy of Oxford University Press:
Young Readers' Dictionary
(large print edition)
Young Readers' Thesaurus
(large print edition)

For further information or a free brochure, please contact us at:
Ulverscroft Large Print Books Ltd.,
The Green, Bradgate Road, Anstey,
Leicester, LE7 7FU, England.
Tel: (00 44) 0116 236 4325
Fax: (00 44) 0116 234 0205

DERBYSHIRE DECEPTION

Ann Barker

When Freya Pascoe accompanies Claudia Bryce to Derbyshire for a bet, the objectionable Miss Bryce is unaware that her paid companion is immensely wealthy, for Freya has promised not to reveal her circumstances to anyone. She is also attracted to Claudia's brother Piers, the handsome mill owner, who seems to reciprocate her feelings. Once in Derbyshire, she meets Lord Ravendale, Claudia's fiance, a man of unsavoury reputation, whose reasons for marrying are wholly mercenary. Almost against her will, Freya finds herself drawn to him. Gradually, she discovers that both Piers Bryce and Lord Ravendale differ from her expectations . . .

THE GRAND TOUR

Ann Barker

When Lord Craythorne dismisses his niece's governess, Flora Chayter, for immoral behaviour he makes two assumptions: that she is a woman of low character, and that he will never come across her again. He is indignant, therefore, when he discovers that Flora is to be the travelling companion of Mrs Wylde, whom he has agreed to escort to Venice. On the journey, Flora attracts the attention of a number of men, but steadfastly rejects every advance. It is not until the travellers reach Venice, where tragedy threatens, that Craythorne is forced to confront his true feelings for Flora.

HIS LORDSHIP'S GARDENER

Ann Barker

Arriving home after three years' absence, Lord Lyddington discovers that his sister is having his garden remodelled. The Earl is pleased to discover a roistering companion in his gardener's nephew, 'Master' Sutcliffe. However, young Sutcliffe is not all he seems, and soon the Earl is obliged to reassess his previous ideas concerning appropriate female behaviour and attire. Meanwhile, someone seeks to sabotage the garden alterations, viciously attacks Sutcliffe senior and even assaults the Earl himself. Who could be responsible? The Earl's happiness depends on a swift resolution of this matter.

THE HIGHCLOUGH LADY

Melinda Hammond

Governess Verity Shore longs for a little adventure, but when Rafe Bannerman arrives to carry her off to Highclough she soon discovers that life can be a little too exciting! An estate on the edge of the wild Yorkshire Moors, Highclough is Verity's inheritance, but the land is coveted, not only by her handsome cousin Luke but also by Rafe. With her very life in danger, whom can she trust?

AN HEIR FOR ASHINGBY

Olga Sinclair

1812. America and Britain are on the brink of war. American-born Sarah Dunthorne is visiting her grandmother in London. Sarah is compromised when she assists her friend, Corinne de Vere, to elope with Forbes Thackstone. Corinne is the ward and heir to Colonel, Lord Wrenningham, who is now determined that the rebellious couple shall never inherit his estate at Ashingby. Physically attracted to Sarah, Wrenningham proposes, but she will not marry without love. Grandmama is furious and sends Sarah home on the same ship as Wrenningham, who is taking reinforcements to Canada. Then war is declared. As the couple journey on through danger and difficulties, will they find love?

DL 5/13
SC 2/15
Hn 9/18